By

By Lawrence Block

OTHER NOVELS

After the First Death
Ariel
Cinderella Sims
Coward's Kiss
Deadly Honeymoon
The Girl with the Long Green
  Heart
Grifter's Game
Not Comin' Home to You

Random Walk
Ronald Rabbit is a Dirty Old
  Man
Small Town
The Specialists
Such Men Are Dangerous
The Triumph of Evil
You Could Call it Murder

COLLECTED SHORT STORIES

Sometimes They Bite
Like a Lamb to Slaughter
Some Days You Get the Bear
Ehrengraf for the Defense

One Night Stands
The Lost Causes of Ed London
Enough Rope

BOOKS FOR WRITERS

Writing the Novel from Plot
  to Print
Telling Lies for Fun & Profit

Write for Your Life
Spider, Spin Me a Web

ANTHOLOGIES CITED

Death Cruise
Master's Choice
Opening Shots
Master's Choice 2
Speaking of Lust

Opening Shots 2
Speaking of Greed
Blood on Their Hands
Gangsters Swindlers Killers &
  Thieves

HIT PARADE

Lawrence Block

An Orion paperback

First published in Great Britain in 2006
by Orion Books
This paperback edition published in 2007
by Orion Books
an imprint of The Orion Publishing Group Ltd,
Carmelite House, 50 Victoria Embankment,
London EC4Y 0DZ

3 5 7 9 10 8 6 4

Portions of this book have appeared in somewhat different form
in the following publications: *Murderer's Row*, *Murder at the
Foul Line* and *Murder at the Race Track*, all edited by Otto Penzler;
Transgressions, edited by Ed McBain; *Playboy*; and audiobookcafe.com

A CIP catalogue record for this book
is available from the British Library.

ISBN 978-0-7528-8153-9

Printed and bound by CPI Group (UK) Ltd, Croydon, CR0 4YY

The Orion Publishing Group's policy is to use papers that
are natural, renewable and recyclable products and
made from wood grown in sustainable forests. The logging
and manufacturing processes are expected to conform to
the environmental regulations of the country of origin.

www.orionbooks.co.uk

This is for

HAROLD K.

who gave Keller some good tips . . .

Zai gezunt, boychik!

KELLER'S DESIGNATED HITTER

CHAPTER ONE

Keller, a beer in one hand and a hot dog in the other, walked up a flight and a half of concrete steps and found his way to his seat. In front of him, two men were discussing the ramifications of a recent trade the Tarpons had made, sending two minor-league prospects to the Florida Marlins in return for a left-handed reliever and a player to be named later. Keller figured he hadn't missed anything, as they'd been talking about the same subject when he left. He figured the player in question would have been long since named by the time these two were done speculating about him.

Keller took a bite of his hot dog, drew a sip of his beer. The fellow on his left said, "You didn't bring me one."

Huh? He'd told the guy he'd be back in a minute, might have mentioned he was going to the refreshment stand, but had he missed something the man had said in return?

"What didn't I bring you? A hot dog or a beer?"

"Either one," the man said.

"Was I supposed to?"

"Nope," the man said. "Hey, don't mind me. I'm just jerking your chain a little."

"Oh," Keller said.

The fellow started to say something else but broke it off after a word or two as he and everybody else in the stadium turned their attention to home plate, where the

Tarpons' cleanup hitter had just dropped to the dirt to avoid getting hit by a high inside fastball. The Yankee pitcher, a burly Japanese with a herky-jerky windup, seemed unfazed by the boos, and Keller wondered if he even knew they were for him. He caught the return throw from the catcher, set himself, and went into his pitching motion.

"Taguchi likes to pitch inside," said the man who'd been jerking Keller's chain, "and Vollmer likes to crowd the plate. So every once in a while Vollmer has to hit the dirt or take one for the team."

Keller took another bite of his hot dog, wondering if he ought to offer a bite to his new friend. That he even considered it seemed to indicate that his chain had been jerked successfully. He was glad he didn't have to share the hot dog, because he wanted every bite of it for himself. And, when it was gone, he had a feeling he might go back for another.

Which was strange, because he never ate hot dogs. A few years back he'd read a political essay on the back page of a news magazine that likened legislation to sausage. You were better off not knowing how it was made, the writer observed, and Keller, who had heretofore never cared how laws were passed or sausages produced, found himself more conscious of the whole business. The legislative aspect didn't change his life, but without making any conscious decision on the matter, he found he'd lost his taste for sausage.

Being at a ballpark somehow made it different. He had a hunch the hot dogs they sold here at Tarpon Stadium were if anything more dubious in their composition than your average supermarket frankfurter, but that seemed to be beside

4

the point. A ballpark hot dog was just part of the baseball experience, along with listening to some flannel-mouthed fan shouting instructions to a ballplayer dozens of yards away who couldn't possibly hear him, or booing a pitcher who couldn't care less, or having one's chain jerked by a total stranger. All part of the Great American Pastime.

He took a bite, chewed, sipped his beer. Taguchi went to three-and-two on Vollmer, who fouled off four pitches before he got one he liked. He drove it to the 396-foot mark in left center field, where Bernie Williams hauled it in. There had been runners on first and second, and they trotted back to their respective bases when the ball was caught.

"One out," said Keller's new friend, the chain jerker.

Keller ate his hot dog, sipped his beer. The next batter swung furiously and topped a roller that dribbled out toward the mound. Taguchi pounced on it, but his only play was to first, and the runners advanced. Men on second and third, two out.

The Tarpon third baseman was next, and the crowd booed lustily when the Yankees elected to walk him intentionally. "They always do that," Keller said.

"Always," the man said. "It's strategy, and nobody minds when their own team does it. But when your guy's up and the other side won't pitch to him, you tend to see it as a sign of cowardice."

"Seems like a smart move, though."

"Unless Turnbull shows 'em up with a grand slam, and God knows he's hit a few of 'em in the past."

"I saw one of them," Keller recalled. "In Wrigley Field, before they had the lights. He was with the Cubs. I forget who they were playing."

"That would have had to be before the lights came in,

if he was with the Cubs. Been all around, hasn't he? But he's been slumping lately, and you got to go with the percentages. Walk him and you put on a .320 hitter to get at a .280 hitter, plus you got a force play at any base."

"It's a game of percentages," Keller said.

"A game of inches, a game of percentages, a game of woulda-coulda-shoulda," the man said, and Keller was suddenly more than ordinarily grateful that he was an American. He'd never been to a soccer match, but somehow he doubted they ever supplied you with a conversation like this one.

"Batting seventh for the Tarpons," the stadium announcer intoned. "Number seventeen, the designated hitter, Floyd Turnbull."

CHAPTER TWO

"**H**e's a designated hitter," Dot had said, on the porch of the big old house on Taunton Place. "Whatever that means."

"It means he's in the lineup on offense only," Keller told her. "He bats for the pitcher."

"Why can't the pitcher bat for himself? Is it some kind of union regulation?"

"That's close enough," said Keller, who didn't want to get into it. He had once tried to explain the infield fly rule to a stewardess, and he was never going to make that sort of mistake again. He wasn't a sexist about it, he knew plenty of women who understood this stuff, but the ones who didn't were going to have to learn it from somebody else.

"I saw him play a few times," he told her, stirring his glass of iced tea. "Floyd Turnbull."

"On television?"

"Dozens of times on TV," he said. "I was thinking of seeing him in person. Once at Wrigley Field, when he was with the Cubs and I happened to be in Chicago."

"You just happened to be there?"

"Well," Keller said. "I don't ever just happen to be any-place. It was business. Anyway, I had a free afternoon and I went to a game."

"Nowadays you'd go to a stamp dealer."

"Games are mostly at night nowadays," he said, "but I

still go every once in a while. I saw Turnbull a couple of times in New York, too. Out at Shea, when he was with the Cubs and they were in town for a series with the Mets. Or maybe he was already with the Astros when I saw him. It's hard to remember."

"And not exactly crucial that you get it right."

"I think I saw him at Yankee Stadium, too. But you're right, it's not important."

"In fact," Dot said, "it would be fine with me if you'd never seen him at all, up close or on TV. Does this complicate things, Keller? Because I can always call the guy back and tell him we pass."

"You don't have to do that."

"Well, I hate to, since they already paid half. I can turn down jobs every day and twice on Sundays, but there's something about giving back money once I've got it in my hands that makes me sick to my stomach. I wonder why that is?"

"A bird in the hand," Keller suggested.

"When I've got a bird in my hand," she said, "I hate like hell to let go of it. But you saw this guy play. That's not gonna make it tough for you to take him out?"

Keller thought about it, shook his head. "I don't see why it should," he said. "It's what I do."

"Right," Dot said. "Same as Turnbull, when you think about it. You're a designated hitter yourself, aren't you, Keller?"

"**D**esignated hitter," Keller said as Floyd Turnbull took a called second strike. "Whoever thought that one up?"

"Some marketing genius," his new friend said. "Some dipstick who came up with research to prove that fans wanted to see more hits and home runs. So they lowered the pitching mound and told the umpires to quit calling the high strike, and then they juiced up the baseball and brought in the fences in the new ballparks, and the ballplayers started lifting weights and swinging lighter bats, and now you've got baseball games with scores like football games. Last week the Tigers beat the A's fourteen to thirteen. First thing I thought, Jeez, who missed the extra point?"

"At least the National League still lets pitchers hit."

"And at least nobody in the pros uses those aluminum bats. They show college baseball on ESPN, and I can't watch it. I can't stand the sound the ball makes when you hit it. Not to mention it travels too goddam far."

The next pitch was in the dirt. Posada couldn't find it, but the third-base coach, suspicious, held the runner. The fans booed, though it was hard to tell whom they were booing, or why. The two in front of Keller joined in the booing, and Keller and the man next to him exchanged knowing glances.

"Fans," the man said and rolled his eyes.

The next pitch was belt high, and Turnbull connected solidly with it. The stadium held its collective breath and the ball sailed toward the left-field corner, hooking foul at the last moment. The crowd heaved a sigh, and the runners trotted back to their bases. Turnbull, looking not at all happy, dug in again at the plate.

He swung at the next pitch, which looked like ball four to Keller, and popped to right. O'Neill floated under it and gathered it in and the inning was over.

"Top of the order for the Yanks," said Keller's friend. "About time they broke this thing wide open, wouldn't you say?"

9

With two out in the Tarpons' half of the eighth inning, with the Yankees ahead by five runs, Floyd Turnbull got all of a Mike Stanton fastball and hit it into the upper deck. Keller watched as he jogged around the bases, getting a good hand from what remained of the crowd.

"Career home run number three ninety-three for the old warhorse," said the man on Keller's left. "And all those people missed it because they had to beat the traffic."

"Number three ninety-three?"

"Leaves him seven shy of four hundred. And, in the hits department, you just saw number twenty-nine eighty-eight."

"You've got those stats at your fingertips?"

"My fingers won't quite reach," the fellow said, and pointed to the scoreboard, where the information he'd cited was posted. "Just twelve hits to go before he joins the magic circle, the Three Thousand Hits club. That's the only thing to be said for the DH rule—it lets a guy like Floyd Turnbull stick around a couple of extra years, long enough to post the kind of numbers that get you into Cooperstown. And he can still do a team some good. He can't run the bases, he can't chase after fly balls, but the son of a bitch hasn't forgotten how to hit a baseball."

The Yankees got the run back with interest in the top of the ninth on a walk to Jeter and a home run by Bernie Williams, and the Tarpons went in order in the bottom of the ninth, with Rivera striking out the first two batters and getting the third to pop to short.

"Too bad there was nobody on when Turnbull got his homer," said Keller's friend, "but that's usually the way it is. He's still good with a stick, but he hits 'em with nobody on, and usually when the team's too far behind or out in front for it to make any difference."

The two men walked down a succession of ramps and out of the stadium. "I'd like to see old Floyd get the numbers he needs," the man said, "but I wish he'd get 'em on some other team. What they need for a shot at the flag's a decent left-handed starter and some help in the bull pen, not an old man with bad knees who hits it out when you don't need it."

"You think they should trade him?"

"They'd love to, but who'd trade for him? He can help a team, but not enough to justify paying him the big bucks. He's got three years left on his contract, three years at six-point-five million a year. There are teams that could use him, but nobody can use him six-point-five worth. And the Tarps can't release him and go out and *buy* the pitching they need, not while they've got Turnbull's salary to pay."

"Tricky business," Keller said.

"And a business is what it is. Well, I'm parked over on Pentland Avenue, so this is where I get off. Nice talking with you."

And off the fellow went, while Keller turned and walked off in the opposite direction. He didn't know the name of the man he had talked to, and would probably never see him again, and that was fine. In fact it was one of the real pleasures of going to a game, the intense conversations you had with strangers whom you then allowed to remain strangers. The man had been good company, and at the end he'd provided some useful information.

Because now Keller had an idea why he'd been hired.

"The Tarpons are stuck with Turnbull," he told Dot. "He draws this huge salary, and they have to pay it whether they play him or not. And I guess that's where I come in."

"I don't know," she said. "Are you sure about this, Keller? That's a pretty extreme form of corporate downsizing. All that just to keep from paying a man his salary? How much could it amount to?"

He told her.

"That much," she said, impressed. "That's a lot to pay a man to hit a ball with a stick, especially when he doesn't have to go out and stand around in the hot sun. He just sits on the bench until it's his turn to bat, right?"

"Right."

"Well, I think you might be on to something," she said. "I don't know who hired us or why, but your guess makes more sense than anything I could come up with off the top of my head. But I feel myself getting a little nervous, Keller."

"Why?"

"Because this is just the kind of thing that could set your milk to curdling, isn't it?"

"What milk? What are you talking about?"

"I've known you a long time, Keller. And I can just see you deciding that this is a hell of a way to treat a faithful employee after long years of service, and how can you allow this to happen, di dah di dah di dah. Am I coming through loud and clear?"

"The di dah part makes more sense than the rest of it," he said. "Dot, as far as who hired us and why, all I am is curious. Curiosity's a long way from righteous indignation."

"Didn't do much for the cat, as I remember."

"Well," he said, "I'm not *that* curious."

"So I've got nothing to worry about?"

"Not a thing," he said. "The guy's a dead man hitting."

The Tarpons closed out the series with the Yankees—and a twelve-game home stand—the following afternoon. They got a good outing from their ace right-hander, who scattered six hits and held the New Yorkers to one run, a bases-empty homer by Brosius. The Tarps won, 3–1, with no help from their designated hitter, who struck out twice, flied to center, and hit a hard liner right at the first baseman.

Keller watched from a good seat on the third-base side, then checked out of his hotel and drove to the airport. He turned in his rental car and flew to Milwaukee, where the Brewers would host the Tarps for a three-game series. He picked up a fresh rental and checked in at a motel half a mile from the Marriott where the Tarpons always stayed.

The Brewers won the first game, 5–2. Floyd Turnbull had a good night at bat, going three for five with two singles and a double, but he didn't do anything to affect the outcome; there was nobody on base when he got his hits, and nobody behind him in the order could drive him in.

The next night the Tarps got to the Brewers' rookie southpaw early and blew the game open, scoring six runs in the first inning and winding up with a 13–4 victory. Turnbull's homer was part of the big first inning, and he collected another hit in the seventh when he doubled into the gap and was thrown out trying to stretch it into a triple.

"Why'd he do that?" the bald guy next to Keller wondered. "Two out, and he tries for third? Don't make the third out at third base, isn't that what they say?"

"When you're up by nine runs," Keller said, "I don't suppose it matters much one way or the other."

"Still," the man said, "it's what's wrong with that prick. Always for himself his whole career. He wanted one more triple in the record book, that's what he wanted. And forget about the team."

After the game Keller went to a German restaurant south of the city on the lake. The place dripped atmosphere, with beer steins hanging from the hand-hewn oak beams, an oompah band in lederhosen, and fifteen different beers on tap. Keller couldn't tell the waitresses apart, they all looked like grown-up versions of Heidi, and evidently Floyd Turnbull had the same problem; he called them all Gretchen and ran his hand up under their skirts whenever they came within reach.

Keller was there because he'd learned the Tarpons favored the place, but the sauerbraten was reason enough to make the trip. He made his beer last until he'd cleaned his plate, then turned down the waitress's suggestion of a refill and asked for a cup of coffee instead. By the time she brought it, several more fans had crossed the room to beg autographs from the Tarpons.

"They all want their menus signed," Keller told the waitress. "You people are going to run out of menus."

"It happens all the time," she said. "Not that we run out of menus, because we never do, but players coming here and our other customers asking for autographs. All the athletes like to come here."

"Well, the food's great," he said.

"And it's free. For the players, I mean. It brings in other customers, so it's worth it to the owner, plus he just likes having his restaurant full of jocks. About it being free for them, I'm not supposed to tell you that."

"It'll be our little secret."

"You can tell the whole world, for all I care. Tonight's my last night. I mean, what do I need with jerks like Floyd Turnbull? I want a pelvic exam, I'll go to my gynecologist, if it's all the same to you."

"I noticed he was a little free with his hands."

"And close with everything else. They eat and drink free, but most of them at least leave tips. Not good tips, ballplayers are cheap bastards, but they leave something. Turnbull always leaves exactly twenty percent."

"Twenty percent's not that bad, is it?"

"It is when it's twenty percent of nothing."

"Oh."

"He said he got a home run tonight, too."

"Number three ninety-four of his career," Keller said.

"Well, he's not getting to first base with me," she said. "The big jerk."

CHAPTER THREE

"**N**ight before last," Keller said, "I was in a German restaurant in Milwaukee."

"Milwaukee, Keller?"

"Well, not exactly in Milwaukee. It was south of the city a few miles, on Lake Michigan."

"That's close enough," Dot said. "It's still a long way from Memphis, isn't it? Although if it's south of the city, I guess it's closer to Memphis than if it was actually inside of Milwaukee."

"Dot . . ."

"Before we get too deep into the geography of it," she said, "aren't you supposed to be in Memphis? Taking care of business?"

"As a matter of fact . . ."

"And don't tell me you already took care of business, because I would have heard. CNN would have had it, and they wouldn't even make me wait until Headline Sports at twenty minutes past the hour. You notice how they never say which hour?"

"That's because of different time zones."

"That's right, Keller, and what time zone are you in? Or don't you know?"

"I'm in Seattle," he said.

"That's Pacific time, isn't it? Three hours behind New York."

"Right."

"But light-years ahead of us," she said, "in coffee. I'll bet you can explain, can't you?"

"They're on a road trip," he said. "They play half their games at home in Memphis, and half the time they're in other cities."

"And you've been tagging along after them."

"That's right. I want to take my time, pick my spot. If I have to spend a few dollars on airline tickets, I figure that's my business. Because nobody said anything about being in a hurry on this one."

"No," she admitted. "If time is of the essence, nobody told me about it. I just thought you were gallivanting around, going to stamp dealers and all. Taking your eye off the ball, so to speak."

"So to speak," Keller said.

"So how can they play ball in Seattle, Keller? Doesn't it rain all the time? Or is it one of those stadiums with a lid on it?"

"A dome," he said.

"I stand corrected. And here's another question. What's Memphis got to do with fish?"

"Huh?"

"Tarpons," she said. "Fish. And there's Memphis, in the middle of the desert."

"Actually, it's on the Mississippi River."

"Spot any tarpons in the Mississippi River, Keller?"

"No."

"And you won't," she said, "unless that's where you stick Turnbull when you finally close the deal. It's a deep-sea fish, the tarpon, so why pick that name for the Memphis team? Why not call them the Gracelanders?"

"They moved," he explained.

"To Milwaukee," she said, "and then to Seattle, and God knows where they'll go next."

"No," he said. "The franchise moved. They started out as an expansion team, the Sarasota Tarpons, but they couldn't sell enough tickets, so a new owner took over and moved them to Memphis. Look at basketball, the Utah Jazz and the L.A. Lakers. What's Salt Lake City got to do with jazz, and when did Southern California get to be the Land of Ten Thousand Lakes?"

"The reason I don't follow sports," she said, "is it's too damn confusing. Isn't there a team called the Miami Heat? I hope they stay put. Imagine if they move to Buffalo."

Why had he called in the first place? Oh, right. "Dot," he said, "I was in the Tarpons' hotel earlier today, and I saw a guy."

"So?"

"A little guy," he said, "with a big nose, and one of those narrow heads that looks as though somebody put it in a vise."

"I heard about a guy once who used to do that to people."

"Well, I doubt that's what happened to this fellow, but that's the kind of face he had. He was sitting in the lobby reading a newspaper."

"Suspicious behavior like that, it's no wonder you noticed him."

"No, that's the thing," he said. "He's distinctive-looking, and he looked wrong. And I saw him just a couple of nights before in Milwaukee at this German restaurant."

"The famous German restaurant."

"I gather it is pretty famous, but that's not the point. He was in both places, and he was alone both times. I noticed him in Milwaukee because I was eating by myself, and feeling a little conspicuous about it, and I saw I wasn't the only lone diner, because there he was."

"You could have asked him to join you."

"He looked wrong there, too. He looked like a Broadway sharpie, out of an old movie. Looked like a weasel, wore a fedora. He could have been in *Guys and Dolls*, saying he's got the horse right here."

"I think I see where this is going."

"And what I think," he said, "is I'm not the only DH in the lineup . . . Hello? Dot?"

"I'm here," she said. "Just taking it all in. I don't know who the client is, the contract came through a broker, but what I do know is nobody seems to be getting antsy. So why would they hire somebody else? You're sure this guy's a hitter? Maybe he's a big fan, hates to miss a game, follows 'em all over the country."

"He looks wrong for the part, Dot."

"Could he be a private eye? Ballplayers cheat on their wives, don't they?"

"Everybody does, Dot."

"So some wife hired him, he's gathering divorce evidence."

"He looks too shady to be a private eye."

"I didn't know that was possible."

"He doesn't have that crooked-cop look private eyes have. He looks more like the kind of guy they used to arrest, and he'd bribe them to cut him loose. I think he's a hired gun, and not one from the A-list, either."

"Or he wouldn't look like that."

"Part of the job description," he said, "is you have to be able to pass in a crowd. And he's a real sore thumb."

"Maybe there's more than one person who wants our guy dead."

"Occurred to me."

"And maybe a second client hired a second hit man. You know, maybe taking your time's a good idea."

"Just what I was thinking."

"Because you could do something and find yourself in a mess because of the heat this ferret-faced joker stirs up. And if he's there with a job to do, and you stay in the background and let him do it, where's the harm? We collect no matter who pulls the trigger."

"So I'll bide my time."

"Why not? Drink some of that famous coffee. Get rained on by some of that famous rain. They have any stamp dealers in Seattle, Keller?"

"There must be. I know there's one in Tacoma."

"So go see him," she said. "Buy some stamps. Enjoy yourself."

"I collect worldwide, 1840 to 1949, and up to 1952 for British Commonwealth."

"In other words, the classics," said the dealer, a square-faced man who was wearing a striped tie with a plaid shirt. "The good stuff."

"But I've been thinking of adding a topic. Baseball."

"Good topic," the man said. "Most topics, you get bogged down in all these phony Olympics issues every little stamp-crazy country prints up to sell to collectors. Soccer's even worse, with the World Cup and all. There's less of that crap with baseball, on account of it's not an Olympic sport. I mean, what do they know about baseball in Guinea-Bissau?"

"I was at the game last night," Keller said.

"Mariners win for a change?"

"Beat the Tarpons."

"About time."

"Turnbull went two for four."

"Turnbull. He on the Mariners?"

"He's the Tarpons' DH."

"They brought in the DH," the man said, "I lost interest in the game. He went two for four, huh? Am I missing something here? Is that significant?"

"Well, I don't know that it's significant," Keller said, "but that puts him just five hits shy of three thousand, and he needs three home runs to reach the four hundred mark."

"You never know," the dealer said. "One of these days, St. Vincent-Grenadines may put his picture on a stamp. Well, what do you say? Do you want to see some baseball topicals?"

Keller shook his head. "I'll have to give it some more thought," he said, "before I start a whole new collection. How about Turkey? There's page after page of early issues where I've got nothing but spaces."

"You sit down," the dealer said, "and we'll see if we can't fill some of them for you."

From Seattle the Tarpons flew to Cleveland for three games at Jacobs Field, then down to Baltimore for four games in three days with the division-leading Orioles. Keller missed the last game against the Mariners and flew to Cleveland ahead of them, getting settled in and buying tickets for all three games. Jacobs Field was one of the new parks and an evident source of pride to the local fans, and the previous year they'd filled the stands more often than not, but this year the Indians weren't doing as well, and Keller had no trouble getting good seats.

Floyd Turnbull managed only one hit against the Indians, a scratch single in the first game. He went oh-for-three with a walk in game two, and rode the bench in the third game, the only one the Tarpons won. His replacement, a skinny kid just up from the minors, had two hits and drove in three runs.

"New kid beat us," said Keller's conversational partner du jour. He was a Cleveland fan and assumed Keller was, too. Keller, who'd bought an Indians cap for the series, had encouraged him in this belief. "Wish they'd stick with old Turnbull," the man went on.

"Close to three thousand hits," Keller said.

"Lots of hits and homers, but he never seems to beat you like this kid just did. Hits for the record book, not for the game—that's Floyd for you."

"Excuse me," Keller said. "I see somebody I better go say hello to."

It was the Broadway sharpie, wearing a Panama fedora with a bright red hatband. That made him easy to spot, but even without it he was hard to miss. Keller had picked him out of the crowd back in the third inning, checked now and then to make sure he was still in the same seat. But now the guy was in conversation with a woman, their heads close together, and she didn't look right for the part. The instant camaraderie of the ballpark notwithstanding, a woman who looked like her didn't figure to be discussing the subtleties of the double steal with a guy who looked like him.

She was tall and slender, and she bore herself regally.

She was wearing a suit, and at first glance you thought she'd come from the office, and then you decided she probably owned the company. If she belonged at a ballpark at all, it was in the sky boxes, not the general-admission seats.

What were they discussing with such urgency? Whatever it was, they were done talking about it before Keller could get close enough to listen in. They separated and headed off in different directions, and Keller tossed a mental coin and set out after the woman. He already knew where the man was staying, and what name he was using.

He tagged the woman to the Ritz-Carlton, which sort of figured. He'd gotten rid of his Indians cap en route, but he still wasn't dressed for the lobby of a five-star hotel, not in the khakis and polo shirt that were just fine for Jacobs Field.

Couldn't be helped. He went in, hoping to spot her in the lobby, but she wasn't there. Well, he could have a drink at the bar. Unless they had a dress code, he could nurse a beer and maybe keep an eye on the lobby without looking out of place. If she was settled in for the night he was out of luck, but maybe she'd just gone to her room to change, maybe she hadn't had dinner yet.

Better than that, as it turned out. He walked into the bar and there she was, all by herself at a corner table, smoking a cigarette in a holder—you didn't see that much anymore—and drinking what looked like a rust-colored cocktail in a stemmed glass. A manhattan or a Rob Roy, he figured. Something like that. Classy, like the woman herself, and slightly out-of-date.

Keller stopped at the bar for a bottle of Tuborg, carried it to the woman's table. Her eyes widened briefly at his approach, but otherwise nothing much showed on her face. Keller drew a chair for himself and sat down as if there was no question that he was welcome.

"I'm with the guy," he said.

"I don't know what you're talking about."

"No names, all right? Straw hat with a red band on it. You were talking to him, what, twenty minutes ago? You want to pretend I'm talking Greek, or do you want to come with me?"

"Where?"

"He needs to see you."

"But he just saw me!"

"Look, there's a lot I don't understand here," Keller said, not untruthfully. "I'm just an errand boy. He coulda come himself, but is that what you want? To be seen in public in your own hotel with Slansky?"

"Slansky?"

"I made a mistake there," Keller said, "using that name, which you wouldn't know him by. Forget I said that, will you?"

"But . . ."

"Far as that goes, *we* shouldn't spend too much time together. I'm going to walk out, and you finish your drink and sign the tab and then follow me. I'll be waiting out front in a blue Honda Accord."

"But . . ."

"Five minutes," he told her, and left.

CHAPTER FOUR

It took her more than five minutes, but under ten, and she got into the front seat of the Honda without any hesitation. He pulled out of the hotel lot and hit the button to lock her door.

While they drove around, ostensibly heading for a meeting with the man in the Panama hat (whose name wasn't Slansky, but so what?), Keller learned that Floyd Turnbull, who'd had an affair with this woman, had sweet-talked her into investing in a real estate venture of his. The way it was set up, she couldn't get her money out without a lengthy and expensive lawsuit—unless Turnbull died, in which case the partnership was automatically dissolved. Keller didn't try to follow the legal part. He got the gist of it, and that was enough. The way she spoke about Turnbull, he got the feeling she'd pay a lot to see him dead, even if there was nothing in it for her.

Funny how people tended not to like the guy.

And now Slansky had all the money in advance, and in return for that she had his sworn promise that Turnbull wouldn't have a pulse by the time the team got back to Memphis. She'd been after him to get it done in Cleveland, but he'd stalled until he'd gotten her to pay him the entire fee up front, and it looked as though he wouldn't do it until they were in Baltimore, but it really better happen in Baltimore, because that was the last stop before the Tarpons returned to Memphis for a long home stand, and—

Jesus, suppose the guy tried to save himself a trip to Baltimore?

"Here we go," he said and turned into a strip mall. All the stores were closed for the night, and the parking area was empty except for a delivery van and a Chevy that wouldn't go anywhere until somebody changed its right rear tire. Keller parked next to the Chevy and cut the engine.

"Around the back," he said, and opened the door for her and helped her out. He led her so that the Chevy screened them from the street. "It gets tricky here," he said and took her arm.

The man he'd called Slansky was staying at a budget motel off an interchange of I-71, where he'd registered as John Carpenter. Keller went and knocked on his door, but that would have been too easy.

Hell.

The Tarpons were staying at a Marriott again, unless they were already on their way to Baltimore. But they'd just finished a night game, and they had a night game tomorrow, so maybe they'd stay over and fly out in the morning. He drove over to the Marriott and walked through the lobby to the bar, and on his way he spotted the shortstop and a middle reliever. So they were staying over, unless someone in the front office had cut those two players, and that seemed unlikely, as they didn't look depressed.

He found two more Tarpons in the bar, where he stayed long enough to drink a beer. One of the pair, the second-string catcher, gave Keller a nod of recognition, and that gave him a turn. Had he been hanging around enough for the players to think of him as a familiar face?

He finished his beer and left. As he was on his way out of the lobby, Floyd Turnbull was on his way in, and not looking very happy. And what did he have to be happy about? A string bean named Anliot had taken his job away from him for the evening, and had won the game for the Tarpons in the process. No wonder Turnbull looked like he wanted to kick somebody's ass, and preferably Anliot's. He also looked to be headed for his room, and Keller figured the man was ready to call it a night.

Keller went back to the budget motel. When his knock again went unanswered, he found a pay phone and called the desk. A woman told him that Mr. Carpenter had checked out.

And gone where? He couldn't have caught a flight to Baltimore, not at this hour. Maybe he was driving. Keller had seen his car, and it looked too old and beat-up to be a rental. Maybe he owned it, and he'd drive all night, from Cleveland to Baltimore.

Keller flew to Baltimore and was in his seat at Camden Yards for the first pitch. Floyd Turnbull wasn't in the line-up, they'd benched him and had Graham Anliot slotted as DH. Anliot got two singles and a walk in his first three trips to the plate, and Keller didn't stick around to see how he ended the evening. He left with the Tarpons coming to bat in the top of the seventh, and leading by four runs.

The clerk at Ace Hardware rang up Keller's purchases—a roll of picture-hanging wire, a packet of screw eyes, a packet of assorted picture hooks—and came to a logical conclusion. With a smile, he said, "Gonna hang a pitcher?"

"A DH," Keller said.

"Huh?"

"Sorry," he said, recovering. "I was thinking of something else. Yeah, right. Hang a picture."

In his motel room, Keller wished he'd bought a pair of wire-cutting pliers. In their absence, he measured out a three-foot length of the picture-hanging wire and bent it back on itself until the several strands frayed and broke. He fashioned a loop at each end, then put the unused portion of the wire back in its box, to be discarded down the next handy storm drain. He'd already rid himself of the screw eyes and the picture hooks.

He didn't know where Slansky was staying, hadn't seen him at the game the previous evening. But he knew the sort of motel the man favored and figured he'd pick one near the ballpark. Would he use the same name when he signed in? Keller couldn't think of a reason why not, and evidently neither could Slansky; when he called the Sweet Dreams Motel on Key Highway, a pleasant young woman with a Gujarati accent told him that yes, they did have a guest named John Carpenter, and would he like her to ring the room?

"Don't bother," he said. "I want it to be a surprise."

And it was. When Slansky—Keller couldn't help it, he thought of the man as Slansky, even though it was a name he'd made up for the guy himself—when Slansky got in his car, there was Keller, sitting in the backseat.

The man stiffened just long enough for Keller to tell that his presence was known. Then, smoothly, Slansky moved to fit the key in the ignition. Let him drive away? No, because Keller's own car was parked here at the Sweet

28

Dreams, and he'd only have to walk all the way back.

And the longer Slansky was around, the more chances he had to reach for a gun or crash the car.

"Hold it right there, Slansky," he said.

"You got the wrong guy," the man said, his voice a mix of relief and desperation. "Whoever Slansky is, I ain't him."

"No time to explain," Keller said, because there wasn't, and why bother? Simpler to use the picture-hook wire as he'd used it so often in the past, simpler and easier. And if Slansky went out thinking he was being killed by mistake, well, maybe that would be a comfort to him.

Or maybe not. Keller, his hands through the loops in the wire, yanking hard, couldn't see that it made much difference.

CHAPTER FIVE

"**A**www, hell," said the fat guy a row behind Keller, as the Oriole center fielder came down from his leap with nothing in his glove but his own hand. On the mound, the Baltimore pitcher shook his head the way pitchers do at such a moment, and Floyd Turnbull rounded first base and settled into his home run trot.

"I thought we caught a break when the new kid got hurt," the fat guy said, "on account of he was hotter'n a pistol, not that he won't cool down some when the rest of the league figures out how to pitch to him. He'll be out what, a couple of weeks?"

"That's what I hear," Keller said. "He broke a toe."

"Got his foot stepped on? Is that how it happened?"

"That's what they're saying," Keller said. "He was in a crowded elevator, and nobody knows exactly what happened, whether somebody stepped on his foot or he'd injured it earlier and only noticed it when he put a foot wrong. They figure he'll be good as new inside of a month."

"Well, he's not hurting us now," the man said, "but Turnbull's picking up the slack. He really got ahold of that one."

"Number three ninety-eight," Keller said.

"That a fact? Two shy of four hundred, and he's getting close to the mark for base hits, isn't he?"

"Four more and he'll have three thousand."

"Well, the best of luck to the guy," the man said, "but does he have to get 'em here?"

"I figure he'll hit the mark at home in Memphis."

"Fine with me. Which one? Hits? Homers?"

"Maybe both," Keller said.

"You didn't bring me one," the man said.

It was the same fellow he'd sat next to the first time he saw the Tarpons play, and that somehow convinced Keller he was going to see history made. At his first at bat in the second inning, Floyd Turnbull had hit a grounder that had eyes, somehow picking out a path between the first and second basemen. It had taken a while, the Tarpons were four games into their home stand, playing the first of three with the Yankees, and Turnbull, who'd been a disappointment against Tampa Bay, was nevertheless closing in on the elusive numbers. He had 399 home runs, and that scratch single in the second inning was hit #2999.

"I got the last hot-dog," Keller said, "and I'd offer to share it with you, but I never share."

"I don't blame you," the fellow said. "It's a selfish world."

Turnbull walked in the bottom of the fourth and struck out on three pitches two innings later, but Keller didn't care. It was a perfect night to watch a ball game, and he enjoyed the banter with his companion as much as the drama on the field. The game was a close one, seesawing back and forth, and the Tarpons were two runs down when Turnbull came up in the bottom of the ninth with runners on first and third.

On the first pitch, the man on first broke for second. The throw was high and he slid in under the tag.

"Shit," Keller's friend said. "Puts the tying run in scoring position, so you got to do it, but it takes the bat out of

31

Turnbull's hands, because now they have to put him on, set up the double play."

And, if the Yankees walked Turnbull, the Tarpon manager would lift him for a pinch runner.

"I was hoping we'd see something special," the man said, "but it looks like we'll have to wait a night or two. . . . Well, what do you know? Torre's letting Rivera pitch to him."

But the Yankee closer only had to throw one pitch. The instant Turnbull swung, you knew the ball was gone. So did Bernie Williams, who just turned and watched the ball sail past him into the upper deck, and Turnbull, who watched from the batter's box, then jumped into the air, pumping both fists in triumph, before setting out on his circuit of the bases. The whole stadium knew, and the stands erupted with cheers.

Four hundred homers, three thousand hits—and the game was over, and the Tarps had won.

"Storybook finish," Keller's friend said, and Keller couldn't have put it better.

"Try that tea," Dot said. "See if it's all right."

Keller took a sip of iced tea and sat back in the slat-backed rocking chair. "It's fine," he said.

"I was beginning to wonder," she said, "if I was ever going to see you again. The last time I heard from you there was another hitter on the case, or at least that's what you thought. I started thinking maybe you were the one he was after, and maybe he took you out."

"It was the other way around," Keller said.

"Oh?"

"I didn't want him getting in the way," he explained,

"and I figured the woman who hired him was a loose cannon. So she slipped and fell and broke her neck in a strip mall parking lot in Cleveland, and the guy she hired—"

"Got his head caught in a vise?"

"That was before I met him. He got all tangled up in some picture wire in Baltimore."

"And Floyd Turnbull died of natural causes," Dot said. "Had the biggest night of his life, and it turned out to be the last night of his life."

"Ironic," Keller said.

"That's the word Peter Jennings used. Celebrated, drank too much, went to bed, and choked to death on his own vomit. They had a medical expert on who explained how that happens more often than you'd think. You pass out, and you get nauseated and vomit without recovering consciousness, and if you're sleeping on your back, you aspirate the stuff and choke on it."

"And never know what hit you."

"Of course not," Dot said, "or you'd do something about it. But I never believe in natural causes, Keller, when you're in the picture. Except to the extent that you're a natural cause of death all by yourself."

"Well," he said.

"How'd you do it?"

"I just helped nature a little," he said. "I didn't have to get him drunk, he did that by himself. I followed him home, and he was all over the road. I was afraid he was going to have an accident."

"So?"

"Well, suppose he just gets banged around a little? And winds up in the hospital? Anyway, he made it home all right. I gave him time to go to sleep, and he didn't make it

33

all the way to bed, just passed out on the couch." He shrugged. "I held a rag over his mouth, and I induced vomiting, and—"

"How? You made him drink warm soapy water?"

"Put a knee in his stomach. It worked, and the vomit didn't have anywhere to go, because his mouth was covered. Are you sure you want to hear all this?"

"Not as sure as I was a minute ago, but don't worry about it. He breathed it in and choked on it, end of story. And then?"

"And then I got out of there. What do you mean, 'and then?' "

"That was a few days ago."

"Oh," he said "Well, I went to see a few stamp dealers. Memphis is a good city for stamps. And I wanted to see the rest of the series with the Yankees. The Tarpons all wore black armbands for Turnbull, but it didn't do them any good. The Yankees won the last two games."

"Hurray for our side," she said. "You want to tell me about it, Keller?"

"Tell you about it? I just told you about it."

"You were gone over a month," she said, "doing what you could have done in two days, and I thought you might want to explain it to me."

"The other hitter," he began, but she was shaking her head.

"Don't give me 'the other hitter.' You could have closed the sale before the other hitter ever turned up."

"You're right," he admitted. "Dot, it was the numbers."

"The numbers?"

"Four hundred home runs," he said. "Three thousand hits. I wanted him to do it."

"Cooperstown," she said.

"I don't even know if the numbers'll get him into the Hall of Fame," he said, "and I don't really care about that part of it. I wanted him to get in the record books, four hundred homers and three thousand hits, and I wanted to be able to say I'd been there to see him do it."

"And to put him away."

"Well," he said, "I don't have to think about that part of it."

She didn't say anything for a while. Then she asked him if he wanted more iced tea, and he said he was fine, and she asked him if he'd bought some nice stamps for his collection.

"I got quite a few from Turkey," he said. "That was a weak spot in my collection, and now it's a good deal stronger."

"I guess that's important."

"I don't know," he said. "It gets harder and harder to say what's important and what isn't. Dot, I spent a month watching baseball. There are worse ways to spend your time."

"I'm sure there are, Keller," she said. "And sooner or later I'm sure you'll find them."

KELLER
BY A NOSE

CHAPTER SIX

"So who do you like in the third?"

Keller had to hear the question a second time before he realized it was meant for him. He turned, and a little guy in a Mets warm-up jacket was standing there, a querulous expression on his lumpy face.

Who did he like in the third? He hadn't been paying any attention and was stuck for a response. This didn't seem to bother the guy, who answered the question himself.

"The Two horse is odds-on, so you can't make any money betting on him. And the Five horse might have an outside chance, but he never finished well on turf. The Three, he's okay at five furlongs, but at this distance? So I got to say I agree with you."

Keller hadn't said a word. What was there to agree with?

"You're like me," the fellow went on. "Not like one of these degenerates, has to bet every race, can't go five minutes without some action. Me, sometimes I'll come here, spend the whole day, not put two dollars down the whole time. I just like to breathe some fresh air and watch those babies run."

Keller, who hadn't intended to say anything, couldn't help himself. He said, "Fresh air?"

"Since they gave the smokers a room of their own," the little man said, "it's not so bad in here. Excuse me, I see somebody I oughta say hello to."

He walked off, and the next time Keller noticed him the guy was at the ticket window, placing a bet. Fresh air, Keller thought. Watch those babies run. It sounded good until you took note of the fact that those babies were out at Belmont, running around a track in the open air, while Keller and the little man and sixty or eighty other people were jammed into a Midtown storefront, watching the whole thing on television.

Keller, holding a copy of the *Racing Form*, looked warily around the OTB parlor. It was on Lexington at Forty-fifth Street, just up from Grand Central, and not much more than a five-minute walk from his First Avenue apartment, but this was his first visit. In fact, as far as he could tell, it was the first time he had ever noticed the place. He must have walked past it hundreds if not thousands of times over the years, but he'd somehow never registered it, which showed the extent of his interest in offtrack betting.

Or on-track betting, or any betting at all. Keller had been to the track three times in his entire life. The first time he'd placed a couple of small bets—two dollars here, five dollars there. His horses had run out of the money, and he'd felt stupid. The other times he hadn't even put a bet down.

He'd been to gambling casinos on several occasions, generally work-related, and he'd never felt comfortable there. It was clear that a lot of people found the atmosphere exciting, but as far as Keller was concerned it was just sensory overload. All that noise, all those flashing lights, all those people chasing all that money. Keller, feeding a slot machine or playing a hand of blackjack to fit in, just wanted to go to his room and lie down.

Well, he thought, people were different. A lot of them clearly got something out of gambling. What some of them got, to be sure, was the attention of Keller or somebody like him. They'd lost money they couldn't pay, or stolen money to gamble with, or had found some other way to make somebody seriously unhappy with them. Enter Keller, and, sooner rather than later, exit the gambler.

For most gamblers, though, it was a hobby, a harmless pastime. And just because Keller couldn't figure out what they got out of it, that didn't mean there was nothing there. Keller, looking around the OTB parlor at all those woulda-coulda-shoulda faces, knew there was nothing feigned about their enthusiasm. They were really into it, whatever it was.

And, he thought, who was he to say their enthusiasm was misplaced? One man's meat, after all, was another man's *poisson*. These fellows, all wrapped up in *Racing Form* gibberish, would be hard put to make sense out of his Scott catalog. If they caught a glimpse of Keller, hunched over one of his stamp albums, a magnifying glass in one hand and a pair of tongs in the other, they'd most likely figure he was out of his mind. Why play with little bits of perforated paper when you could bet money on horses?

"They're off!"

And so they were. Keller looked at the wall-mounted television screen and watched those babies run.

It started with stamps.

He collected worldwide, from the first postage stamps, Great Britain's Penny Black and Two-Penny Blue of 1840, up to shortly after the end of World War Two. (Just when he stopped depended upon the country. He collected

41

most countries through 1949, but his British Empire issues stopped at 1952, with the death of George VI. The most recent stamp in his collection was over fifty years old.)

When you collected the whole world, your albums held spaces for many more stamps than you would ever be able to acquire. Keller knew he would never completely fill any of his albums, and he found this not frustrating but comforting. No matter how long he lived or how much money he got, he would always have more stamps to look for. You tried to fill in the spaces, of course—that was the point—but it was the trying that brought you pleasure, not the accomplishment.

Consequently, he never absolutely had to have any particular stamp. He shopped carefully, and he chose the stamps he liked, and he didn't spend more than he could afford. He'd saved money over the years, he'd even reached a point where he'd been thinking about retiring, but when he got back into stamp collecting his hobby gradually ate up his retirement fund—which, all things considered, was fine with him. Why would he want to retire? If he retired, he'd have to stop buying stamps.

As it was, he was in a perfect position. He was never desperate for money, but he could always find a use for it. If Dot came up with a whole string of jobs for him, he wound up putting a big chunk of the proceeds into his stamp collection. If business slowed down, no problem— he'd make small purchases from the dealers who shipped him stamps on approval, send some small checks to others who mailed him their monthly lists, but hold off on anything substantial until business picked up.

It worked fine. Until the Bulger & Calthorpe auction catalog came along and complicated everything.

Bulger & Calthorpe were stamp auctioneers based in Omaha. They advertised regularly in *Linn's* and the other stamp publications, and traveled extensively to examine collectors' holdings. Three or four times a year they would rent a hotel suite in downtown Omaha and hold an auction, and for a few years now Keller had been receiving their well-illustrated catalogs. Their catalog featured an extensive collection from France and the French colonies, and Keller leafed through it on the off chance that he might find himself in Omaha around that time. He was thinking of something else when he hit the first page of color photographs, and whatever it was, he forgot it forever.

Martinique #2. And, right next to it, Martinique #17.

On the screen, the Two horse led wire to wire, winning by four and a half lengths. "Look at that," the little man said, once again at Keller's elbow. "What did I tell you? Pays three-fucking-forty for a two-dollar ticket. Where's the sense in that?"

"Did you bet him?"

"I didn't bet on him," the man said, "and I didn't bet against him. What I had, I had the Eight horse to place, which is nothing but a case of getting greedy, because look what he did, will you? He came in third, right behind the Five horse, so if I bet him to show, or if I semiwheeled the trifecta, playing a Two-Five-Eight and a Two-Eight-Five . . ."

Woulda-coulda-shoulda, thought Keller.

CHAPTER SEVEN

He'd spent half an hour with the Bulger & Calthorpe catalog, reading the descriptions of the two Martinique lots, seeing what else was on offer, and returning more than once for a further look at Martinique #2 and Martinique #17. He interrupted himself to check the balance in his bank account, frowned, pulled out the album that ran from Leeward Islands to Netherlands, opened it to Martinique, and looked first at the couple hundred stamps he had and then at the two empty spaces, spaces designed to hold—what else?—Martinique #2 and Martinique #17.

He closed the album but didn't put it away, not yet, and he picked up the phone and called Dot.

"I was wondering," he said, "if anything came in."

"Like what, Keller?"

"Like work," he said.

"Was your phone off the hook?"

"No," he said. "Did you try to call me?"

"If I had," she said, "I'd have reached you, since your phone wasn't off the hook. And if a job came in I'd have called, the way I always do. But instead you called me."

"Right."

"Which leads me to wonder why."

"I could use the work," he said. "That's all."

"You worked when? A month ago?"

"Closer to two."

"You took a little trip, went like clockwork, smooth as silk. Client paid me and I paid you, and if that's not silken clockwork I don't know what is. Say, is there a new woman in the picture, Keller? Are you spending serious money on earrings again?"

"Nothing like that."

"Then why would you . . . Keller, it's stamps, isn't it?"

"I could use a few dollars," he said. "That's all."

"So you decided to be proactive and call me. Well, I'd be proactive myself, but who am I gonna call? We can't go looking for our kind of work, Keller. It has to come to us."

"I know that."

"We ran an ad once, remember? And remember how it worked out?" He remembered and made a face. "So we'll wait," she said, "until something comes along. You want to help it a little on a metaphysical level, try thinking proactive thoughts."

There was a horse in the fourth race named Going Postal. That didn't have anything to do with stamps, Keller knew, but was a reference to the propensity of disgruntled postal employees to exercise their Second Amendment rights by bringing a gun to work, often with dramatic results. Still, the name was guaranteed to catch the eye of a philatelist.

"What about the Six horse?" Keller asked the little man, who consulted in turn the *Racing Form* and the tote board on the television.

"Finished in the money three times in his last five starts," he reported, "but now he's moving up in class. Likes to come from behind, and there's early speed here, because the Two horse and the Five horse both like to get out in front." There was more that Keller couldn't follow, and then the man said, "Morning line had him at twelve-to-one, and he's up to eighteen-to-one now, so the good news is he'll pay a nice price, but the bad news is nobody thinks he's got much of a chance."

Keller got in line. When it was his turn, he bet two dollars on Going Postal to win.

Keller didn't know much about Martinique beyond the fact that it was a French possession in the West Indies, and he knew the postal authorities had stopped issuing special stamps for the place a while ago. It was now officially a department of France, and used regular French stamps. The French did that to avoid being called colonialists. By designating Martinique a part of France, the same as Normandy or Provence, they obscured the fact that the island was full of black people who worked in the fields, fields that were owned by white people who lived in Paris.

Keller had never been to Martinique—or to France, as far as that went—and had no special interest in the place. It was a funny thing about stamps; you didn't need to be interested in a country to be interested in the country's stamps. And he couldn't say what was so special about the stamps of Martinique, except that one way or another he had accumulated quite a few of them, and that made him seek out more, and now, remarkably, he had all but two.

The two he lacked were among the colony's first issues, created by surcharging stamps originally printed for general use in France's overseas empire. The first, #2 in the Scott catalog, was a twenty-centime stamp surcharged "MARTINIQUE" and "5c" in black. The second, #17, was similar: "MARTINIQUE / 15c" on a four-centime stamp.

According to the catalog, #17 was worth $7,500 mint, $7,000 used. #2 was listed at $11,000, mint or used. The listings were in italics, which was Scott's way of indicating that the value was difficult to determine precisely.

Keller bought most of his stamps at around half the Scott valuation. Stamps with defects went much cheaper, and stamps that were particularly fresh and well centered could command a premium. With a true rarity, however, at a well-publicized auction, it was very hard to guess what price might be realized. Bulger & Calthorpe described #2—it was lot #2144 in their sales catalog—as "mint with part OG, F-VF, the nicest specimen we've seen of this genuine rarity." The description of #17—lot #2153—was almost as glowing. Both stamps were accompanied by Philatelic Foundation certificates attesting that they were indeed what they purported to be. The auctioneers estimated that #2 would bring $15,000, and pegged the other at $10,000.

But those were just estimates. They might wind up selling for quite a bit less, or a good deal more.

Keller wanted them.

Going Postal got off to a slow start, but Keller knew that was to be expected. The horse liked to come from behind. And in fact he did rally, and was running third at one point, fading in the stretch and finishing seventh in a field of nine. As the little man had predicted, the Two and Five horses had both gone out in front, and had both been overtaken, though not by Going Postal. The winner, a dappled horse named Doggen Katz, paid $19.20.

"Son of a bitch," the little man said. "I almost had him. The only thing I did wrong was decide to bet on a different horse."

What he needed, Keller decided, was fifty thousand dollars. That way he could go as high as twenty-five for #2 and fifteen for #17 and, after buyer's commission, still have a few dollars left for expenses and other stamps.

Was he out of his mind? How could a little piece of perforated paper less than an inch square be worth $25,000? How could two of them be worth a man's life?

He thought about it and decided it was just a question of degree. Unless you planned to use it to mail a letter, any expenditure for a stamp was basically irrational. If you could swallow a gnat, why gag at a camel? A hobby, he suspected, was irrational by definition. As long as you kept it in proportion, you were all right.

And he was managing that. He could, if he wanted, mortgage his apartment. Bankers would stand in line to lend him fifty grand, since the apartment was worth ten times that figure. They wouldn't ask him what he wanted the money for, either, and he'd be free to spend every dime of it on the two Martinique stamps.

He didn't consider it, not for a moment. It would be nuts, and he knew it. But what he did with a windfall was something else, and it didn't matter, anyway, because there wasn't going to be any windfall. You didn't need a weatherman, he thought, to note that the wind was not blowing. There was no wind, and there would be no windfall, and someone else could mount the Martinique overprints in his album. It was a shame, but—

The phone rang.

Dot said, "Keller, I just made a pitcher of iced tea. Why don't you come up here and help me drink it?"

In the fifth race, there was a horse called Happy Trigger and another called Hit the Boss. If Going Postal had resonated with his hobby, these seemed to suggest his profession. He mentioned them to the little fellow. "I sort of like these two," he said, "but I don't know which one I like better."

"Wheel them," the man said and explained that Keller should buy two exacta tickets, Four-Seven and Seven-Four. That way Keller would only collect if the two horses finished first and second. But, since the tote board indicated long odds on each of them, the potential payoff was a big one.

"What would I have to bet?" Keller asked him. "Four dollars? Because I've only been betting two dollars a race."

"You want to keep it to two dollars," his friend said, "just bet it one way. Thing is, how are you going to feel if you bet the Four-Seven and they finish Seven-Four?"

"It's right up your alley," Dot told him. "Comes through another broker, so there's a good solid firewall between us and the client. And the broker's reliable, and if the client was a corporate bond he'd be rated triple-A."

"What's the catch?"

"Keller," she said, "what makes you think there's a catch?"

"I don't know," he said. "But there is, isn't there?"

She frowned. "The only catch," she said, "if you want to call it that, is there might not be a job at all."

"I'd call that a catch."

49

"I suppose."

"If there's no job," he said, "why did the client call the broker, and why did the broker call you, and what am I doing out here?"

Dot pursed her lips, sighed. "There's this horse," she said.

CHAPTER EIGHT

The fifth race was reasonably exciting. Bunk Bed Betty, a big brown horse with a black mane, led all the way, only to be challenged in the stretch and overtaken at the wire by a thirty-to-one shot named Hypertension.

Hit the Boss was dead last, which made him the only horse that Happy Trigger beat.

Keller's new friend got very excited toward the end of the race, and showed a ten-dollar win ticket on Hypertension. "Oh, look at that," he said, when they posted the payoff. "Gets me even for the day, plus yesterday and the day before. That was Alvie Jurado on Hypertension, and didn't he ride a gorgeous race there?"

"It was exciting," Keller allowed.

"A lot more exciting with ten bucks on that sweetie's nose. Sorry about your exacta. I guess it cost you four bucks."

Keller gave a shrug that he hoped was ambiguous. In the end, he'd been uncomfortable betting four dollars and unable to decide which way to bet his usual two dollars. So he hadn't bet anything. There was nothing wrong with that, as a matter of fact he'd saved himself two dollars, or maybe four, but he'd feel like a piker admitting as much to a man who'd just won over three hundred dollars.

"The horse's name is Kissimmee Dudley," Dot told him, "and he's running in the seventh race at Belmont Saturday.

It's the feature race, and the word is that Dudley hasn't got a prayer."

"I don't know much about horses."

"They've got four legs," she said, "and if the one you bet on comes in ahead of the others, you make money. That's as much as I know about them, but I know something about Kissimmee Dudley. Our client thinks he's going to win."

"I thought you said he didn't have a prayer."

"That's the word. Our client doesn't see it that way."

"Oh?"

"Evidently Dudley's a better horse than anybody realizes," she said, "and they've been holding him back, waiting for the right race. That way they'll get long odds and be able to clean up. And, just so nothing goes wrong, the other jockeys are getting paid to make sure they don't finish ahead of Dudley."

"The race is fixed," Keller said.

"That's the plan."

"But?"

"But a plan is what things don't always go according to, Keller, which is probably a good thing, because otherwise the phone would never ring. You want some more iced tea?"

"No thanks."

"They'll have the race on Saturday, and Dudley'll run. And if he wins you get two thousand dollars."

"For what?"

"For standing by. For making yourself available."

"I think I get it," he said. "And if Kissimmee Dudley should happen to lose—where'd they come up with a name like that, do you happen to know?"

"Not a clue."

"If he loses," Keller said, "I suppose I have work to do."

She nodded.

"The jockey who beats him?"

"Is toast," she said, "and you're the toaster."

None of the horses in the sixth race had a name that meant anything to Keller. Then again, picking them by name hadn't done him much good so far. This time he looked at the odds. A long shot wouldn't win, he decided, and a favorite wouldn't pay enough to make it worthwhile, so maybe the answer was to pick something in the middle. The Five horse, Mogadishy, was pegged at six-to-one.

He got in line, thinking. Of course, sometimes a long shot came in. Take the preceding race, for instance, with its big payoff for Keller's OTB buddy. There was a long shot in this race, and it would pay a lot more than the twelve bucks he'd win on his six-to-one shot.

On the other hand, no matter what horse he bet on, the return on his two-dollar bet wasn't going to make any real difference to him. And it would be nice to cash a winning ticket for a change.

"Sir?"

He put down his two dollars and bet the odds-on favorite to show.

Dot lived in White Plains, in a big old Victorian house on Taunton Place. She gave him a ride to the train station, and a little over an hour later he was back in his apartment, looking once again at the Bulger & Calthorpe catalog.

If Kissimmee Dudley ran and lost, he'd have a job to do. And his fee for the job would be just enough to fill the two spaces in his album. And, since the horse was racing at Belmont, it stood to reason that all of the jockeys lived within easy commuting distance of the Long Island race-track. Keller wouldn't have to get on a plane to find his man.

If Kissimmee Dudley won, Keller got to keep the two-thousand-dollar standby fee. That was a decent amount of money for not doing a thing, and there were times when he'd have been happy to see it play out that way.

But this wasn't one of those times. He really wanted those stamps. If the horse lost, well, he'd go out and earn them. But what if the damned horse won?

The sixth race ended with Pass the Gas six lengths ahead of the field. Keller cashed his ticket and ran into his friend, who'd been talking with a fellow who bore a superficial resemblance to Jerry Orbach.

"Saw you in line to get paid," the little man said. "What did you have, the exacta or the trifecta?"

"I don't really understand those fancy bets," Keller admitted. "I just put my money on Pass the Gas."

"Paid even money, didn't he? That's not so bad."

"I had him to show."

"Well, if you had enough of a bet on him—"

"Just two dollars."

"So you got back two-twenty," the man said.

"I just felt like winning," Keller said.

"Well," the man said, "you won."

*

54

He'd put down the catalog, picked up the phone. When Dot answered he said, "I was thinking. If that Dudley horse wins, the client wins his bet and I don't have any work to do."

"Right."

"But if one of the other jockeys crosses him up—"

"It's the last time he'll ever do it."

"Well," he said, "why would he do it? The jockey, I mean. What would be the point?"

"Does it matter?"

"I'm just trying to understand it," he said. "I mean, I could understand if it was boxing. Like in the movies. They want the guy to throw a fight. But he can't do it, something in him recoils at the very idea, and he has to go on and win the fight, even if it means he'll get his legs broken."

"And never play the piano again," Dot said. "I think I saw that movie, Keller."

"All the boxing movies are like that, except the ones with Sylvester Stallone running up flights of steps. But how would that apply with horses?"

"I don't know," she said. "It's been years since I saw *National Velvet*."

"If you were a jockey, and they paid you to throw a race, and you didn't—I mean, where's the percentage in it?"

"You could bet on yourself."

"You'd make more money betting on Kissimmee Dudley. He's the long shot, right?"

"That's a point."

"And that way nobody'd have a reason to take out a contract on you, either."

"Another point," Dot said, "and if the jockeys are all as

55

reasonable as you and I, Keller, you're not going to see a dime beyond the two grand. But they're very small."

"The jockeys?"

"Uh-huh. Short and scrawny little bastards, every last one of them. Who the hell knows what somebody like that is going to do?"

Keller's friend was short enough to be a jockey, but a long way from scrawny. Facially, he looked a little like Jerry Orbach. It was beginning to dawn on Keller that everybody in the OTB parlor, even the blacks and the Asians, looked a little like Jerry Orbach. It was sort of a generic horseplayer look, and they all had it.

"Kissimmee Dudley," Keller said. "Where'd somebody come up with a name like that?"

The little man consulted his *Racing Form*. "By Florida Cracker out of Dud Avocado," he said. "Kissimmee's in Florida, isn't it?"

"Is it?"

"I think so." The fellow shrugged. "The name's the least of that horse's problems. You take a look at his form?"

The man reeled off a string of sentences, and Keller just let the words wash over him. If he tried to follow it he'd only wind up feeling stupid. Well, so what? How many of these Jerry Orbach clones would know what to do with a perforation gauge?

"Look at the morning line," the man went on. "Hell, look at the tote board. Old Dudley's up there at forty-to-one."

"That means he doesn't have a chance?"

"A long shot'll come in once in a while," the man

56

allowed. "Look at Hypertension. With him, though, his past performance charts showed he had a chance. A slim one, but slim's better than no chance at all."

"And Kissimmee Dudley? No chance at all?"

"He'd need a tailwind and a whole lot of luck," the man said, "before he could rise to the level of no chance at all."

Keller slipped away, and when he came back from the ticket window his friend asked him what horse he'd bet on. Keller's response was mumbled, and the man had to ask him to repeat it.

"Kissimmee Dudley," he said.

"That right?"

"I know what you said, and I suppose you're right, but I just had a feeling."

"A hunch," the man said.

"Sort of, yes."

"And you're a man on a lucky streak, aren't you? I mean, you just won twenty cents betting the favorite to show."

The line was meant to be sarcastic, but something funny happened; by the time the man got to the end of the sentence, his manner had somehow changed. Keller was wondering what to make of it—had he just been insulted or not?

"The trick," the fellow said, "is doing the wrong thing at the right time." He went away and came back, and told Keller he probably ought to have his head examined, but what the hell.

"Kissimmee Dudley," he said, savoring each syllable. "I can't believe I bet on that animal. Only way he's gonna win the seventh race is if he was entered in the sixth, but it'll be some sweet payoff if he does. Not forty-to-one, though. Price is down to thirty-to-one."

"That's too bad," Keller said.

"Except it's a good sign, because it means some late bets are coming in on the horse. You see a horse drop just before post time from, say, five-to-one to three-to-one, that's a good sign." He shrugged. "When you start at forty-to-one, you need more than good signs. You need a rocket up your ass, either that or you need all the other horses to drop dead."

CHAPTER NINE

Keller wasn't sure what to watch for. He knew what you did to get your horse to run faster. You hit him with the whip, and dug your heels into his flanks.

But suppose you wanted to slow him down? You could sit back in the saddle and yank on the reins, but wouldn't that be a little on the obvious side? Could you just hold off on the whip and cool it a little with the heel-digging? Would that be enough to keep your mount from edging out Kissimmee Dudley?

The horses were entering the starting gate, and he picked out Dudley and decided he looked like a winner. But then they all looked like winners to Keller, big well-bred horses, some taking their positions without a fuss, others showing a little spirit and giving their riders a hard time, but all of them sooner or later going where they were supposed to go.

Two of the jockeys were girls, Keller noticed, including the one riding the second favorite. Except you were probably supposed to call them women, you had to stop calling them girls these days around the time they entered kindergarten, from what Keller could tell. Still, when they were jockey-size, it seemed a stretch to call them women. Was he being sexist? Maybe, or maybe he was being sizeist, or heightist. He wasn't sure.

"They're off!"

And so they were, bursting out of the starting gate.

Neither of the girl jockeys was riding Kissimmee Dudley, so if one of them won, well, she'd live to regret it, albeit briefly. Some people in Keller's line of work didn't like to take out women, while others were supposed to get a special satisfaction out of it. Keller didn't care one way or the other. He wasn't a sexist when it came to business, although he wasn't sure that was enough to make him a hero in the eyes of the National Organization for Women.

"Will you look at that!"

Keller had been looking at the screen but without registering what he was seeing. Now he realized that Kissimmee Dudley was out in front, with a good lead on the rest of the field.

Keller's little friend was urging him on. "Oh, you beauty," he said. "Oh, run, you son of a bitch. Oh, yes. Oh, yes!"

Were any of the horses being held back? If so, Keller couldn't see it. If he didn't know better, he'd swear Kissimmee Dudley was simply outrunning all of the other horses, proving himself to be superior to the competition.

But wait a damn minute. That piebald horse—what did he think he was doing? Why was he gaining ground on Dudley?

"No!" cried the little man. "Where'd the Two horse come from? It's that fucking Alvie Jurado. Fade, you cocksucker! Die, will you? Come on, Dudley!"

The guy had liked Jurado well enough when he was making money for him on Hypertension. Now, riding a horse called Steward's Folly, he'd become the enemy. Maybe, Keller thought, the jockey was just trying to make it look good. Maybe he'd ease up at the very end, settling for the place money and avoiding any suspicion that he'd thrown the race.

But it was a hell of a show Jurado was putting on, standing up in the stirrups, flailing away with the whip, apparently doing everything he possibly could to get Steward's Folly to the wire ahead of Kissimmee Dudley.

"It's Kissimmee Dudley and Steward's Folly," the announcer cried. "Steward's Folly and Kissimmee Dudley. They're neck and neck, nose to nose as they hit the wire—"

"Shit on toast," Keller's friend said.

"Who won?"

"Who fucking knows? See? It's a photo finish." And indeed the word *photo* flashed on and off on the television screen. "Son of a *bitch*. Where did that fucking Jurado come from?"

"He gained a lot of ground in a hurry," Keller said.

"The little prick. Now we have to wait for the photo. I wish they'd hurry. See, I really got behind that hunch of yours." He showed a ticket, and Keller leaned over and squinted at it.

"A hundred dollars?"

"On the nose," the little man said, "plus I got him wheeled in the five-dollar exacta. You got a hunch, and I bet a bunch. And he went off at twenty-eight to one, and if it's a Six-Two exacta with him and Steward's Folly, Jesus, I'm rich. I'm fucking rich. And you got two bucks on him yourself, so you'll win yourself fifty-six dollars. Unless you went and played him to show, which would explain why you're so calm, 'cause it'd be the same to you if he comes in first or second. Is that what you went and did?"

"Not exactly," Keller said and fished out a ticket.

"A hundred bucks to win! Man, when you get a hunch you really back it, don't you?"

Keller didn't say anything. He had nineteen other tickets just like it in his pocket, but the little man didn't have to know about them. If the photo of the two horses crossing the finish line showed Dudley in front, his tickets would be worth $58,000.

If not, well, Alvie Jurado would be worth almost as much.

"I got to hand it to you," the little man said. "All that dough on the line, and you're calm as a cucumber."

Ten days later, Keller sat at his dining room table. He was holding a pair of stainless steel stamp tongs, and they in turn were holding a little piece of paper worth—

Well, it was hard to say just how much it was worth. The stamp was Martinique #2, and Keller had wound up bidding $18,500 for it. The lot had opened at $9,000, and there was a bidder in the third row on the right who dropped out around the $12,000 mark, and then there was a phone bidder who hung on like grim death. When the auctioneer pounded the gavel and said, "Sold for eighteen five to JPK," Keller's heart was pounding harder than the gavel.

It was still racing eight lots later when the second stamp, Martinique #17, went on the block. It had a lower Scott value than #2, and was estimated lower in the Bulger & Calthorpe sales catalog, and the starting bid was lower, too, at an even $6,000.

And then, remarkably, it had wound up sailing all the way to $21,250 before Keller prevailed over another phone bidder. (Or the same one, irritated at having lost #2 and unwilling to miss out on #17.) That was too much, it was three times the Scott value, but what could you do? He wanted the stamp, and he could afford it, and when would he get a chance at another one like it?

With buyer's commission, the two lots had cost him $43,725.

He admired the stamp through his magnifier. It looked beautiful to him, although he couldn't say why; aesthetically, it wasn't discernibly different from other Martinique overprints worth less than twenty dollars. Carefully, he cut a mount to size, slipped the stamp into it, and secured it in his album.

Not for the first time, he thought of the little man at the OTB parlor. Keller hadn't seen him since that afternoon, and doubted he'd ever cross paths with him again. He remembered the fellow's excitement, and how impressed he'd been by Keller's own coolness.

Cool? Naturally he'd been cool. Either way he won. If he didn't cash the winning tickets on Kissimmee Dudley, he'd do just about as well when he punched Alvie Jurado's ticket. It was interesting, waiting to see how the photo came out, but he couldn't say it was all that nerve-racking.

Not when you compared it to sitting in a hotel suite in Omaha, waiting for hours while lot after lot was auctioned off, until finally the stamps you'd been waiting for came up for bids. And then sitting there with your pencil lifted to indicate you were bidding, sitting there while the price climbed higher and higher, not knowing where it would stop, not knowing if you had enough cash in the belt around your waist. How high would you have to go for the first lot? And would you have enough left for the other one? And what was the matter with that phone bidder?

Would the man never quit?

Now that was excitement, he thought, as he cut a second mount for Martinique #17. That was true edge-of-the-chair tension, unlike anything those Jerry Orbach look-alikes in the OTB parlor would ever know.

He felt sorry for them.

What difference did it make, really, how the photo finish turned out? What did he care who won the race? If Kissimmee Dudley held on to win by a nose or a nose hair, it was up to Keller to work out a tax-free way to cash twenty $100 tickets. If Steward's Folly made it home first, Alvie Jurado moved to the top of Keller's list of Things to Make and Do. Whichever chore Keller wound up with, he had to pull it off in a hurry; he had to have his money in hand—or, more accurately, in belt—when his flight took off for Omaha.

And now it was over, and he'd done what he had to, so did it matter what it was he'd done?

Hell, no. He had the stamps.

KELLER'S
ADJUSTMENT

CHAPTER TEN

Keller, waiting for the traffic light to turn from red to green, wondered what had happened to the world. The traffic light wasn't the problem. There'd been traffic lights for longer than he could remember, longer than he'd been alive. For almost as long as there had been automobiles, he supposed, although the automobile had clearly come first, and would in fact have necessitated the traffic light. At first they'd have made do without them, he supposed, and then, when there were enough cars around for them to start slamming into one another, someone would have figured out that some form of control was necessary, some device to stop east-west traffic while allowing north-south traffic to proceed, and then switching.

He could imagine an early motorist fulminating against the new regimen. *Whole world's going to hell. They're taking our rights away one after another. Light turns red because some damn timer tells it to turn red, a man's supposed to stop what he's doing and hit the brakes. Don't matter if there ain't another car around for fifty miles, he's gotta stop and stand there like a god-dam fool until the light turns green and tells him he can go again. Who wants to live in a country like that? Who wants to bring children into a world where that kind of crap goes on?*

A horn sounded, jarring Keller abruptly from the early days of the twentieth century to the early days of the twenty-first. The light, he noted, had turned from red to green, and the fellow in the SUV just behind him felt a need to bring this fact to Keller's attention. Keller, without feeling much in the way of actual irritation or anger, allowed himself a moment of imagination in which he shifted into park, engaged the emergency brake, got out of the car, and walked back to the SUV, whose driver would already have begun to regret leaning on the horn. Even as the man (pig-faced and jowly in Keller's fantasy) was reaching for the button to lock the door, Keller was opening the door, taking hold of the man (sweating now, fulminating, making simultaneous threats and excuses) by the shirtfront, yanking him out of the car, sending him sprawling on the pavement. Then, while the man's child (no, make it his wife, a fat shrew with dyed hair and rheumy eyes) watched in horror, Keller bent from the waist and dispatched the man with a movement learned from the Burmese master U Minh U, one in which the adept's hands barely appeared to touch the subject, but death, while indescribably painful, was virtually instantaneous.

Keller, satisfied by the fantasy, drove on. Behind him, the driver of the SUV—an unaccompanied young woman, Keller now noted, her hair secured by a bandana, and a sack of groceries on the seat beside her—followed along for half a block, then turned off to the right, seemingly unaware of her close brush with death.

How you do go on, he thought.

It was all the damned driving. Before everything went to hell, he wouldn't have had to drive clear across the country. He'd have taken a cab to JFK and caught a flight to Phoenix, where he'd have rented a car, driven it around for the day or two it would take to do the job, then turned it in and flown back to New York. In and out, case closed, and he could get on with his life.

And leave no traces behind, either. They made you show ID to get on the plane, they'd been doing that for a few years now, but it didn't have to be terribly good ID. Now they all but fingerprinted you before they let you board, and they went through your checked baggage and gave your carry-on luggage a lethal dose of radiation. God help you if you had a nail clipper on your key ring.

He hadn't flown at all since the new security procedures had gone into effect, and he didn't know that he'd ever get on a plane again. Business travel was greatly reduced, he'd read, and he could understand why. A business traveler would rather hop in his car and drive five hundred miles than get to the airport two hours early and go through all the hassles the new system imposed. It was bad enough if your business consisted of meeting with groups of salesmen and giving them pep talks. If you were in Keller's line of work, well, it was out of the question.

Keller rarely traveled other than for business, but sometimes he'd go somewhere for a stamp auction, or because it was the middle of a New York winter and he felt the urge to lie in the sun somewhere. He supposed he could still fly on such occasions, showing valid ID and clipping his nails before departure, but would he want to? Would it still be pleasure travel if you had to go through all that in order to get there?

He felt like that imagined motorist, griping about red lights. *Hell, if that's what they're gonna make me do, I'll just walk. Or I'll stay home. That'll show them!*

It all changed, of course, on a September morning, when a pair of airliners flew into the twin towers of the World

Trade Center. Keller, who lived on First Avenue not far from the UN building, had not been home at the time. He was in Miami, where he had already spent a week, getting ready to kill a man named Rubén Olivares. Olivares was a Cuban, and an important figure in one of the Cuban exile groups, but Keller wasn't sure that was why someone had been willing to spend a substantial amount of money to have him killed. It was possible, certainly, that he was a thorn in the side of the Castro government, and that someone had decided it would be safer and more cost-effective to hire the work done than to send a team of agents from Havana. It was also possible that Olivares had turned out to be a spy for Havana, and it was his fellow exiles who had it in for him.

Then, too, he might be sleeping with the wrong person's wife, or muscling in on the wrong person's drug trade. With a little investigative work, Keller might have managed to find out who wanted Olivares dead, and why, but he'd long since determined that such considerations were none of his business. What difference did it make? He had a job to do, and all he had to do was do it.

Monday night, he'd followed Olivares around, watched him eat dinner at a steak house in Coral Gables, then tagged along when Olivares and two of his dinner companions hit a couple of titty bars in Miami Beach. Olivares left with one of the dancers, and Keller tailed him to the woman's apartment and waited for him to come out. After an hour and a half, Keller decided the man was spending the night. Keller, who'd watched lights go on and off in the apartment house, was reasonably certain he knew which apartment the couple was occupying, and didn't think it would prove difficult to get into the building. He thought about going in and getting it over with. It was too late to catch a flight to New York, it was the middle of the night, but he could get the work done and stop at his motel to shower and collect his luggage, then go straight to the airport and try to get on the first flight home.

Or he could sleep late and fly home sometime in the early afternoon. Several airlines flew from New York to Florida, and there were flights all day long. Miami International was not his favorite airport—it was not anybody's favorite airport—but he could skip it if he wanted, turning in his rental car at Fort Lauderdale or West Palm Beach and flying home from there.

No end of options, once the work was done.

But he'd have to kill the woman, the topless dancer.

He'd do that if he had to, but he didn't like the idea of killing people just because they were in the way. A higher body count drew more police and media attention, but that wasn't it, nor was the notion of slaughtering the innocent. How did he know the woman was innocent? For that matter, who was to say Olivares was guilty of anything?

Later, when he thought about it, it seemed to him that the deciding factor was purely physical. He'd slept poorly the night before, rising early and spending the whole day driving around unfamiliar streets. He was tired, and he didn't much feel like forcing a door and climbing a flight of stairs and killing one person, let alone two. And suppose she had a roommate, and suppose the roommate had a boyfriend, and—

He went back to his motel, took a long hot shower, and went to bed.

When he woke up he didn't turn on the TV but went across the street to the place where he'd been having his

71

breakfast every morning. He walked in the door and saw that something was different. They had a television set on the back counter, and everybody was staring at it. He watched for a few minutes, then picked up a container of coffee and took it back to his room. He sat in front of his own TV and watched the same scenes, over and over and over.

If he'd done his work the night before, he realized, he might have been in the air when it happened. Or maybe not, because he'd probably have decided to get some sleep instead, so he'd be right where he was, in his motel room, watching the plane fly into the building. The only certain difference was that Rubén Olivares, who as things stood was probably watching the same footage everybody else in America was watching (except that he might well be watching it on a Spanish-language station)—well, Olivares wouldn't be watching TV. Nor would he be on it. A garden-variety Miami homicide wasn't worth airtime on a day like this, not even if the deceased was of some importance in the Cuban exile community, not even if he'd been murdered in the apartment of a topless dancer, with her own death a part of the package. A newsworthy item any other day, but not on this day. There was only one sort of news today, one topic with endless permutations, and Keller watched it all day long.

It was Wednesday before it even occurred to him to call Dot, and late Thursday before he finally got a call through to her in White Plains. "I've been wondering about you, Keller," she said. "There are all these planes on the ground in Newfoundland, they were in the air when it happened and got rerouted there, and God knows when they're

72

gonna let them come home. I had the feeling you might be there."

"In Newfoundland?"

"The local people are taking the stranded passengers into their homes," she said. "Making them welcome, giving them cups of beef bouillon and ostrich sandwiches, and—"

"Ostrich sandwiches?"

"Whatever. I just pictured you there, Keller, making the best of a bad situation, which I guess is what you're doing in Miami. God knows when they're going to let you fly home. Have you got a car?"

"A rental."

"Well, hang on to it," she said. "Don't give it back, because the car rental agencies are emptied out, with so many people stranded and trying to drive home. Maybe that's what you ought to do."

"I was thinking about it," he said. "But I was also thinking about, you know. The guy."

"Oh, him."

"I don't want to say his name, but—"

"No, don't."

"The thing is, he's still, uh . . ."

"Doing what he always did."

"Right."

"Instead of doing like John Brown."

"Huh?"

"Or John Brown's body," Dot said. "Moldering in the grave, as I recall."

"Whatever *moldering* means."

"We can probably guess, Keller, if we put our minds to it. You're wondering is it still on, right?"

73

"It seems ridiculous even thinking about it," he said. "But on the other hand—"

"On the other hand," she said, "they sent half the money. I'd just as soon not have to give it back."

"No."

"In fact," she said, "I'd just as soon have them send the other half. If they're the ones to call it off, we keep what they sent. And if they say it's still on, well, you're already in Miami, aren't you? Sit tight, Keller, while I make a phone call."

Whoever had wanted Olivares dead had not changed his mind as a result of several thousand deaths fifteen hundred miles away. Keller, thinking about it, couldn't see why he should be any less sanguine about the prospect of killing Olivares than he had been Monday night. On the television news, there was a certain amount of talk about the possible positive effects of the tragedy. New Yorkers, someone suggested, would be brought closer together, aware as never before of the bonds created by their common humanity.

Did Keller feel a bond with Rubén Olivares of which he'd been previously unaware? He thought about it and decided he did not. If anything, he was faintly aware of a grudging resentment against the man. If Olivares had spent less time over dinner and hurried through the foreplay of the titty bar, if he'd gone directly to the topless dancer's apartment and left the premises in the throes of postcoital bliss, Keller could have taken him out in time to catch the last flight back to the city. He might have been in his own apartment when the attack came.

And what earthly difference would that have made? None, he had to concede. He'd have watched the hideous

74

rama unfold on his own television set, just as he'd watched on the motel's unit, and he'd have been no more capable of influencing events whatever set he watched.

Olivares, with his steak dinners and topless dancers, made a poor surrogate for the heroic cops and firemen, the doomed office workers. He was, Keller conceded, a fellow member of the human race. If all men were brothers, a possibility Keller, an only child, was willing to entertain, well, brothers had been killing each other for a good deal longer than Keller had been on the job. If Olivares was Abel, Keller was willing to be Cain.

If nothing else, he was grateful for something to do.

And Olivares made it easy. All over America, people were writing checks and inundating blood banks, trying to do something for the victims in New York. Cops and firemen and ordinary citizens were piling into cars and heading north and east, eager to join in the rescue efforts. Olivares, on the other hand, went on leading his life of self-indulgence, going to an office in the morning, making a circuit of bars and restaurants in the afternoon and early evening, and finishing up with rum drinks in a room full of bare breasts.

Keller tagged him for three days and three nights, and by the third night he'd decided not to be squeamish about the topless dancer. He waited outside the titty bar until a call of nature led him into the bar, past Olivares's table (where the man was chatting up three silicone-enhanced young ladies), and on to the men's room. Standing at the urinal, Keller wondered what he'd do if the Cuban took all three of them home.

He washed his hands, left the restroom, and saw Olivares counting out bills to settle his tab. All three women were

75

still at the table, and playing up to him, one clutching his arm and leaning her breasts against it, the others just as coquettish. Keller, who'd been ready to sacrifice one bystander, found himself drawing the line at three.

But wait—Olivares was on his feet, his body language suggesting he was excusing himself for a moment. And yes, he was on his way to the men's room, clearly aware of the disadvantage of attempting a night of love on a full bladder.

Keller slipped into the room ahead of him, ducked into an empty stall. There was an elderly gentleman at the urinal, talking soothingly in Spanish to himself, or perhaps to his prostate. Olivares entered the room, stood at the adjoining urinal, and began chattering in Spanish to the older man, who spoke slow sad sentences in response.

Shortly after arriving in Miami, Keller had gotten hold of a gun, a .22-caliber revolver. It was a small gun with a short barrel, and fit easily in his pocket. He took it out now, wondering if the noise would carry.

If the older gentleman left first, Keller might not need the gun. But if Olivares finished first, Keller couldn't let him leave, and would have to do them both, and that would mean using the gun, and a minimum of two shots. He watched them over the top of the stall, wishing that something would happen before some other drunken voyeur felt a need to pee. Then the older man finished up, tucked himself in, and headed for the door.

And paused at the threshold, returning to wash his hands, and saying something to Olivares, who laughed heartily at it, whatever it was. Keller, who'd returned the gun to his pocket, took it out again, and replaced it a moment later when the older gentleman left. Olivares waited until the door closed after him, then produced a little blue glass bottle and a tiny spoon. He treated each of his cavernous nostrils to two quick hits of what Keller could only presume to be cocaine, then returned the bottle and spoon to his pocket and turned to face the sink.

Keller burst out of the stall. Olivares, washing his hands, evidently couldn't hear him with the water running; in any event he didn't react before Keller reached him, one hand cupping his jowly chin, the other taking hold of his greasy mop of hair. Keller had never studied the martial arts, not even from a Burmese with an improbable name, but he'd been doing this sort of thing long enough to have learned a trick or two. He broke Olivares's neck and was dragging him across the floor to the stall he'd just vacated when, damn it to hell, the door burst open and a little man in shirtsleeves got halfway to the urinal before he suddenly realized what he'd just seen. His eyes widened, his jaw dropped, and Keller got him before he could make a sound.

The little man's bladder, unable to relieve itself in life, could not be denied in death. Olivares, having emptied his bladder in his last moments of life, voided his bowels. The men's room, no garden spot to begin with, stank to the heavens. Keller stuffed both bodies into one stall and got out of there in a hurry, before some other son of a bitch could rush in and join the party.

Half an hour later he was heading north on I-95. Somewhere north of Stuart he stopped for gas, and in the men's room—empty, spotless, smelling of nothing but pine-scented disinfectant—he put his hands against the smooth white tiles and vomited. Hours later, at a rest area just across the Georgia line, he did so again.

He couldn't blame it on the killing. It had been a bad idea,

77

lurking in the men's room. The traffic was too heavy, with all those drinkers and cocaine sniffers. The stench of the corpses he'd left there, on top of the reek that had permeated the room to start with, could well have turned his stomach, but it would have done so then, not a hundred miles away when it no longer existed outside of his memory.

Some members of his profession, he knew, typically threw up after a piece of work, just as some veteran actors never failed to vomit before a performance. Keller had known a man once, a cheerfully cold-blooded little murderer with dainty little-girl wrists and a way of holding a cigarette between his thumb and forefinger. The man would chatter about his work, excuse himself, throw up discreetly into a basin, and resume his conversation in midsentence.

A shrink would probably argue that the body was expressing a revulsion that the mind was unwilling to acknowledge, and that sounded about right to Keller. But it didn't apply to him, because he'd never been one for puking. Even early on, when he was new to the game and hadn't found ways to deal with it, his stomach had remained serene.

This particular incident had been unpleasant, even chaotic, but he could if pressed recall others that had been worse.

But there was a more conclusive argument, it seemed to him. Yes, he'd thrown up outside of Stuart, and again in Georgia, and he'd very likely do so a few more times before he reached New York. But it hadn't begun with the killings.

He'd thrown up every couple of hours ever since he sat in front of his television set and watched the towers fall.

CHAPTER ELEVEN

A week or so after he got back, there was a message on his answering machine. Dot, wanting him to call. He checked his watch, decided it was too early. He made himself a cup of coffee, and when he'd finished it he dialed the number in White Plains.

"Keller," she said. "When you didn't call back, I figured you were out late. And now you're up early."

"Well," he said.

"Why don't you get on a train, Keller? My eyes are sore, and I figure you're a sight for them."

"What's the matter with your eyes?"

"Nothing," she said. "I was trying to express myself in an original fashion, and it's a mistake I won't make again in a hurry. Come see me, why don't you?"

"Now?"

"Why not?"

"I'm beat," he said. "I was up all night, I need to get to sleep."

"What were you . . . never mind, I don't need to know. All right, I'll tell you what. Sleep all you want and come out for dinner. I'll order something from the Chinese. Keller? You're not answering me."

"I'll come out sometime this afternoon," he said.

He went to bed, and early that afternoon he caught a train to White Plains and a cab from the station. She was on the porch of the big old Victorian on Taunton Place, with a pitcher of iced tea and two glasses on the tin-topped table. "Look," she said, pointing to the lawn. "I swear the trees are dropping their leaves earlier than usual this year. What's it like in New York?"

"I haven't really been paying attention."

"There was a kid who used to come around to rake them, but I guess he must have gone to college or something. What happens if you don't rake the leaves, Keller? You happen to know?"

He didn't.

"And you're not hugely interested, I can see that. There's something different about you, Keller, and I've got a horrible feeling I know what it is. You're not in love, are you?"

"In love?"

"Well, are you? Out all night, and then when you get home all you can do is sleep. Who's the lucky girl, Keller?"

He shook his head. "No girl," he said. "I've been working nights."

"Working? What the hell do you mean, working?"

He let her drag it out of him. A day or two after he got back to the city and turned in his rental car, he'd heard something on the news and went to one of the Hudson River piers, where they were enlisting volunteers to serve food for the rescue workers at Ground Zero. Around ten every evening they'd all get together at the pier, then sail down the river and board another ship anchored near the site. Top chefs supplied the food, and Keller and his fellows dished it out to men who'd worked up prodigious appetites laboring at the smoldering wreckage.

"My God," Dot said. "Keller, I'm trying to picture this. You stand there with a big spoon and fill their plates for them? Do you wear an apron?"

80

"Everybody wears an apron."

"I bet you look cute in yours. I don't mean to make fun, Keller. What you're doing's a good thing, and of course you'd wear an apron. You wouldn't want to get marinara sauce all over your shirt. But it seems strange to me, that's all."

"It's something to do," he said.

"It's heroic."

He shook his head. "There's nothing heroic about it. It's like working in a diner, dishing out food. The men we feed, they work long shifts doing hard physical work and breathing in all that smoke. That's heroic, if anything is. Though I'm not sure there's any point to it."

"What do you mean?"

"Well, they call them rescue workers," he said, "but they're not rescuing anybody, because there's nobody to rescue. Everybody's dead."

She said something in response but he didn't hear it. "It's the same as with the blood," he said. "The first day, everybody mobbed the hospitals, donating blood for the wounded. But it turned out there weren't any wounded. People either got out of the buildings or they didn't. If they got out, they were okay. If they didn't, they're dead. All that blood people donated? They've been throwing it out."

"It seems like a waste."

"It's all a waste," he said and frowned. "Anyway, that's what I do every night. I dish out food, and they try to rescue dead people. That way we all keep busy."

"The longer I know you," Dot said, "the more I realize I don't."

"Don't what?"

"Know you, Keller. You never cease to amaze me.

Somehow I never pictured you as Florence Nightingale."

"I'm not nursing anybody. All I do is feed them."

"Betty Crocker, then. Either way, it seems like a strange role for a sociopath."

"You think I'm a sociopath?"

"Well, isn't that part of the job description, Keller? You're a hit man, a contract killer. You leave town and kill strangers and get paid for it. How can you do that without being a sociopath?"

He thought about it.

"Look," she said, "I didn't mean to bring it up. It's just a word, and who even knows what it means? Let's talk about something else, like why I called you and got you to come out here."

"Okay."

"Actually," she said, "there's two reasons. First of all, you've got money coming. Miami, remember?"

"Oh, right."

She handed him an envelope. "I thought you'd want this," she said, "although it couldn't have been weighing on your mind, because you never asked about it."

"I hardly thought about it."

"Well, why would you want to think about blood money while you were busy doing good works? But you can probably find a use for it."

"No question."

"You can always buy stamps with it. For your collection."

"Sure."

"It must be quite a collection by now."

"It's coming along."

"I'll bet it is. The other reason I called, Keller, is somebody called me."

"Oh?"

She poured herself some more iced tea, took a sip. "There's work," she said. "If you want it. In Portland, something to do with labor unions."

"Which Portland?"

"You know," she said, "I keep forgetting there's one in Maine, but there is, and I suppose they've got their share of labor problems there, too. But this is Portland, Oregon. As a matter of fact, it's Beaverton, but I think it's a suburb. The area code's the same as Portland."

"Clear across the country," he said.

"Just a few hours in a plane."

They looked at each other. "I can remember," he said, "when all you did was step up to the counter and tell them where you wanted to go. You counted out bills, and they were perfectly happy to be paid in cash. You had to give them a name, but you could make it up on the spot, and the only way they asked for identification was if you tried to pay them by check."

"The world's a different place now, Keller."

"They didn't even have metal detectors," he remembered, "or scanners. Then they brought in metal detectors, but the early ones didn't work all the way down to the ground. I knew a man who used to stick a gun into his sock and walk right onto the plane with it. If they ever caught him at it, I never heard about it."

"I suppose you could take a train."

"Or a clipper ship," he said. "Around the Horn."

"What's the matter with the Panama Canal? Metal detectors?" She finished the tea in her glass, heaved a sigh. "I think you answered my question. I'll tell Portland we have to pass."

83

After dinner she gave him a lift to the station and joined him on the platform to wait for his train. He broke the silence to ask her if she really thought he was a sociopath.

"Keller," she said, "it was just an idle remark, and I didn't mean anything by it. Anyway, I'm no psychologist. I'm not even sure what the word means."

"Someone who lacks a sense of right and wrong," he said. "He understands the difference but doesn't see how it applies to him personally. He lacks empathy, doesn't have any feeling for other people."

She considered the matter. "It doesn't sound like you," she said, "except when you're working. Is it possible to be a part-time sociopath?"

"I don't think so. I've done some reading on the subject. Case histories, that sort of thing. The sociopaths they write about, almost all of them have the same three things in their childhood background. Setting fires, torturing animals, and wetting the bed."

"You know, I heard that somewhere. Some TV program about FBI profilers and serial killers. Do you remember your childhood, Keller?"

"Most of it," he said. "I knew a woman once who claimed she could remember being born. I don't go back that far, and some of it's spotty, but I remember it pretty well. And I didn't do any of those three things. Torture animals? God, I loved animals. I told you about the dog I had."

"Nelson. No, sorry, that was the one you had a couple of years ago. You told me the name of the other one, but I can't remember it."

"Soldier."

"Soldier, right."

"I loved that dog," he said. "And I had other pets from time to time, the way kids do. Goldfish, baby turtles. They all died."

"They always do, don't they?"

"I suppose so. I used to cry."

"When they died."

"When I was little. When I got older I took it more in stride, but it still made me sad. But torture them?"

"How about fires?"

"You know," he said, "when you talked about the leaves, and what happens if you don't rake them, I remembered raking leaves when I was a kid. It was one of the things I did to make money."

"You want to make twenty bucks here and now, there's a rake in the garage."

"What we used to do," he remembered, "was rake them into a pile at the curb, and then burn them. It's illegal nowadays, because of fire laws and air pollution, but back then it's what you were supposed to do."

"It was nice, the smell of burning leaves on the autumn air."

"And it was satisfying," he said. "You raked them up and put a match to them and they were gone. Those were the only fires I remember setting."

"I'd say you're oh-for-two. How'd you do at wetting the bed?"

"I never did, as far as I can recall."

"Oh-for-three. Keller, you're about as much of a sociopath as Albert Schweitzer. But if that's the case, how come you do what you do? Never mind, here's your train. Have fun dishing out the lasagna tonight. And don't torture any animals, you hear?"

CHAPTER TWELVE

Two weeks later he picked up the phone on his own and told her not to turn down jobs automatically. "Now you tell me," she said. "You at home? Don't go anywhere, I'll make a call and get back to you." He sat by the phone, and picked it up when it rang. "I was afraid they'd found somebody by now," she said, "but we're in luck, if you want to call it that. They're sending us something by Airborne Express, which always sounds to me like paratroopers ready for battle. They swear I'll have it by nine tomorrow morning, but you'll just be getting home around then, won't you? Do you figure you can make the 2:04 from Grand Central? I'll pick you up at the station."

"There's a 10:08," he said. "Gets to White Plains a few minutes before eleven. If you're not there, I'll figure you had to wait for the paratroopers, and I'll get a cab."

It was a cold, dreary day, with enough rain so that she needed to use the windshield wipers but not enough to keep the blades from squeaking. She put him at the kitchen table, poured him a cup of coffee, and let him read the notes she'd made and study the Polaroids that had come in the Airborne Express envelope, along with the initial payment in cash. He held up one of the pictures, which showed a man in his seventies, with a round face and a small white mustache, holding up a golf club as if in the hope that someone would take it from him.

He said the fellow didn't look much like a labor leader, and Dot shook her head. "That was Portland," she said. "This is Phoenix. Well, Scottsdale, and I bet it's nicer there today than it is here. Nicer than Portland, too, because I understand it always rains there. In Portland, I mean. It never rains in Scottsdale. I don't know what's the matter with me, I'm starting to sound like the Weather Channel. You could fly, you know. Not all the way, but to Denver, say."

"Maybe."

She tapped the photo with her fingernail. "Now according to them," she said, "the man's not expecting anything, and not taking any security precautions. Other hand, his life is a security precaution. He lives in a gated community."

"Sundowner Estates, it says here."

"There's an eighteen-hole golf course, with individual homes ranged around it. And each of them has a state-of-the-art home security system, but the only thing that ever triggers an alarm is when some clown hooks his tee shot through your living room picture window, because the only way into the compound is past a guard. No metal detector, and they don't confiscate your nail clippers, but you have to belong there for him to let you in."

"Does Mr. Egmont ever leave the property?"

"He plays golf every day. Unless it rains, and we've already established that it never does. He generally eats lunch at the clubhouse, they've got their own restaurant. He has a housekeeper who comes in a couple of times a week—they know her at the guard shack, I guess. Aside from that, he's all alone in his house. He probably gets invited out to dinner a lot. He's unattached, and there's always six women for every man in those Geezer Leisure communities. You're staring at his picture, and I bet I know why. He looks familiar, doesn't he?"

"Yes, and I can't think why."

"You ever play Monopoly?"

"By God, that's it," he said. "He looks like the drawing of the banker in Monopoly."

"It's the mustache," she said, "and the round face. Don't forget to pass Go, Keller. And collect two hundred dollars."

She drove him back to the train station, and because of the rain they waited in her car instead of on the platform. He said he'd pretty much stopped working on the food ship. She said she hadn't figured it was something he'd be doing for the rest of his life.

"They changed it," he said. "The Red Cross took it over. They do this all the time, their specialty's disaster relief, and they're pros at it, but it transformed the whole thing from a spontaneous New York affair into something impersonal. I mean, when we started we had name chefs knocking themselves out to feed these guys something they'd enjoy eating, and then the Red Cross took over, and we were filling their plates with macaroni and cheese and chipped beef on toast. Overnight we went from Bobby Flay to Chef Boyardee."

"Took the joy out of it, did it?"

"Well, would you like to spend ten hours shifting scrap metal and collecting body parts and then tuck into something you'd expect to find in an army chow line? I got so I couldn't look them in the eye when I ladled the slop onto their plates. I skipped a night and felt guilty about it, and I went in the next night and felt worse, and I haven't been back since."

"You were probably ready to give it up, Keller."

"I don't know. I still felt good doing it, until the Red Cross showed up."

"But that's why you were there," she said. "To feel good."

"To help out."

She shook her head. "You felt good because you were helping out," she said, "but you kept going back and doing it because it made you feel good."

"Well, I suppose so."

"I'm not impugning your motive, Keller. You're still a hero, as far as I'm concerned. All I'm saying is that volunteerism only goes so far. When it stops feeling good, it tends to run out of steam. That's when you need the professionals. They do their job because it's their job, and it doesn't matter whether they feel good about it or not. They buckle down and get it done. It may be macaroni and cheese, and the cheese may be Velveeta, but nobody winds up holding an empty plate. You see what I mean?"

"I guess so," Keller said.

Back in the city, he called one of the airlines, thinking he'd take Dot's suggestion and fly to Denver. He worked his way through their automated answering system, pressing numbers when prompted, and wound up on hold, because all of their agents were busy serving other customers. The music they played to pass the time was bad enough all by itself, but they kept interrupting it every fifteen seconds to tell him how much better off he'd be using their website. After a few minutes of this he called Hertz, and the phone was answered right away by a human being.

He picked up a Ford Taurus first thing the next morning and beat the rush hour traffic through the tunnel and onto the New Jersey Turnpike. He'd rented the car under his own name, showing his own driver's license and using his own American Express card, but he had a cloned card in another name that Dot had provided, and he used it in the motels where he stopped along the way.

It took him four long days to drive to Tucson. He would drive until he was hungry, or the car needed gas, or he needed a restroom, then get behind the wheel again and drive some more. When he got tired he'd find a motel and register under the name on his fake credit card, take a shower, watch a little TV, and go to bed. He'd sleep until he woke up, and then he'd take another shower and get dressed and look for someplace to have breakfast. And so on.

While he drove he played the radio until he couldn't stand it, then turned it off until he couldn't stand the silence. By the third day the solitude was getting to him, and he couldn't figure out why. He was used to being alone, he lived his whole life alone, and he certainly never had or wanted company while he was working. He seemed to want it now, though, and at one point turned the car's radio to a talk show on a clear-channel station in Omaha. People called in and disagreed with the host, or a previous caller, or some schoolteacher who'd given them a hard time in the fifth grade. Gun control was the announced topic for the day, but the real theme, as far as Keller could tell, was resentment, and there was plenty of it to go around.

Keller listened, fascinated at first, and before very long he reached the point where he couldn't stand another minute of it. If he'd had a gun handy, he might have put a bullet in the radio, but all he did was switch it off.

The last thing he wanted, it turned out, was someone talking to him. He had the thought, and realized a moment later that he'd not only thought it but had actually spoken the words aloud. He was talking to himself, and wondered—wondered in silence, thank God—if this was something new. It was like snoring, he thought. If you slept alone, how would you know if you did it? You wouldn't, not unless you snored so loudly that you woke yourself up.

He started to reach for the radio, stopped himself before he could turn it on again. He checked the speedometer, saw that the cruise control was keeping the car at three miles an hour over the posted speed limit. Without cruise control you found yourself going faster or slower than you wanted to, wasting time or risking a ticket. With it, you didn't have to think about how fast you were going. The car did the thinking for you.

The next step, he thought, would be steering control. You got in the car, keyed the ignition, set the controls, and leaned back and closed your eyes. The car followed the turns in the road, and a system of sensors worked the brake when another car loomed in front of you, swung out to pass when such action was warranted, and knew to take the next exit when the gas gauge dropped below a certain level.

It sounded like science fiction, but no less so in Keller's boyhood than cruise control, or auto-response telephone answering systems, or a good 95 percent of the things he nowadays took for granted. Keller didn't doubt for a minute that right this instant some bright young man in Detroit or Osaka or Bremen was working on steering control. There'd be some spectacular head-on collisions before they got the bugs out of the system, but before long every car would have it, and the accident rate would plummet and the state troopers wouldn't have anybody to give tickets to, and everybody would be crazy about technology's newest break-through, except for a handful of cranks in England who were convinced you had more control and got better mileage the old-fashioned way.

Meanwhile, Keller kept both hands on the steering wheel.

CHAPTER THIRTEEN

Sundowner Estates, home of William Wallis Egmont, was in Scottsdale, an upscale suburb of Phoenix. Tucson, a couple hundred miles to the east, was as close as Keller wanted to bring the Taurus. He followed the signs to the airport and left the car in long-term parking. Over the years he'd left other cars in long-term parking, but they'd been other men's cars, with their owners stuffed in the trunk, and Keller, having no need to find the cars again, had gotten rid of the claim checks at the first opportunity. This time was different, and he found a place in his wallet for the check the gate attendant had supplied, and noted the lot section and the number of the parking space.

He went into the terminal, found the car rental counters, and picked up a Toyota Camry from Avis, using his fake credit card and a matching Pennsylvania driver's license. It took him a few minutes to figure out the cruise control. That was the trouble with renting cars, you had to learn a new system with every car, from lights and windshield wipers to cruise control and seat adjustment. Maybe he should have gone to the Hertz counter and picked up another Taurus. Was there an advantage in driving the same model car throughout? Was there a disadvantage that offset it, and was some intuitive recognition of that disadvantage what had led him to the Avis counter?

"You're thinking too much," he said and realized he'd spoken the words aloud. He shook his head, not so much annoyed as amused, and a few miles down the road realized that what he wanted, what he'd been wanting all along, was not someone to talk to him but someone to listen.

A little ways past an exit ramp, a kid with a duffel bag had his thumb out, trying to hitch a ride. For the first time that he could recall, Keller had the impulse to stop for him. It was just a passing thought; if he'd had his foot on the gas, he'd have barely begun to ease up on the gas pedal before he'd overruled the thought and sped onward. Since he was running on cruise control, his foot didn't even move, and the hitchhiker slipped out of sight in the rearview mirror, unaware what a narrow escape he'd just had.

Because the only reason to pick him up was for someone to talk to, and Keller would have told him everything. And, once he'd done that, what choice would he have?

Keller could picture the kid, listening wide-eyed to everything Keller had to tell him. He pictured himself, his soul unburdened, grateful to the youth for listening, but compelled by circumstance to cover his tracks. He imagined the car gliding to a stop, imagined the brief struggle, imagined the body left in a roadside ditch, the Camry heading west at a thoughtful three miles an hour above the speed limit.

The motel Keller picked was an independent mom-and-pop operation in Tempe, which was another suburb of Phoenix. He counted out cash and paid a week in advance, plus a twenty-dollar deposit for phone calls. He didn't plan to make any calls, but if he needed to use the phone he wanted it to work.

He registered as David Miller of San Francisco and fabricated an address and zip code. You were supposed to include your license plate number, and he mixed up a couple of digits and put CA for the state instead of AZ. It was hardly worth the trouble, nobody was going to look at the registration card, but there were certain things he did out of habit, and this was one of them.

He always traveled light, never took along more than a small carry-on bag with a shirt or two and a couple changes of socks and underwear. That made sense when you were flying, and less sense when you had a car with an empty trunk and backseat at your disposal. By the time he got to Phoenix, he'd run through his socks and underwear. He picked up two three-packs of briefs and a six-pack of socks at a strip mall, and was looking for a trash bin for his dirty clothes when he spotted a Goodwill Industries collection box. He felt good dropping his soiled socks and underwear in the box, though not quite as good as he'd felt dishing out designer food to the smoke-stained rescue workers at Ground Zero.

Back at his motel, he called Dot on the prepaid cell phone he'd picked up on Twenty-third Street. He'd paid cash for it, and hadn't even been asked his name, so as far as he could tell it was completely untraceable. At best someone could identify calls made from it as originating with a phone manufactured in Finland and sold at Radio Shack. Even if they managed to pin down the specific Radio Shack outlet, so what? There was nothing to tie it to Keller, or to Phoenix.

On the other hand, cell phone communications were about as secure as shouting. Any number of listening devices could pick up your conversation, and whatever you said was very likely being heard by half a dozen people on their car radios and one old fart who was catching every word on the fillings in his teeth. That didn't bother Keller, who figured every phone was tapped, and acted accordingly.

He phoned Dot, and the phone rang seven or eight times, and he broke the connection. She was probably out, he decided, or in the shower. Or had he misdialed? Always a chance, he thought, and pressed Redial, then caught himself and realized that, if he had in fact misdialed, redialing would just repeat the mistake. He broke the connection again in midring and punched in the number afresh, and this time he got a busy signal.

He redialed, got another busy signal, frowned, waited, and tried again. It had barely begun to ring when she picked up, barking "Yes?" into the phone, and somehow fitting a full measure of irritation into the single syllable.

"It's me," he said.

"What a surprise."

"Is something wrong?"

"I had somebody at the door," she said, "and the teakettle was whistling, and I finally got to the phone and picked it up in time to listen to the dial tone."

"I let it ring a long time."

"That's nice. So I put it down and turned away, and it rang again, and I picked it up in the middle of the first ring, and I was just in time to hear you hang up."

He explained about pressing Redial, and realizing that wouldn't work.

"Except it worked just fine," she said, "since you hadn't misdialed in the first place. I figured it had to be you, so I pressed star sixty-nine. But whatever phone you're on, star sixty-nine doesn't work. I got one of those weird tones and a canned message saying return calls to your number were blocked."

"It's a cell phone."

"Say no more. Hello? Where'd you go?"

"I'm here. You said *Say no more,* and . . ."

"It's an expression. Tell me it's all wrapped up and you're heading for home."

"I just got here."

"That's what I was afraid of. How's the weather?"

"Hot."

"Not here. They say it might snow, but then again it might not. You're just calling to check in, right?"

"Right."

"Well, it's good to hear your voice, and I'd love to chat, but you're on a cell phone."

"Right."

"Call anytime," she said. "It's always a treat to hear from you."

Keller didn't know the population or acreage of Sundowner Estates, although he had a hunch neither figure would be hard to come by. But what good would the information do him? The compound was large enough to contain a full-size eighteen-hole golf course, and enough homes adjacent to it to support the operation.

And there was a ten-foot adobe wall encircling the entire affair. Keller supposed it was easier to sell homes if you called it Sundowner Estates, but Fort Apache would have better conveyed the stockadelike feel of the place.

He drove around the compound a couple of times, establishing that there were in fact two gates, one at the east and the other not quite opposite, at the southwest corner. He parked where he could keep an eye on the southwest gate, and couldn't tell much beyond the fact that every vehicle entering or leaving the compound had to stop for some sort of exchange with the uniformed guard. Maybe you flashed a pass at him, maybe he called to make sure you were expected, maybe they wanted a thumbprint and a semen sample. No way to tell, not from where Keller was watching, but he was pretty sure he couldn't just drive up and bluff his way through. People who willingly lived behind a thick wall almost twice their own height probably expected a high level of security, and a guard who failed to provide that would be looking for a new job.

He drove back to his motel, sat in front of the TV, and watched a special on the Discovery Channel about scuba diving at Australia's Great Barrier Reef. Keller didn't think it looked like something he wanted to do. He'd tried snorkeling once, on a vacation in Aruba, and kept having to stop because he was getting water in his snorkel, and under his mask. And he hadn't been able to see much of anything, anyhow.

The divers on the Discovery Channel were having much better luck, and there were plenty of colorful fish for them (and Keller) to look at. After fifteen minutes, though, he'd seen as much as he wanted to and was ready to change the channel. It seemed like a lot of trouble to go through, flying all the way to Australia, then getting in the water with a mask and fins. Couldn't you get pretty much the same effect staring into a fish tank at a pet shop or a Chinese restaurant?

"I'll tell you this," the woman said. "If you do make a decision to buy at Sundowner, you won't regret it. Nobody ever has."

"That's quite a recommendation," Keller said.

"Well, it's quite an operation, Mr. Miller. I don't suppose I have to ask if you play golf."

"It's somewhere between a pastime and an addiction," he said.

"I hope you brought your clubs. Sundowner's a championship course, you know. Robert Walker Wilson designed it, and Clay Bunis was a consultant. We're in the middle of the desert, but you wouldn't know it inside the walls at Sundowner. The course is as green as a pasture in the Irish midlands."

Her name, Keller learned, was Michelle Prentice, but everyone called her Mitzi. And what about him? Did he prefer Dave or David?

That was a stumper, and Keller realized he was taking too long to answer it. "It depends," he said, finally. "I answer to either one."

"I'll bet business associates call you Dave," she said, "and really close friends call you David."

"How on earth did you know that?"

She smiled broadly, delighted to be right. "Just a guess," she said. "Just a lucky guess, David."

So they were going to be close friends, he thought. Toward that end she proceeded to tell him a few things about herself, and by the time they reached the guard shack at the east gate of Sundowner Estates, he learned that she was thirty-nine years old, that she'd divorced her rat bastard of a husband three years ago and moved out here from Frankfort, Kentucky, which happened to be the state capital, although most people would guess it was Louisville. She'd sold houses in Frankfort, so she'd picked up an Arizona realtor's license first chance she got, and it was a lot better selling houses here than it had ever been in

Kentucky, because they just about sold themselves. The entire Phoenix area was growing like a house on fire, she assured him, and she was just plain excited to be a part of it all.

At the east gate she moved her sunglasses up onto her forehead and gave the guard a big smile. "Hi, Harry," she said. "Mitzi Prentice, and this here's Mr. Miller, come for a look at the Lattimore house on Saguaro Circle."

"Miz Prentice," he said, returning her smile and nodding at Keller. He consulted a clipboard, then slipped into the shack and picked up a telephone. After a moment he emerged and told Mitzi she could go ahead. "I guess you know how to get there," he said.

"I guess I ought to," she told Keller, after they'd driven away from the entrance. "I showed the house two days ago, and he was there to let me by. But he's got his job to do, and they take it seriously, let me tell you. I know not to joke with him, or with any of them, because they won't joke back. They can't, because it might not look good on camera."

"There are security cameras running?"

"Twenty-four hours a day. You don't get in unless your name's on the list, and the camera's got a record of when you came and went, and what car you were driving, license plate number and all."

"Really."

"There are some very affluent people at Sundowner," she said, "and some of them are getting along in years. That's not to say you won't find plenty of people your age here, especially on the golf course and around the pool, but you do get some older folks, too, and they tend to be a little more concerned about security. Now just look,

David. Isn't that a beautiful sight?"

She pointed out her window at the golf course, and it looked like a golf course to him. He agreed it sure looked gorgeous.

The living room of the Lattimore house had a cathedral ceiling and a walk-in fireplace. Keller thought the fireplace looked nice, but he didn't quite get it. A walk-in closet was one thing, you could walk into it and pick what you wanted to wear, but why would anybody want to walk into a fireplace?

For that matter, who'd want to hold a prayer service in the living room?

He thought of raising the point with Mitzi. She might find either question provocative, but would it fit the Serious Buyer image he was trying to project? So he asked instead what he figured were more typical questions, about heating and cooling systems and financing, good basic home-buyer questions.

There was, predictably enough, a big picture window in the living room, and it afforded the predictable view of the golf course, overlooking what Mitzi told him were the fifth green and the sixth tee. There was a man taking practice swings who might have been W. W. Egmont himself, although from this distance and angle it was hard to say one way or the other. But if the guy turned a little to his left, and if Keller could look at him not with his naked eye but through a pair of binoculars—

Or, he thought, a telescopic sight. That would be quick and easy, wouldn't it? All he had to do was buy the place and set up in the living room with a high-powered rifle, and Egmont's state-of-the-art home burglar alarm wouldn't do him a bit of good. Keller could just perch there like a vulture, and sooner or later Egmont would finish up the fifth hole by four-putting for a triple bogey, and Keller could take him right there and save the poor duffer a stroke, or wait until he came even closer and teed up his ball for the sixth hole (525 yards, par five). Keller was no great shakes as a marksman, but how hard could it be to center the crosshairs on a target and squeeze the trigger?

"I bet you're picturing yourself on that golf course right now," Mitzi said, and he grinned and told her she got that one right.

From the bedroom window in the back of the house, you could look out at a desert garden, with cacti and succulents growing in sand. The plantings, like the bright green lawn in front, were all the responsibility of the Sundowner Estates association, who took care of all maintenance. They kept it beautiful year-round, she told him, and you never had to lift a finger.

"A lot of people think they want to garden when they retire," she said, "and then they find out how much work it can be. And what happens when you want to take off for a couple of weeks in Maui? At Sundowner, you can walk out the door and know everything's going to be beautiful when you come back."

He said he could see how that would be a comfort. "I can't see the fence from here," he said. "I was wondering about that, if you'd feel like you were walled in. I mean, it's nice-looking, being adobe and earth-colored and all, but it's a pretty high fence."

"Close to twelve feet," she said.

Even higher than he'd thought. He said he wondered

what it would be like living next to it, and she said none of the houses were close enough to the fence for it to be a factor.

"The design was very well thought out," she said. "There's the twelve-foot fence, and then there's a big space, anywhere from ten to twenty yards, and then there's an inner fence, also of adobe, that stands about five feet tall, and there's cactus and vines in front of it for landscaping, so it looks nice and decorative."

"That's a great idea," he said. And he liked it; all he had to do was clear the first fence and follow the stretch of no-man's-land around to wherever he felt like vaulting the shorter wall. "About the taller fence, though. I mean, it's not really terribly secure, is it?"

"What makes you say that?"

"Well, I don't know. I guess it's because I'm used to the Northeast, where security's pretty up front and obvious, but it's just a plain old mud fence, isn't it? No razor wire on top, no electrified fencing. It looks as though all a person would have to do is lean a long ladder up against it and he'd be over the top in a matter of seconds."

She laid a hand on his arm. "David," she said, "you asked that very casually, but I have the sense that security's a real concern of yours."

"I have a stamp collection," he said. "It's not worth a fortune, and collections are hard to sell, but the point is I've been collecting since I was a kid and I'd hate to lose it."

"I can understand that."

"So security's a consideration, yes. And the fellow at the gate's enough to put anybody's mind at rest, but if any jerk with a ladder can just pop right over the fence—"

It was, she told him, a little more complicated than that. There was no razor or concertina wire, because that made a place look like a concentration camp, but there were sensors that set up some kind of force field, and no one could begin to climb the fence without setting off all kinds of alarms. Nor were you home free once you cleared the fence, because there were dogs that patrolled the belt of no-man's-land, Dobermans, swift and silent.

"And there's an unmarked patrol car that circles the perimeter at regular intervals twenty-four hours a day," she said, "so if they spotted you on your way to the fence with a ladder under your arm—"

"It wouldn't be me," he assured her. "I like dogs okay, but I'd just as soon not meet those Dobermans you just mentioned."

It was, he decided, a good thing he'd asked. Earlier, he'd found a place to buy an aluminum extension ladder. He could have been over the fence in a matter of seconds, just in time to keep a date with Mr. Swift and Mr. Silent.

In the Lattimore kitchen, they sat across a table topped with butcher block while Mitzi went over the fine points with him. The furniture was all included, she told him, and as he could see it was in excellent condition. He might want to make some changes, of course, as a matter of personal taste, but the place was in turnkey condition. He could buy it today and move in tomorrow.

"In a manner of speaking," she said, and touched his arm again. "Financing takes a little time, and even if you were to pay cash it would take a few days to push the paperwork through. Were you thinking in terms of cash?"

"It's always simpler," he said.

"It is, but I'm sure you wouldn't have trouble with a mortgage. The banks love to write mortgages on Sundowner properties, because the prices only go up." Her fingers encircled his wrist. "I'm not sure I should tell you this, David, but now's a particularly good time to make an offer."

"Mr. Lattimore's eager to sell?"

"Mr. Lattimore couldn't care less," she said. "About selling or anything else. It's his daughter who'd like to sell. She had an offer of ten percent under the asking price, but she'd just listed the property and she turned it down, thinking the buyer'd boost it a little, but instead the buyer went and bought something else, and that woman's been kicking herself ever since. What *I* would do, I'd offer fifteen percent under what she's asking. You might not get it for that, but the worst you'd do is get it for ten percent under, and that's a bargain in this market."

He nodded thoughtfully, and asked what happened to Lattimore. "It was very sad," she said, "although in another sense it wasn't, because he died doing what he loved."

"Playing golf," Keller guessed.

"He hit a very nice tee shot on the thirteenth hole," she said, "which is a par four with a dogleg to the right. 'That's a sweet shot,' his partner said, and Mr. Lattimore said, 'Well, I guess I can still hit one now and then, can't I?' And then he just went and dropped dead."

"If you've got to go . . ."

"That's what everyone said, David. The body was cremated, and then they had a nice nondenominational service in the clubhouse, and afterward his daughter and son-in-law rode golf carts to the sixteenth hole and put his ashes in the water hazard." She laughed involuntarily, and let go of his wrist to cover her mouth with her hand. "Pardon me for laughing, but I was thinking what somebody said. How his balls were already there, and now he could go look for them."

Her hand returned to his wrist. He looked at her, and her eyes were looking back at him. "Well," he said. "My car's at your office, so you'd better run me back there. And then I'll want to get back to where I'm staying and freshen up, but after that I'd love to take you to dinner."

"Oh, I wish," she said.

"You have plans?"

"My daughter lives with me," she said, "and I like to be home with her on school nights, and especially tonight because there's a program on television we never miss."

"I see."

"So you're on your own for dinner," she said, "but what do you and I care about dinner, David? Why don't you just take me into old Mr. Lattimore's bedroom and fuck me senseless?"

CHAPTER FOURTEEN

She had a nice body and used it eagerly and imaginatively. Keller, his mind on his work, had been only vaguely aware of the sexual possibilities, and had in fact surprised himself by asking her to dinner. In the Lattimore bedroom he surprised himself further.

Afterward she said, "Well, I had high expectations, but I have to say they were exceeded. Isn't it a good thing I'm busy tonight? Otherwise it'd be a couple of hours before we even got to the restaurant, and ages before we got to bed. I mean, why waste all that time?"

He tried to think of something to say, but she didn't seem to require comment. "For all those years," she said, "I was the most faithful wife since Penelope. And it's not like nobody was interested. Men used to hit on me all the time. David, I even had girls hitting on me."

"Really."

"But I was never interested, and if I was, if I felt a little itch, a little tickle, well, I just pushed it away and put it out of my mind. Because of a little thing called marriage. I'd made some vows, and I took them seriously.

"And then I found out the son of a bitch was cheating on me, and it turned out it was nothing new. On our wedding day? It was years before I knew it, but that son of a bitch got lucky with one of my bridesmaids. And over the years he was catting around all the time. Not just my friends, but my sister."

"Your sister?"

"Well, my half-sister, really. My daddy died when I was little, and my mama remarried, and that's where she came from." She told him more than he needed to know about her childhood, and he lay there with his eyes closed and let the words wash over him. He hoped there wasn't going to be a test, because he wasn't paying close attention. . . .

So I decided to make up for lost time," she said.

He'd dozed off, and after she woke him they'd showered in separate bathrooms. Now they were dressed again, and he'd followed her into the kitchen, where she opened the refrigerator and seemed surprised to find it empty.

She closed it and turned to him and said, "When I meet someone I feel like sleeping with, well, I go ahead and do it. I mean, why wait?"

"Works for me," he said.

"The only thing I don't like to do," she said, "is mix business and pleasure. So I made sure not to commit myself until I knew you weren't going to buy this place. And you're not, are you?"

"How did you know?"

"A feeling I got, when I said how you should make an offer. Instead of trying to think how much to offer, you were looking for a way out—or at least that was what I picked up. Which was okay with me, because by then I was more interested in getting laid than in selling a house. I didn't have to tell you about a whole lot of tax advantages, and how easy it is to rent the place out during the time you spend somewhere else. It's all pretty persuasive, and I could give you that whole rap now, but you don't really want to hear it, do you?"

"I might be in the market in a little while," he said, "but you're right, I'm nowhere near ready to make an offer at the present time. I suppose it was wrong of me to drag you out here and waste your time, but—"

"Do you hear me complaining, David?"

"Well, I just wanted to see the place," he said. "So I exaggerated my interest somewhat. Whether or not I'll be serious about settling in here depends on the outcome of a couple of business matters, and it'll be a while before I know how they're going to turn out."

"Sounds very mysterious," she said.

"I wish I could talk about it, but you know how it is."

"You could tell me," she said, "but then you'd have to kill me. In that case, don't you say a word."

He ate dinner by himself in a Mexican restaurant that reminded him of another Mexican restaurant. He was lingering over a second cup of café con leche before he figured it out. Years ago work had taken him to Roseburg, Oregon, and before he got out of there he'd picked out a real estate agent and spent an afternoon driving around looking at houses for sale.

He hadn't gone to bed with the Oregon realtor, or even considered it, nor had he used her as a way to get information on an approach to his quarry. That man, whom the Witness Protection Program had imperfectly protected, had been all too easy to find, but Keller, who ordinarily knew well enough to keep his business and personal life separate, had somehow let himself befriend the poor bastard. Before he knew it he was having fantasies about moving to Roseburg himself, buying a house, getting a dog, settling down.

He'd looked at houses, but that was as far as he'd let it go. The night came when he got a grip on himself, and the next thing he got a grip on was the man who'd brought him there. He used a garrote, and what he got a grip on was the guy's throat, and then it was time to go back to New York.

He remembered the Mexican café in Roseburg now. The food had been good, though he didn't suppose it was all that special, and he'd had a mild crush on the waitress, about as realistic as the whole idea of moving there. He thought of the man he'd killed, an accountant who'd become the proprietor of a quick-print shop.

You could learn the business in a couple of hours, the man had said of his new career. *You could buy the place and move in the same day,* Mitzi had said of the Lattimore house.

Patterns . . .

You could tell me, she'd said, thinking she was joking, *but then you'd have to kill me.* Oddly, in the languor that followed their lovemaking, he'd had the impulse to confide in her, to tell her what had brought him to Scottsdale.

Yeah, right.

He drove around for a while, then found his way back to his motel and surfed the TV channels without finding anything that caught his interest. He turned off the set and sat there in the dark.

He thought of calling Dot. There were things he could talk about with her, but others he couldn't, and anyway he didn't want to do any talking on a cell phone, not even an untraceable one.

He found himself thinking about the guy in Roseburg. He tried to picture him and couldn't. Early on he'd worked out a way to keep people from the past from flooding the present with their faces. You worked with their images in your mind, leached the color out of them, made the features grow dimmer, shrank the picture as if viewing it through the wrong end of a telescope. You made them grow smaller and darker and hazier until they disappeared, and if you did it correctly you forgot everything but the barest of facts about them. There was no emotional charge, no weight to them, and they became more and more difficult to recall to mind.

But now he'd bridged a gap and closed a circuit, and the man's face was there in his memory, the face of an aging chipmunk. *Jesus,* Keller thought, *get out of my memory, will you? You've been dead for years. Leave me the hell alone.*

If you were here, he told the face, *I could talk to you. And you'd listen, because what the hell else could you do? You couldn't talk back, you couldn't judge me, you couldn't tell me to shut up. You're dead, so you couldn't say a goddam word.*

He went outside, walked around for a while, came back in and sat on the edge of the bed. Very deliberately he set about getting rid of the man's face, washing it of color, pushing it farther and farther away, making it disappear. The process was more difficult than it had been in years, but it worked, finally, and the little man was gone to wherever the washed-out faces of dead people went. Wherever it was, Keller prayed he'd stay there.

He took a long hot shower and went to bed.

In the morning he found someplace new to have breakfast. He read the paper and had a second cup of coffee, then drove pointlessly around the perimeter of Sundowner Estates.

Back at the motel, he called Dot on his cell phone.

"Here's what I've been able to come up with," he said. "I park where I can watch the entrance. Then, when some resident drives out, I follow them."

"Them?"

"Well, him or her, depending which it is. Or them, if there's more than one in the car. Sooner or later, they stop somewhere and get out of the car."

"And you take them out, and you keep doing this, and sooner or later it's the right guy."

"They get out of the car," he said, "and I hang around until nobody's watching, and I get in the trunk."

"The trunk of their car."

"If I wanted to get in the trunk of my own car," he said, "I could go do that right now. Yes, the trunk of their car."

"I get it," she said. "Their car morphs into the Trojan Chrysler. They sail back into the walled city, and you're in there, and hoping they'll open the trunk eventually and let you out."

"Car trunks have a release mechanism built in these days," he said. "So kidnap victims can escape."

"You're kidding," she said. "The automakers added something for the benefit of the eight people a year who get stuffed into car trunks?"

"I think it's probably more than eight a year," he said, "and then there are the people, kids mostly, who get locked in accidentally. Anyway, it's no problem getting out."

"How about getting in? You real clever with auto locks?"

"That might be a problem," he admitted. "Does everybody lock their car nowadays?"

"I bet the ones who live in gated communities do. Not when they're home safe, but when they're out and about in a dangerous place like the suburbs of Phoenix. How crazy are you about this plan, Keller?"

"Not too," he admitted.

"Because how would you even know they were going back? Your luck, they're on their way to spend two weeks in Las Vegas."

"I didn't think of that."

"Of course you'd know right away," she said, "when you tried to get in the trunk and it was full of suitcases and copies of *Beat the Dealer*."

"It's not a great plan," he allowed, "but you wouldn't believe the security. The only other thing I can think of is to buy a place."

"Buy a house there, you mean. I don't think the budget would cover it."

"I could keep it as an investment," he said, "and rent it out when I wasn't using it."

"Which would be what, fifty-two weeks a year?"

"But if I could afford to do all that," he said, "I could also afford to tell the client to go roll his hoop, which I'm thinking I might have to go and do anyway."

"Because it's looking difficult."

"It's looking impossible," he said, "and then on top of everything else . . ."

"Yes? Keller? Where'd you go? Hello?"

"Never mind," he said. "I just figured out how to do it."

"**A**s you can see," Mitzi Prentice said, "the view's nowhere near as nice as the Lattimore house. And there's just two bedrooms instead of three, and the furnishing's a little on the generic side. But compared to spending the next two weeks in a motel—"

"It's a whole lot more comfortable," he said.

"And more secure," she said, "just in case you've got your stamp collection with you."

"I don't," he said, "but a little security never hurt anybody. I'd like to take it."

"I don't blame you, it's a real good deal, and nice income for Mr. and Mrs. Sundstrom, who're in the Galapagos Islands looking at blue-footed boobies. That's where all the crap on their walls comes from. Not the Galapagos, but other places they go to on their travels."

"I was wondering."

"Well, they could tell you about each precious piece, but they're not here, and if they were then their place wouldn't be available, would it? We'll go to the office and fill out the paperwork, and then you can give me a check and I'll give you a set of keys and some ID to get you past the guard at the gate. And a pass to the clubhouse, and information on greens fees and all. I hope you'll have some time for golf."

"Oh, I should be able to fit in a few rounds."

"No telling what you'll be able to fit in," she said. "Speaking of which, let's fit in a quick stop at the Lattimore house before we start filling out lease agreements. And no, silly, I'm not trying to get you to buy that place. I just want you to take me into that bedroom again. I mean, you don't expect me to do it in Cynthia Sundstrom's bed, do you? With all those weird masks on the wall? It'd give me the jimjams for sure. I'd feel like primitive tribes were watching me."

The Sundstrom house was a good deal more comfortable than his motel, and he found he didn't mind being surrounded by souvenirs of the couple's travels. The second bedroom, which evidently served as Harvey Sundstrom's den, had a collection of edged weapons hanging on the walls, knives and daggers and what he supposed were battle-axes, and there was no end of carved masks and tapestries in the other rooms. Some of the masks looked god-awful, he supposed, but they weren't the sort of things to give him the jimjams, whatever the jimjams might be, and he got in the habit of acknowledging one of them, a West African mask with teeth like tombstones and a lot of rope fringe for hair. He found himself giving it a nod when he passed it, even raising a hand in a salute.

Pretty soon, he thought, he'd be talking to it.

Because it was becoming clear to him that he felt the need to talk to someone. It was, he supposed, a need he'd had all his life, but for years he'd led an existence that didn't much lend itself to sharing confidences. He'd spent virtually all his adult life as a paid assassin, and it was no line of work for a man given to telling his business to strangers—or to friends, for that matter. You did what they paid you to do and you kept your mouth shut, and that was about it. You didn't talk about your work, and it got so you didn't talk about much of anything else, either. You could go to a sports bar and discuss the game with the fellow on the next barstool, you could gripe about the weather to the woman standing alongside you at the bus stop, you could complain about the mayor to the waitress at the corner coffee shop, but if you wanted a conversation with a little more substance to it, well, you were pretty much out of luck.

Once, a few years ago, he'd let someone talk him into going to a psychotherapist. He'd taken what struck him as reasonable precautions, paying cash, furnishing a false name and address, and essentially limiting disclosures to his childhood. It was productive, too, and he developed some useful insights, but in the end it went bad, with the therapist drawing some unwelcome inferences and eventually following Keller, and learning things he wasn't supposed to know about him. The man wanted to become a client himself, and of course Keller couldn't allow that, and made him a quarry instead. So much for therapy. So much for shared confidences.

Then, for some months after the therapist's exit, he'd had a dog. Not Soldier, the dog of his boyhood years, but Nelson, a fine Australian cattle dog. Nelson had turned out to be not only the perfect companion but also the perfect confidant. You could tell him anything, secure in the knowledge that he'd keep it to himself, and it wasn't like talking to yourself or talking to the wall, because the dog was real and alive and gave every indication of paying close attention. There were times when he could swear Nelson understood every word.

He wasn't judgmental, either. You could tell him anything and he didn't love you any the less for it.

If only it had stayed that way, he thought. But it hadn't, and he supposed it was his own fault. He'd found someone to take care of Nelson when work took him out of town, and that was better than putting him in a kennel, but then he wound up falling for the dog walker, and she moved in, and he only really got to talk to Nelson when Andria was somewhere else. That wasn't too bad, and she was fun to have around, but then one day it was time for her to move on, and on she moved. He'd bought her no end of earrings during their time together, and she took the earrings along with her when she left, which was okay. But she also took Nelson, and there he was, right back where he'd started.

Another man might have gone right out and got himself another dog—and then, like as not, gone looking for a woman to walk it for him. Keller figured enough was enough. He hadn't replaced the therapist, and he hadn't replaced the dog, and, although women drifted in and out of his life, he hadn't replaced the girlfriend. He had, after all, lived alone for years, and it worked for him.

Most of the time, anyway.

CHAPTER FIFTEEN

"**N**ow this is nice," Keller said. "The suburbs go on for a ways, but once you get past them you're out in the desert, and as long as you stay off the interstate you've pretty much got the whole place to yourself. It's pleasant, isn't it?"

There was no answer from the passenger seat.

"I paid cash for the Sundstrom house," he went on. "Two weeks, a thousand dollars a week. That's more than a motel, but I can cook my own meals and save on restaurant charges. Except I like to go out for my meals. But I didn't drag you all the way out here to listen to me talk about stuff like that."

Again, his passenger made no response, but then he hadn't expected one.

"There's a lot I have to figure out," he said. "Like what I'm going to do with the rest of my life, for starters. I don't see how I can keep on doing what I've been doing all these years. If you think of it as killing people, taking lives, well, how could a person go on doing it year after year after year?

"But the thing is, see, you don't have to dwell on that aspect of the work. I mean, face it, that's what it is. These people are walking around, doing what they do, and then I come along, and whatever it is they've been doing, they don't get to do it anymore. Because they're dead, because I killed them."

He glanced over, looking for a reaction. Yeah, right.

"What happens," he said, "is you wind up thinking of each subject not as a person to be killed but as a problem to be solved. Here's this piece of work you have to do, and how do you get it done? How do you carry out the contract as expediently as possible, with the least stress all around?

"Now there are guys doing this," he went on, "who cope with it by making it personal. They find a reason to hate the guy they have to kill. They're mad at him, they're angry with him, because it's his fault that they've got to do this bad thing. If it weren't for him, they wouldn't be committing this sin. He's going to be the cause of them going to hell, the son of a bitch, so of course they're mad at him, of course they hate him, and that makes it easier for them to kill him, which is what they made up their minds to do in the first place.

"But that always struck me as silly. I don't know what's a sin and what isn't, or if one person deserves to go on living and another deserves to have his life ended. Sometimes I think about stuff like that, but as far as working it all out in my mind, well, I never seem to get anywhere.

"I could go on like this, but the thing is I'm okay with the moral aspects of it, if you want to call it that. I just think I'm getting a little old to be still at it, that's part of it, and the other's that the business has changed. It's the same in that there are still people who are willing to pay to have other people killed. You never have to worry about running out of clients. Sometimes business drops off for a while, but it always comes back again. Whether it's a guy like that Cuban in Miami, who must have had a hundred guys with a reason to want him dead, or this Egmont with his potbelly and his golf clubs, who you'd think would be unlikely to inspire strong feelings in anybody. All kinds of subjects, and all kinds of clients, and you never run out of either one."

The road curved, and he took the curve a little too fast and had to reach over with his right hand to reposition his silent companion.

"You should be wearing your seat belt," he said. "Where was I? Oh, the way the business is changing. It's the world, really. Airport security, having to show ID everywhere you go. And gated communities, and all the rest of it. You think of Daniel Boone, who knew it was time to head west when he couldn't cut down a tree without giving some thought to which direction it was going to fall.

"I don't know, it seems to me that I'm just running off at the mouth, not making any sense. Well, that's okay. What do you care? Just so long as I take it easy on the curves so you don't wind up on the floor, you'll be perfectly willing to sit there and listen as long as I want to talk. Won't you?"

No response.

"If I played golf," he said, "I'd be out on the course every day, and I wouldn't have to burn up a tankful of gas driving around the desert. I'd spend all my time within the Sundowner walls, and I wouldn't have been walking around the mall, wouldn't have seen you in the display next to the cash register. A batch of different breeds on sale, and I'm not sure what you're supposed to be, but I guess you're some kind of terrier. They're good dogs, terriers. Feisty, lots of personality.

"I used to have an Australian cattle dog. I called him Nelson. Well, that was his name before I got him, and

I didn't see any reason to change it. I don't think I'll give you a name. I mean, it's nutty enough, buying a stuffed animal, taking it for a ride and having a conversation with it. It's not as if you're going to answer to a name, or as if I'll relate to you on a deeper level if I hang a name on you. I mean, I may be crazy, but I'm not stupid. I realize I'm talking to polyester and foam rubber, or whatever the hell you're made out of. Made in China, it says on the tag. That's another thing, everything's made in China or Indonesia or the Philippines, nothing's made in America anymore. It's not that I'm paranoid about it, it's not that I'm worried about all the jobs going overseas. What do I care, anyway? It's not affecting my work. As far as I know, nobody's flying in hired killers from Thailand and Korea to take jobs away from good homegrown American hit men.

"It's just that you have to wonder what people in this country are doing. If they're not making anything, if everything's imported from someplace else, what the hell do Americans do when they get to the office?"

He talked for a while more, then drove around some in silence, then resumed the one-sided conversation. Eventually he found his way back to Sundowner Estates, circling the compound and entering by the southwestern gate.

Hi, Mr. Miller. Hello, Harry. Hey, whatcha got there? Cute little fella, isn't he? A present for my sister's little girl, my niece. I'll ship it to her tomorrow.

The hell with that. Before he got to the guard shack, he reached into the backseat for a newspaper and spread it over the stuffed dog in the passenger seat.

CHAPTER SIXTEEN

In the clubhouse bar, Keller listened sympathetically as a fellow named Monty went over his round of golf, stroke by stroke. "What kills me," Monty said, "is that I just can't put it all together. Like on the seventh hole this afternoon, my drive's smack down the middle of the fairway, and my second shot with a three iron is hole high and just off the edge of the green on the right. I'm not in the bunker, I'm past it, and I've got a good lie maybe ten, twelve feet from the edge of the green."

"Nice," Keller said, his voice carefully neutral. If it wasn't nice, Monty could assume he was being ironic.

"Very nice," Monty agreed, "and I'm lying two, and all I have to do is run it up reasonably close and sink the putt for a par. I could use a wedge, but why screw around? It's easier to take this little chipping iron I carry and run it up close."

"Uh-huh."

"So I run it up close, all right, and it doesn't miss the cup by more than two inches, but I played it too strong, and it picks up speed and rolls past the pin and all the way off the green, and I wind up farther from the cup than when I started."

"Hell of a thing."

"So I chip again, and pass the hole again, though not quite as badly. And by the time I'm done hacking away with my goddam putter I'm three strokes over par with a seven.

Takes me two strokes to cover four hundred and forty yards and five more strokes to manage the last fifty feet."

"Well, that's golf," Keller said.

"By God, you said a mouthful," Monty said. "That's golf, all right. How about another round of these, Dave, and then we'll get ourselves some dinner? There're a couple of guys you ought to meet."

He wound up at a table with four other fellows. Monty and a man named Felix were residents of Sundowner Estates, while the other two men were Felix's guests, seasonal residents of Scottsdale who belonged to one of the other local country clubs. Felix told a long joke, involving a hapless golfer driven to suicide by a bad round of golf. For the punch line, Felix held his wrists together and said, "What time?" and everybody roared. They all ordered steaks and drank beer and talked about golf and politics and how screwed-up the stock market was these days, and Keller managed to keep up his end of the conversation without anybody seeming to notice that he didn't know what the hell he was talking about.

"So how'd you do out there today?" someone asked him, and Keller had his reply all ready.

"You know," he said thoughtfully, "it's a hell of a thing. You can hack away like a man trying to beat a ball to death with a stick, and then you hit one shot that's so sweet and true that it makes you feel good about the whole day."

He couldn't even remember when or where he'd heard that, but it evidently rang true with his dinner companions. They all nodded solemnly, and then someone changed the subject and said something disparaging about Democrats, and it was Keller's turn to nod in agreement.

Nothing to it.

"So we'll go out tomorrow morning," Monty said to Felix. "Dave, if you want to join us . . ."

Keller pressed his wrists together, said, "What time?" When the laughter died down he said, "I wish I could, Monty. I'm afraid tomorrow's out. Another time, though."

"You could take a lesson," Dot said. "Isn't there a club pro? Doesn't he give lessons?"

"There is," he said, "and I suppose he does, but why would I want to take one?"

"So you could get out there and play golf. Protective coloration and all."

"If anyone sees me swinging a golf club," he said, "with or without a lesson, they'll wonder what the hell I'm doing here. But this way they just figure I fit in a round earlier in the day. Anyway, I don't want to spend too much time around the clubhouse. Mostly I get the hell out of here and go for drives."

"On the driving range?"

"Out in the desert," he said.

"You just ride around and look at the cactus."

"There's a lot of it to look at," he said, "although they have a problem with poachers."

"You're kidding."

"No," he said, and explained how the cacti were protected, but criminals dug them up and sold them to florists.

"Cactus rustlers," Dot said. "That's the damnedest thing I ever heard of. I guess they have to be careful of the spines."

"I suppose so."

"Serve them right if they get stuck. You just drive around, huh?"

"And think things out."

"Well, that's nice. But you don't want to lose sight of the reason you moved in there in the first place."

"I won't."

"Besides," she said, "I miss you. I got this phone call."

"Oh?"

"It was sort of weird. Well, atypical, anyway. I don't know who it was from, or why he called."

"Maybe it was a wrong number."

"No, it wasn't that. The hell with it. If you were here we could talk about it, but not over the phone."

He stayed away from the clubhouse the next day, and the day after. Then, on a Tuesday afternoon, he got in his car and drove around, staying within the friendly confines of Sundowner. He passed the Lattimore house and wondered if Mitzi Prentice had shown it to anyone lately. He drove past William Egmont's house, which looked to be pretty much the same model as the Sundstrom place. Egmont's Cadillac was parked in the carport, but the man owned his own golf cart, and Keller couldn't see it there. He'd probably motored over to the first tee on his cart, and might be out there now, taking big divots, slicing balls deep into the rough.

Keller went home, parked his Toyota in the Sundstrom carport. He'd worried, after taking the house for two weeks, that Mitzi would call all the time, or, worse, start turning up without calling first. But in fact he hadn't heard a word from her, for which he'd been deeply grateful, and now he found himself thinking about calling her, at work or at home, and figuring out a place to meet. Not at his place, because of the masks, and not at her place, because of her daughter, and—

That settled it. If he was starting to think like that, well, it was time he got on with it. Or the next thing you knew he'd be taking golf lessons, and buying the Lattimore house, and trading in the stuffed dog for a real one.

He went outside. The afternoon had already begun fading into early evening, and it seemed to Keller that the darkness came quicker here than it did in New York. That stood to reason, it was a good deal closer to the equator, and that would account for it. Someone had explained why to him once, and he'd understood it at the time, but now all that remained was the fact: the farther you were from the equator, the more extended twilight became.

In any event, the golfers were through for the day. He took a walk along the edge of the golf course, and passed Egmont's house. The car was still there, and the golf cart was not. He walked on for a while, then turned around and headed toward the house again, coming from the other direction, and saw someone gliding along on a motorized golf cart. Was it Egmont, on his way home? No, as the cart came closer he saw that the rider was thinner than Keller's quarry, and had a fuller head of hair. And the cart turned off before it reached Egmont's house, which pretty much cinched things.

Besides, he was soon to discover, Egmont had already returned. His cart was parked in the carport, alongside his car, and the bag of golf clubs was slung over the back of the cart. Something about that last touch reminded Keller of a song, though he couldn't pin down the song or figure out how it hooked up to the golf cart. Something mournful, something with bagpipes, but Keller couldn't put his finger on it.

There were lights on in Egmont's house. Was he alone? Had he brought someone home with him?

One easy way to find out. He walked up the path to the front door, poked the doorbell. He heard it ring, then didn't hear anything and considered ringing it again. First he tried the door, and found it locked, which was no great surprise, and then he heard footsteps, but just barely, as if someone was walking lightly on deep carpet. And then the door opened a few inches until the chain stopped it, and William Wallis Egmont looked out at him, a puzzled expression on his face.

"Mr. Egmont?"

"Yes?"

"My name's Miller," he said. "David Miller. I'm staying just over the hill, I'm renting the Sundstrom house for a couple of weeks . . ."

"Oh, of course," Egmont said, visibly relaxing. "Of course, Mr. Miller. Someone was mentioning you just the other day. And I do believe I've seen you around the club. And out on the course, if I'm not mistaken."

It was a mistake Keller saw no need to correct. "You probably have," he said. "I'm out there every chance I get."

"As am I, sir. I played today, and I expect to play tomorrow."

Keller pressed his wrists together, said, "What time?"

"Oh, very good," Egmont said. " 'What time?' That's a golfer for you, isn't it? Now how can I help you?"

"It's delicate," Keller said. "Do you suppose I could come in for a moment?"

"Well, I don't see why not," Egmont said, and slipped the chain lock to let him in.

CHAPTER SEVENTEEN

The keypad for the burglar alarm was mounted on the wall, just to the right of the front door. Immediately adjacent to it was a sheet of paper headed *HOW TO SET THE BURGLAR ALARM* with the instructions printed by hand in block capitals large enough to be read easily by elderly eyes. Keller read the directions, followed them, and let himself out of Egmont's house. A few minutes later he was back in his own house—the Sundstrom house. He made himself a cup of coffee in the Sundstrom kitchen and sat with it in the Sundstrom living room, and while it cooled he let himself remember the last moments of William Wallis Egmont.

He practiced the exercises that were automatic for him by now, turning the images that came to mind from color to black and white, then watching them fade to gray, willing them farther and farther away so that they grew smaller and smaller until they were vanishing pinpoints, gray dots on a gray field, disappearing into the distance, swallowed up by the past.

When his coffee cup was empty he went into the Sundstrom bedroom and undressed, then showered in the Sundstrom bathroom, only to dry off with a Sundstrom towel. He went into the den, Harvey Sundstrom's den, and took a Fijian battle-ax from the wall. It was fashioned of black wood, and heavier than it looked, and its elaborate geometric shape suggested it would be of more use as wall decoration than weapon. But Keller worked out how to grip it and swing it, and took a few experimental whiffs with it, and he could see how the islanders would have found it useful.

He could have taken it with him to Egmont's house, and he let himself imagine it now, saw himself clutching the device in both hands and swinging around in a 360-degree arc, whipping the business end of the ax into Egmont's skull. He shook his head, returned the battle-ax to the wall, and resumed where he'd left off earlier, summoning up Egmont's image, reviewing the last moments of Egmont's life, and making it all gray and blurry, making it all smaller and smaller, making it all go away.

In the morning he went out for breakfast, returning in time to see an ambulance leaving Sundowner Estates through the east gate. The guard recognized Keller and waved him through, but he braked and rolled down the window to inquire about the ambulance. The guard shook his head soberly and reported the sad news.

He went home and called Dot. "Don't tell me," she said. "You've decided you can't do it."

"It's done."

"It's amazing how I can just sense these things," she said. "You figure it's psychic powers or old-fashioned feminine intuition? That was a rhetorical question, Keller. You don't have to answer it. I'd say I'll see you tomorrow, but I won't, will I?"

"It'll take me a while to get home."

"Well, no rush," she said. "Take your time, see the sights. You've got your clubs, haven't you?"

"My clubs?"

"Stop along the way, play a little golf. Enjoy yourself, Keller. You deserve it."

The day before his two-week rental was up, he walked over to the clubhouse, settled his account, and turned in his keys and ID card. He walked back to the Sundstrom house, where he put his suitcase in the trunk and the little stuffed dog in the passenger seat. Then he got behind the wheel and drove slowly around the golf course, leaving the compound by the east gate.

"It's a nice place," he told the dog. "I can see why people like it. Not just the golf and the weather and the security. You get the feeling nothing really bad could happen to you there. Even if you die, it's just part of the natural order of things."

He set cruise control and pointed the car toward Tucson, lowering the visor against the morning sun. It was, he thought, good weather for cruise control. Just the other day, he'd had NPR on the car radio, and listened as a man with a professionally mellow voice cautioned against using cruise control in wet weather. If the car were to hydroplane on the slick pavement, cruise control would think the wheels weren't turning fast enough, and would speed up the engine to compensate. And then, when the tires got their grip again, wham!

Keller couldn't recall the annual cost in lives from this phenomenon, but it was higher than you'd think. At the time all he did was resolve to make sure he took the car out of cruise control whenever he switched on the windshield wipers. Now, cruising east across the Arizona desert, he found himself wondering if there might be any practical application for this new knowledge. Accidental death was a useful tool, it had most recently claimed the life of William Wallis Egmont, but Keller couldn't see how cruise control in inclement weather could become part of his bag of tricks. Still, you never knew, and he let himself think about it.

In Tucson he stuck the dog in his suitcase before he turned in the car, then walked out into the heat and managed to locate his original car in long-term parking. He tossed his suitcase in the backseat and stuck the key in the ignition, wondering if the car would start. No problem if it wouldn't, all he'd have to do was talk to somebody at the Hertz counter, but suppose they'd just spotted him at the Avis counter, turning in another car. Would they notice something like that? You wouldn't think so, but airports were different these days. There were people standing around noticing everything.

He turned the key, and the engine turned over right away. The woman at the gate figured out what he owed and sounded apologetic when she named the figure. He found himself imagining what the charges would have added up to on other cars he'd left in long-term lots, cars he'd never returned to claim, cars with bodies in their trunks. Probably a lot of money, he decided, and nobody to pay it. He figured he could afford to pick up the tab for a change. He paid cash, took the receipt, and got back on the interstate.

As he drove, he found himself figuring out just how he'd have handled it if the car hadn't started. "For God's sake," he said, "look at yourself, will you? Something could have happened but didn't, it's over and done with, and you're figuring out what you would have done, developing a coping strategy when there's nothing to cope with.

What the hell's the matter with you?"

He thought about it. Then he said, "You want to know what's the matter with you? You're talking to yourself, that's what's the matter with you."

He stopped doing it. Twenty minutes down the road he pulled into a rest area, leaned over the seat back, opened his suitcase, and returned the dog to its position in the passenger seat.

"And away we go," he said.

In New Mexico he got off the interstate and followed the signs to an Indian pueblo. A plump woman, her hair braided and her face expressionless, sat in a room with pots she had made herself. Keller picked out a little black pot with scalloped edges. She wrapped it carefully for him, using sheets of newspaper, and put the wrapped pot in a brown paper bag, and the paper bag into a plastic bag. Keller tucked the whole thing away in his suitcase and got back behind the wheel.

"Don't ask," he told the dog.

Just over the Colorado state line it started to rain. He drove through the rain for ten or twenty miles before he remembered the guy on NPR. He tapped the brake, which made the cruise control cut out, but just to make sure he used the switch, too.

"Close one," he told the dog.

In Kansas he took a state road north and visited a roadside attraction, a house that had once been a hideout of the Dalton boys. They were outlaws, he knew, contemporaries of Jesse James and the Youngers. The place was tricked out as a minimuseum, with memorabilia and news clippings, and there was an underground passage leading from the house to the barn in back, so that the brothers, when surprised by the law, could hurry through the tunnel and escape that way. He'd have liked to see the passage, but it was sealed off.

"Still," he told the woman attendant, "it's nice to know it's there."

If he was interested in the Daltons, she told him, there was another museum at the other end of the state. At Coffeyville, she said, where as he probably knew most of the Daltons were killed, trying to rob two banks in one day. He had in fact known that, but only because he'd just read it on the information card for one of the exhibits.

He stopped at a gas station, bought a state map, and figured out the route to Coffeyville. Halfway there he stopped for the night at a Red Roof Inn, had a pizza delivered, and ate it in front of the television set. He ran the cable channels until he found a western that looked promising, and damned if it didn't turn out to be about the Dalton boys. Not just the Daltons—Frank and Jesse James were in it, too, and Cole Younger and his brothers.

They seemed like real nice fellows, too, the kind of guys you wouldn't mind hanging out with. Not a sadist or pyromaniac in the lot, as far as he could tell. And did you think Jesse James wet the bed? Like hell he did.

In the morning he drove on to Coffeyville and paid the admission charge and took his time studying the exhibits. It was a pretty bold act, robbing two banks at once, but it might not have been the smartest move in the history of American crime. The local citizens were just waiting for them, and they riddled the brothers with bullets. Most of them were dead by the time the shooting stopped, or died of their wounds before long.

Emmett Dalton wound up with something like a dozen bullets in him, and went off to prison. But the story didn't end there. He recovered, and eventually got released, and wound up in Los Angeles, where he wrote films for the young motion picture industry and made a small fortune in real estate.

Keller spent a long time taking that in, and it gave him a lot to think about.

Most of the time he was quiet, but now and then he talked to the dog.

"Take soldiers," he said, on a stretch of I-80 east of Des Moines. "They get drafted into the army, they go through basic training, and before you know it they're aiming at other soldiers and pulling the trigger. Maybe they have to force themselves the first couple of times, and maybe they have bad dreams early on, but then they get used to it, and before you know it they sort of enjoy it. It's not a sex thing, they don't get that kind of a thrill out of it, but it's sort of like hunting. Except you just pull the trigger and leave it at that. You don't have to track wounded soldiers to make sure they don't suffer. You don't have to dress your kill and pack it back to camp. You just pull the trigger and get on with your life.

"And these are ordinary kids," he went on. "Eighteen-year-old boys, drafted fresh out of high school. Or I guess it's volunteers now, they don't draft them anymore, but it amounts to the same thing. They're just ordinary American boys. They didn't grow up torturing animals or starting fires. Or wetting the bed.

"You know something? I still don't see what wetting the bed has to do with it."

Coming into New York on the George Washington Bridge, he said, "Well, they're not there."

The towers, he meant. And of course they weren't there, they were gone, and he knew that. He'd been down to the site enough times to know it wasn't trick photography, that the twin towers were in fact gone. But somehow he'd half expected to see them, half expected the whole thing to turn out to have been a dream. You couldn't make part of the skyline disappear, for God's sake.

He drove to the Hertz place, returned the car. He was walking away from the office with his suitcase in hand when an attendant rushed up, brandishing the little stuffed dog. "You forgot somethin'," the man said, smiling broadly.

"Oh, right," Keller said. "You got any kids?"

"Me?"

"Give it to your kid," Keller told him. "Or some other kid."

"You don't want him?"

He shook his head, kept walking. When he got home he showered and shaved and looked out the window. His window faced east, not south, and had never afforded a view of the towers, so it was the same as it had always been. And that's why he'd looked, to assure himself that everything was still there, that nothing had been taken away.

It looked okay to him. He picked up the phone and called Dot.

CHAPTER EIGHTEEN

She was waiting for him on the porch, with the usual pitcher of iced tea. "You had me going," she said. "You didn't call and you didn't call and you didn't call. It took you the better part of a month to get home. What did you do, walk?"

"I didn't leave right away," he said. "I'd paid for two weeks."

"And you wanted to make sure you got your money's worth."

"I thought it'd be suspicious, leaving early. 'Oh, I remember that guy, he left four days early, right after Mr. Egmont died.'"

"And you thought it'd be safer to hang around the scene of a homicide?"

"Except it wasn't a homicide," he said. "The man came home after an afternoon at the golf course, locked his door, set the burglar alarm, got undressed, and drew a hot bath. He got into the tub and lost consciousness and drowned."

"Most accidents happen in the home," Dot said. "Isn't that what they say? What did he do, hit his head?"

"He may have smacked it on the tile on the way down, after he lost his balance. Or maybe he had a little stroke. Hard to say."

"You undressed him and everything?"

He nodded. "Put him in the tub. He came to in the

water, but I picked up his feet and held them in the air, and his head went under, and, well, that was that."

"Water in the lungs."

"Right."

"Death by drowning."

He nodded.

"You okay, Keller?"

"Me? Sure, I'm fine. Anyway, I figured I'd wait the four days, leave when my time was up."

"Just like Egmont."

"Huh?"

"He left when his time was up," she said. "Still, how long does it take to drive home from Phoenix? Four, five days?"

"I got sidetracked," he said, and told her about the Dalton Boys.

"Two museums," she said. "Most people have never been to one Dalton Boys museum, and you've been to two."

"Well, they robbed two banks at once."

"What's that got to do with it?"

"I don't know. Nothing, I guess. You ever hear of Nashville, Indiana?"

"I've heard of Nashville," she said, "and I've heard of Indiana, but I guess the answer to your question is no. What have they got in Nashville, Indiana? The Grand Ole Hoosier Opry?"

"There's a John Dillinger museum there."

"Jesus, Keller. What were you taking, an outlaw's tour of the Midwest?"

"There was a flyer for the place in the museum in Coffeyville, and it wasn't that far out of my way. It was interesting. They had the fake gun he used to break out of prison. Or it may have been a replica. Either way, it was pretty interesting."

"I'll bet."

"They were folk heroes," he said. "Dillinger and Pretty Boy Floyd and Baby Face Nelson."

"And Bonnie and Clyde. Have those two got a museum?"

"Probably. They were heroes the same as the Daltons and Youngers and Jameses, but they weren't brothers. Back in the nineteenth century it was a family thing, but then that tradition died out."

"Kids today," Dot said. "What about Ma Barker? Wasn't that around the same time as Dillinger? And didn't she have a whole houseful of bank-robbing brats? Or was that just in the movies?"

"No, you're right," he said. "I forgot about Ma Barker."

"Well, let's forget her all over again, so you can get to the point."

He shook his head. "I'm not sure there is one. I just took my time getting back, that's all. I had some thinking to do."

"And?"

He reached for the pitcher, poured himself more iced tea. "Okay," he said. "Here's the thing. I can't do this anymore."

"I can't say I'm surprised."

"I was going to retire a while ago," he said. "Remember?"

"Vividly."

"At the time," he said, "I figured I could afford it. I had

money put aside. Not a ton, but enough for a little bunga-low somewhere in Florida."

"And you could get to Denny's in time for the early bird special, which helps keep food costs down."

"You said I needed a hobby, and that got me interested in stamp collecting again. And before I knew it I was spending serious money on stamps."

"And that was the end of your retirement fund."

"It cut into it," he agreed. "And it's kept me from sav-ing money ever since then, because any extra money just goes into stamps."

She frowned. "I think I see where this is going," she said. "You can't keep on doing what you've been doing, but you can't retire, either."

"So I tried to think what else I could do," he said. "Emmett Dalton wound up in Hollywood, writing movies and dealing in real estate."

"You working on a script, Keller? Boning up for the realtor's exam?"

"I couldn't think of a single thing I could do," he said. "Oh, I suppose I could get some kind of minimum-wage job. But I'm used to living a certain way, and I'm used to not having to work many hours. Can you see me clerking in a 7-Eleven?"

"I couldn't even see you sticking up a 7-Eleven, Keller."

"It might be different if I were younger."

"I guess armed robbery is a young man's job."

"If I were just starting out," he said, "I could take some entry-level job and work my way up. But I'm too old for that now. Nobody would hire me in the first place, and the jobs I'm qualified for, well, I wouldn't want them."

"'Do you want fries with that?' You're right, Keller.

Somehow it just doesn't sound like you."

"I started at the bottom once. I started coming around, and the old man found things for me to do. 'Richie's gotta see a man, so why don't you ride along with him, keep him company.' Or go see this guy, tell him we're not happy with the way he's been acting. Or he used to send me to the store to pick up candy bars for him. What was that candy bar he used to like?"

"Mars bars."

"No, he switched to those, but early on it was something else. They were hard to find, only a few stores had them. I think he was the only person I ever met who liked them. What the hell was the name of them? It's on the tip of my tongue."

"Hell of a place for a candy bar."

"Powerhouse," he said. "Powerhouse candy bars."

"The dentist's best friend," she said. "I remember them now. I wonder if they still make them."

" 'Do me a favor, kid, see if they got any of my candy bars downtown.' Then one day it was do me a favor, here's a gun, go see this guy and give him two in the head. Out of the blue, more or less, except by then he probably knew I'd do it. And you know something? It never occurred to me not to. 'Here's a gun, do me a favor.' So I took the gun and did him a favor."

"Just like that?"

"Pretty much. I was used to doing what he told me, and I just did. And that let him know I was somebody who could do that kind of thing. Because not everybody can."

"But it didn't bother you."

"I've been thinking about this," he said. "Reflecting, I guess you'd call it. I didn't let it bother me."

"That thing you do, fading the color out of the image and pushing it off in the distance . . ."

"It was later that I taught myself to do that," he said. "Earlier, well, I guess you'd just call it denial. I told myself it didn't bother me and made myself believe it. And then there was this sense of accomplishment. Look what I did, see what a man I am. Bang, and he's dead and you're not, there's a certain amount of exhilaration that comes with it."

"Still?"

He shook his head. "There's the feeling that you've got the job done, that's all. If it was difficult, well, you've accomplished something. If there are other things you'd rather be doing, well, now you can go home and do them."

"Buy stamps, see a movie."

"Right."

"You just pretended it didn't bother you," she said, "and then one day it didn't."

"And it was easy to pretend, because it never bothered me all that much. But yes, I just kept on doing it, and then I didn't have to pretend. This place where I stayed in Scottsdale, there were all these masks on the walls. Tribal stuff, I guess they were. And I thought about how I started out wearing a mask, and before long it wasn't a mask, it was my own face."

"I guess I follow you."

"It's just a way of looking at it," he said. "Anyway, how I got here's not the point. Where do I go from here? That's the question."

"You had a lot of time to think up an answer."

"Too much time."

"I guess, with all the stops in Nashville and Coffee Pot."

"Coffeyville."

"Whatever. What did you come up with, Keller?"

"Well," he said, and drew a breath. "One, I'm ready to stop doing this. The business is different, with the airline security and people living behind stockade fences. And I'm different. I'm older, and I've been doing this for too many years."

"Okay."

"Two, I can't retire. I need the money, and I don't have any other way to earn what I need to live on."

"I hope there's a three, Keller, because one and two don't leave you much room to swing."

"What I had to do," he said, "was figure out how much money I need."

"To retire on."

He nodded. "The figure I came up with," he said, "is a million dollars."

"A nice round sum."

"That's more than I had when I was thinking about retirement the last time. I think this is a more realistic figure. Invested right, I could probably get a return of around fifty thousand dollars a year."

"And you can live on that?"

"I don't want that much," he said. "I'm not thinking in terms of around-the-world cruises and expensive restaurants. I don't spend a lot on clothes, and when I buy something I wear it until it's worn out."

"Or even longer."

"If I had a million in cash," he said, "plus what I could get for the apartment, which is probably another half million."

143

"Where would you move?"

"I don't know. Someplace warm, I suppose."

"Sundowner Estates?"

"Too expensive. And I wouldn't care to be walled in, and I don't play golf."

"You might, just to have something to do."

He shook his head. "Some of those guys loved golf," he said, "but others, you had the feeling they had to keep selling themselves on the idea, telling one another how crazy they were about the game. 'What time?'"

"How's that?"

"It's the punch line of a joke. It's not important. No, I wouldn't want to live there. But there are these little towns in New Mexico north of Albuquerque, up in the high desert, and you could buy a shack there or just pick up a mobile home and find a place to park it."

"And you think you could stand it? Out in the boonies like that?"

"I don't know. The thing is, say I netted half a million from the apartment, plus the million I saved. Say five percent, comes to seventy-five thousand a year, and yes, I could live fine on that."

"And your apartment's worth half a million?"

"Something like that."

"So all you need is a million dollars, Keller. Now I'd lend it to you myself, but I'm a little short this month. What are you going to do, sell your stamps?"

"They're not worth anything like that. I don't know what I've spent on the collection, but it certainly doesn't come to a million dollars, and you can't get back what you put into them, anyway."

"I thought they were supposed to be a good investment."

"They're better than spending the money on caviar and champagne," he said, "because you get something back when you sell them, but dealers have to make a profit, too, and if you get half your money back you're doing well. Anyway, I wouldn't want to sell them."

"You want to keep them. And keep on collecting?"

"If I had seventy-five thousand a year coming in," he said, "and if I lived in some little town in the desert, I could afford to spend ten or fifteen thousand a year on stamps."

"I bet northern New Mexico's full of people doing just that."

"Maybe not," he said, "but I don't see why I couldn't do it."

"You could be the first, Keller. Now all you need is a million dollars."

"That's what I was thinking."

"Okay, I'll bite. How're you going to get it?"

"Well," he said, "that pretty much answers itself, doesn't it? I mean, there's only one thing I know how to do."

CHAPTER NINETEEN

"I think I get it," Dot said. "You can't do this anymore, so you've got to do it with a vengeance. You have to depopulate half the country in order to get out of the business of killing people."

"When you put it that way . . ."

"Well, there's a certain irony operating, wouldn't you say? But there's a certain logic there, too. You want to grab every high-ticket job that comes along, so that you can salt away enough cash to get out of the business once and for all. You know what it reminds me of?"

"What?"

"Cops," she said. "Their pensions are based on what they make the last year they work, so they grab all the overtime they can get their hands on, and then when they retire they can live in style. Usually we sit back and pick and choose, and you take time off between jobs, but that's not what you want to do now, is it? You want to do a job, come home, catch your breath, then turn around and do another one."

"Right."

"Until you can cash in at an even million."

"That's the idea."

"Or maybe a few dollars more, to allow for inflation."

"Maybe."

"A little more iced tea, Keller?"

"No, I'm fine."

"Would you rather have coffee? I could make coffee."

"No thanks."

"You sure?"

"Positive."

"You took a lot of time in Scottsdale. Did he really look just like the man in Monopoly?"

"In the photo. Less so in real life."

"He didn't give you any trouble?"

He shook his head. "By the time he had a clue what was happening, it was pretty much over."

"He wasn't on his guard at all, then."

"No. I wonder why he got on somebody's list."

"An impatient heir would be my guess. Did it bother you much, Keller? Before, during, or after?"

He thought about it, shook his head.

"And then you took your time getting out of there."

"I thought it made sense to hang around a few days. One more day and I could have gone to the funeral."

"So you left the day they buried him?"

"Except they didn't," he said. "He had the same kind of funeral as Mr. Lattimore."

"Am I supposed to know who that is?"

"He had a house I could have bought. He was cremated, and after a nondenominational service his ashes were placed in the water hazard."

"Just a five-iron shot from his front door."

"Well," Keller said. "Anyway, yes, I took my time getting home."

"All those museums."

"I had to think it all through," he said. "Figuring out what I want to do with the rest of my life."

"Of which today is the first day, if I remember correctly. Let me make sure I've got this straight. You're done feeding rescue workers at Ground Zero, and you're done going to museums for dead outlaws, and you're ready to get out there and kill one for the Gipper. Is that about it?"

"It's close enough."

"Because I've been turning down jobs left and right, Keller, and what I want to do is get on the horn and spread the word that we're ready to do business. We're not holding any two-for-one sales, but we're very much in the game. Am I clear on that?" She got to her feet. "Which reminds me. Don't go away."

She came back with a pair of envelopes and dropped one on the table in front of him. "They paid up right away, and it took you so long to get home I was beginning to think of it as my money. What's this?"

"Something I picked up on the way home."

She opened the package, took the little black clay pot in her hands. "That's really nice," she said. "What is it, Indian?"

"From a pueblo in New Mexico."

"And it's for me?"

"I got the urge to buy it," he said, "and then afterward I wondered what I was going to do with it. And I thought maybe you'd like it."

"It would look nice on the mantel," she said. "Or it would be handy to keep paper clips in. But it'll have to be one or the other, because there's no point in keeping paper clips on the mantel. You said you got it in New Mexico? In the town you're figuring to wind up in?"

He shook his head. "It was a pueblo. I think you have to be an Indian."

"Well, they do nice work. I'm very pleased to have it."

"Glad you like it."

"What's not to like? It's beautiful. And I think you'll like this," she said, brandishing the second envelope. "But maybe not. I told you I got a strange telephone call."

"This was a while ago."

"Right."

"And you didn't want to talk about it over the phone."

"Partly because it was the phone, and partly because I didn't know what to say about it."

"Oh."

She leaned back in her chair. "This guy called," she said, "and it wasn't a voice I recognized, and the only name he gave me was Al."

"Al."

"'Al who?' I said. 'Just Al,' he said."

"Just Al."

"He said he wanted to send me something," she said, "and wanted to know where to send it."

"What did he want to send you?"

"My question precisely. Something on account, he said."

"On account?"

"On account of what, is what I wanted to know. On account of it's Tuesday? Just something on account, he said, and where would I like him to send it."

"He wanted to find out your address."

"My first thought," she said, "and I wanted to tell him to shit in his hat. I'm not telling you my address, I said, and he said he already knew it, but maybe I'd rather receive the parcel at another location. What parcel? I asked him. The parcel I'm going to send you, he said."

"On account."

"Right. At this point I was confused."

"I can understand why."

"I told him to let me think about it, and he said he'd call in a day or two. And that's where it stood when I spoke to you that time."

"When you said you had a weird conversation. You weren't kidding."

"He called back in a couple of days," she went on, "and by then I had just about decided I wouldn't hear from him again, which would have been fine with me, but there he was on the other end of the phone. 'It's Al,' he said."

"And?"

"I'd had some time to think. You know, a couple of times over the years I've used a post office box, or one of those private mailboxes. When we were dealing with somebody we didn't know who didn't know us, the box let us keep our distance. But if he already knew the address here on Taunton Place, why make a trip to a post office?"

"If he knew the address."

"Well, he'd have to know it, wouldn't he? He knew the phone number, and any four-year-old can Google a reverse directory and find an address to go with the number."

"I didn't think of that."

"So I told him to go ahead and send it here, whatever it was. I mean, say it was a letter bomb. What's the advantage of picking it up at Mailboxes 'R' Us as opposed to getting it right here?"

"So you told him to send it." He nodded at the envelope. "Is that it?"

She shook her head. "What I got," she said, "came by overnight FedEx."

"And it wasn't a letter bomb."

"I didn't really think it would be. I thought it would be money, and it was."

"Money."

"Cash," she said. "Fifty thousand dollars."

"On account."

"Uh-huh."

"That's . . . substantial."

"It is," she said, "and I don't know what it's for, but I could probably make an educated guess. I figured I'd get a phone call to explain it."

"And did you?"

"I got a phone call, but not much of an explanation. 'This is Al. I hope the parcel arrived in good order.' I said it did, but I didn't understand what was involved. 'You'll hear from me,' he said, 'when the time comes.' That was all I could get out of him."

"Fifty thousand dollars."

"Hundred-dollar bills," she said, "used and out of sequence. Five hundred of them."

"That's a lot better than a letter bomb," he said. "Still . . ."

"It makes you think."

"It does."

"Sooner or later," she said, "Al's gonna expect us to earn it. Like the Godfather, talking to that undertaker. 'Someday I'll need a favor.'"

"I guess that was supposed to be Marlon Brando."

"If I could do imitations," she said, "I'd be on the Comedy Channel. Whoever he is, Al's got a credit balance with us. My guess is we'll hear from him. In the meantime, you get your share."

He weighed the envelope in his hand. "You don't really have to split this with me," he said. "I mean, there are other people you've used from time to time. Who's to say you won't use somebody else for Al's job?"

"And keep you from reaching your million-dollar goal? Not likely. No, I got fifty large on account, and you're getting half of it, also on account. With both of those envelopes, I'd say you're off to a good start. Though I suppose you'll want to spend some of it on stamps."

CHAPTER TWENTY

Two days later he was working on his stamps when the phone rang. "I'm in the city," she said. "Right around the corner from you, as a matter of fact."

She told him the name of the restaurant, and he went there and found her in a booth at the back, eating an ice cream sundae. "When I was a kid," she said, "they had these at Wohler's drugstore for thirty-five cents. It was five cents extra if you wanted walnuts on top. I'd hate to tell you what they get for this beauty, and walnuts weren't part of the deal, either."

"Nothing's the way it used to be."

"You're right about that," she said, "and a philosophical observation like that is worth the trip. But it's not why I came in. Here's the waitress, Keller. You want one of these?"

He shook his head, ordered a cup of coffee. The waitress brought it, and when she was out of earshot Dot said, "I had a call this morning."

"From Al?"

"Al? No, not Al. I haven't heard a thing from Al. This was somebody else."

"Oh?"

"And I was going to call you, but it wasn't anything to discuss on the phone, and I didn't feel right about telling you to come out to White Plains because I was pretty sure you'd be wasting your time. So I figured I'd come in, and have an ice cream sundae while I'm at it. It's worth the trip, incidentally, even if they do charge the earth for it. You sure you don't want one?"

"Positive."

"I got a call," she said, "from a guy we've worked with before, a broker, very solid type. And there's some work to be done, a nice upscale piece of work, which would put a nice piece of change in your retirement fund and one in mine, too."

"What's the catch?"

"It's in Santa Barbara, California," she said, "and there's a very narrow window operating. You'd have to do it Wednesday or Thursday, which makes it impossible, because it would take longer than that for you to drive there even if you left right away and only stopped for gas. I mean, suppose you drove it in three days, which is ridiculous anyway. You'd be wiped out when you got there, and you'd get there when, Thursday afternoon at the earliest? Can't be done."

"No."

"So I'll tell them no," she said, "but I wanted to check with you first."

"Tell them we'll do it," he said.

"Really?"

"I'll fly out tomorrow morning. Or tonight, if I can get something."

"You weren't ever going to fly again."

"I know."

"And then a job comes along."

"And all at once not flying just doesn't seem that important," he said. "Don't ask me why."

"Actually," she said, "I have a theory."

"Oh?"

"When the towers came down," she said, "it was very traumatic for you. Same as it was for everybody else. You had to adjust to a new reality, and that's not easy to do. Your whole world went tilt, and for a while there you stayed off airplanes, and you went downtown and fed the hungry, and you bided your time and tried to figure out a way to get along without doing your usual line of work."

"And?"

"And time passed," she said, "and things settled down, and you adjusted to the way the world is now. While you were at it, you realized what you'll have to do if you're going to be in a position to retire. You thought things through and came up with a plan."

"Well, sort of a plan."

"And a lot of things which seemed very important a while ago, like not flying with all this security and ID checks and all, turn out to be just an inconvenience and not something to make you change your life around. You'll get a second set of ID, or you'll use real ID and find some other way to cover your tracks. One way or another, you'll work it out."

"I suppose," he said. "Santa Barbara. That's between L.A. and San Francisco, isn't it?"

"Closer to L.A. They have their own airport."

He shook his head. "They can keep it," he said. "I'll fly to LAX. Or Burbank, that's even better, and I'll rent a car and drive up to Santa Barbara. Wednesday or Thursday, you said?" He pressed his wrists together. " 'What time?' "

"What time? What do you mean, 'what time'? What's so funny, anyway?"

"Oh, it's a joke one of the golfers told in the clubhouse in Scottsdale. This golfer goes out and he has the worst round of his life. He loses balls in the rough, he can't get out of sand traps, he hits ball after ball into the water hazard. Nothing goes right for him. By the time he gets to the eighteenth green all he's got left is his putter, because he's broken every other club over his knee, and after he four-putts the final hole he breaks the putter, too, and sends it flying.

"He marches into the locker room, absolutely furious, and he unlocks his locker and takes out his razor and opens it up and gets the blade in his hand and slashes both his wrists. And he stands there, watching the blood flow, and someone calls to him over the bank of lockers. 'Hey, Joe,' the guy says, 'we're getting up a foursome for tomorrow morning. You interested?'

"And the guy says"—Keller raised his hands to shoulder height, pressed his wrists together—"'What time?'"

"'What time?'"

"Right."

"'What time?'" She shook her head. "I like it, Keller. And any old time you want'll be just fine."

PROACTIVE
KELLER

CHAPTER TWENTY-ONE

Keller's flight, from New York to Detroit, was bumpy. That was okay, he didn't mind a little turbulence, but the pilot kept announcing every patch of rough air over the intercom and, worse, apologizing for it. By itself the turbulence wasn't that bad, and he could have dozed through it well enough, if the son of a bitch hadn't kept waking him up with announcements. At least the landing was smooth.

Santa Barbara had been almost anticlimactically simple. A flight to L.A., a flight home from San Francisco, and a quick and easy assignment between the two. He got home ready for another job, and the time crawled by, and nothing came along. Until now, finally, here he was in Detroit.

He hadn't checked a bag, so he hoisted his carry-on and walked straight to where the drivers were waiting and scanned the signs for one bearing the name BOGART. He didn't know why they'd picked that name, which could only invite unnecessary conversational overtures from strangers, twisted-lip imitations: "Play it again, Sam. You played it for her, now you can play it for me." But that was their choice, Bogart, and there'd been no time to talk them out of it, let alone to rent a car and drive to Detroit.

Time, Dot had told him, was of the essence. So here he was, fresh off a bumpy flight, and looking for a sign with BOGART on it. He found it right off the bat, and when his eyes moved from the sign to the man who was holding it, the man was looking right back at him, with an expression on his face that Keller found hard to read.

He was a short, stocky guy, who looked as though he spent a lot of time at the gym, lifting heavy objects. He said, "Mr. Bogart? Right this way, sir."

Was the guy sneering at him? Keller wasn't quite sure how you defined a sneer, whether it tended to be facial or verbal, but he generally knew it when he encountered it, and this time he wasn't sure. Often, he'd found, people didn't know what to say to a person like him. The nature of his work put them off balance, and made them nervous, and sometimes they adopted a pose of cockiness to mask the nervousness.

But this didn't quite feel like that, either.

Well, what difference did it make? He followed the guy out of the terminal and across a few lanes of traffic to short-term parking and past a row of cars until they reached a late-model Lincoln with an Ontario plate. The guy triggered a remote to unlock the doors and then opened and held the passenger-side door for Keller, which was unexpected.

So was the presence of the big guy in the backseat.

Keller was already getting into the car when he saw him. He froze, and felt a hand on his shoulder, urging him forward.

If you get in, he thought, you're defenseless. But wasn't he defenseless already? He was about as unarmed as you could be, unarmed enough to pass through airport security, with not even a nail clipper at his command. Action scenarios ran unbidden through his mind—his elbows swinging, his legs kicking out—but they were somehow unconvincing, and all he did was stand there.

The big guy chuckled, which wasn't what he much wanted to hear, and the short guy—he was too wide and muscular to be thought of as the little guy—told him there was nothing to worry about. "There's a gentleman wants to meet you," he said. "That's all."

His tone was reassuring, but Keller wasn't reassured. But he got in, and the short guy closed the door and walked around the car and got behind the wheel. He fastened his seat belt and suggested that Keller do the same.

And give himself even less maneuverability? "I never use it," he said. "Claustrophobia."

Which was nonsense, he always used a seat belt. And it didn't work anyway, because the guy told him it was the law in Detroit, and all he needed was a fucking traffic ticket, so buckle the belt, will you?

So he did.

They drove to a house somewhere in the suburbs. They hadn't blindfolded him, so he could have paid attention to the route, but what good was that going to do? He didn't really know the area, and even if he did, geography wasn't likely to be a big factor here.

He'd flown out because somebody was paying him to kill a man, and now it was beginning to look as though he was the one who was going to get killed. That was one of the risks in his business. He didn't dwell on it, he rarely gave it any thought whatsoever, but there was no getting around the fact that it was always a possibility. He sat in his seat, the seat belt snug around him, and figured there were two possibilities—either they intended to kill him or they didn't. If they didn't, he had nothing to worry about. If they did, there were two possibilities—either he'd be able to do something about it or he wouldn't, and he'd only find that out when the time came.

So he relaxed. The big Lincoln provided a smooth ride, so there was no turbulence, and no pain-in-the-ass pilot to apologize for it. Neither the driver nor the man in the backseat said a word, and Keller matched their silence with silence of his own.

They got off the beltway and into a suburb, and after several left and right turns wound up on a tree-shaded dead-end street—the DEAD END sign gave him a turn—full of large homes on large lots. The driver pulled into a semi-circular driveway and braked at the entrance of an oversize center hall Colonial.

This time the big guy from the backseat opened the door for him. The driver went on ahead and unlocked the front door. The two of them escorted him through a large living room with a fire in the fireplace, down a broad hallway, and into what he supposed was a den. It held an enormous TV set, on which a tennis match was being played with the sound off. There were bookshelves artfully equipped with sets of leather-bound books, decorative ceramics that looked vaguely pre-Columbian, a couple of leather chairs, and, in one of the chairs, a man with a broad face, pockmarked cheeks, hair like gray Brillo, thin lips, abundant eyebrows, and an expression that, like everyone else's since he'd left New York, Keller found hard to read.

But it was a familiar face, somehow. He'd never met this man, so where had he seen his face?

Oh, right.

"I don't suppose your name is Bogart," the man said.

Keller agreed that it wasn't.

"Well, I don't necessarily have to know your name," the man said. "My guess is you already know mine."

"I believe so, yes."

"Prove it."

Prove it? "I believe you're Mr. Horvath," he said.

"Len Horvath," the man said. "You recognize me, or you just make a good guess?"

"I, uh, recognized you."

"Wha'd they do, send you a picture?" Keller nodded. "And then someone was gonna meet you at the airport, point me out?"

"I think so. The arrangements got a little vague after I was to meet up with the man with the sign."

"Bogart," said the driver, who was stationed at Keller's right, with the big man on his other side. Keller couldn't see the driver's face, but the sneer in his voice was unmistakable.

"Not a name I would have picked," Keller said.

"I always liked Bogart," Horvath said. "But I wouldn't want to be looking for a sign with his name on it, or holding one, either. You were supposed to kill me."

Keller didn't say anything.

"Awww, relax," Horvath said. "You think I've got a beef with you? You took a job, for Chrissake. You couldn't help who hired you. You even *know* who hired you?"

"They never tell me."

"Well, I can tell you. A little prick named Kevin Dealey hired you. Guess what happened to him."

Keller had a pretty good idea.

"The point is," Horvath told him, "you don't have a client anymore. So the job's canceled. You're no longer required to kill me."

163

"Good," Keller said.

Somehow that struck Horvath funny, and the men flanking Keller joined in the laughter. When it died down Horvath said, "He talked a little, Kevin Dealey did, before we fixed it so he couldn't. Told us what flight you'd be on and all about the Bogart bullshit. First thought I had, Phil and Norman here meet you at the airport, turn you around, and send you back to New York. *Hi there, Mr. Bogart, services no longer required, have a nice return flight, blah blah blah*. Put you on the plane, wave good-bye, and you go back to your quotidian life."

Keller's face must have shown something, because Horvath grinned at him. "*Quotidian*. Means ordinary, everyday. I read books. Not all the ones you see, but plenty. You a reader yourself?"

"Some."

"Yeah? What else do you do? When you're not flying off to Detroit."

Keller told him.

"Stamps," Horvath said. "I had a collection when I was a kid. I don't know what the hell ever happened to it. That's a great pastime, collecting stamps."

They talked a little about stamps, and Keller was beginning to believe they weren't going to kill him. You were planning on killing a man, would you start telling him about the stamps you collected as a kid?

"Where was I?" Horvath said and answered his own question. "Oh, right, meet you at the airport, turn you around and send you home. Thing is, why would you believe Phil and Normie? But if you meet the putative victim in his own house, that makes it clear-cut. So now I'll shake your hand, because for all I know the day may come when

I have to hire you myself, and I got no hard feelings against you, and hope you don't resent me for keeping you from completing your job. You get paid something in front?"

"Half."

"That's what Dealey said, but he was never the kind of fellow whose word you could take to the bank. Well, that's all you get, but the bright side is you get to keep it without having to earn it. You can buy yourself some stamps."

CHAPTER TWENTY-TWO

"**Y**ou say that all the time," Keller said.

"I do?"

" 'You can buy yourself some stamps.' When you hand me my share, or when you let me know the money's arrived. 'Here you go, Keller—buy yourself some stamps.' "

"It does have a familiar ring to it," Dot allowed. "I didn't realize I said it all the time."

"Well, a lot of the time."

"Because I'd hate to be a bore, you know? There's not all that many people I talk to besides you, and if I'm tossing the same catchphrases at you all the damn time—"

"Actually, it's nice," he said. "And it'll echo in my mind when I'm looking over a price list and trying to decide whether to order something. I hear your voice in my head, telling me I can buy myself some stamps, and it gives me permission to be extravagant."

"The roles we play in each other's lives," Dot said, "and we're not even aware of it. Who says there's no divine order to the universe?"

"Not me," said Keller.

They were in White Plains, sitting across the kitchen table in Dot's big old house on Taunton Place. She'd made coffee for him and was herself sipping her usual glass of iced tea.

"Well," she said. "Must have been scary."

"What I was afraid of," he said, "was that there was a

way out of it but that I couldn't see it. So if I got killed, on top of being dead it'd be my own fault."

"I think I see what you mean."

"But it turned out I was worried about nothing, because all he wanted to do was let me know the game had changed. Between the time we got the contract and the time I got off the plane, our client stopped having a pulse."

"And here you are," she said. "And I've evidently said this before, but I'll say it again, Keller. Now you can buy yourself some stamps."

"But not as many as I'd like."

"Oh?"

"It's nice we got half the money," he said, "but it would have been nice to get the other half. Even if I had to earn it."

"Half a loaf may be better than none," she agreed, "but it's not as good as the whole enchilada. Are you hurting for dough?"

"I wouldn't say hurting. But I was sort of counting on the money."

"I know the feeling. I flat hate it when we're supposed to get money and then we don't."

"Plus I wanted the work. You go too long between jobs and you start to lose your edge. And it's been a while. Maybe if I'd worked more recently I'd have reacted quicker to Phil and Norman."

"Which would have been the worst thing to do, because you might have gotten yourself killed, when you weren't in any real danger in the first place."

He frowned, thinking it over, then shrugged. "Maybe. It's all pretty hypothetical. What's that you say sometimes about my grandmother's tea cart?"

"Huh? Oh, I know what you mean. 'If your grandmother had wheels she'd be a tea cart, but she'd still be your grandmother.'"

"That's it."

"Is that something else I say all the time?"

"No, just once in a while."

"Christ, I'm glad I don't have to listen to myself. I'd bore myself to tears. I wish I had work for you, Keller, but all I can do is sit back like a good spider and see what flies into the web. The jobs have to come to us."

"Maybe."

She gave him a look.

"On the trip to Detroit," he said, "I flew first-class. They were sold out in coach, and that was the flight I wanted, especially since we'd arranged for them to be meeting it. So I spent the extra money."

"Cuts into the profit, doesn't it?"

"It does," he said, "but that's not the point. It's a funny thing about sitting in the front of the plane. You've got more leg room, and the seats are wider, with more space between you and the person sitting next to you. You'd think that would be a distancing factor, but people in first are much more likely to get into conversations. In coach you sit there with your knees jammed against the seat in front of you, and trying to keep your elbows from pushing the other guy's elbows off the shared armrest, and you crawl in a cocoon and stay there until the plane's back on the ground."

"But in first class you turn into Chatty Cathy?"

"Not on the flight out," he said. "The woman sitting next to me had her laptop up and running, and she might as well have been in her office cubicle, the way she was all wrapped up in her work."

"That's a shame, if she was cute. Was she?"

"Not really. On the way back, well, I was still in first class, because it was simpler to just go ahead and book the whole flight that way. And the guy next to me started talking the minute we got off the ground."

"**T**his is when I get to relax," the man had said for openers. "When I'm in a plane and the plane's in the air. I never even think about crashing. Never even consider the possibility. Do you?"

"Not until just now," Keller said.

"What I do," the man went on, "is I leave my troubles on the ground. Because I'm up here and they're down there, and while I'm here there's not a damn thing I can do about them, so why carry them around with me?"

"I see what you mean."

"Except," the man said, "this is one of those days when I just don't think it's gonna work. Because I just can't shake the thought that in two hours we'll be back on the ground and I'm in the same pile of crap as always."

The fellow didn't look like someone who spent much time in a pile of crap. He was dressed for success in a dark pinstripe suit, his button-down shirt was a Wedgwood blue, his tie gold with dark blue fleurs-de-lis. Like Keller, he was wearing loafers; if they were going to make you take off your shoes at airport security, you didn't want to have to untie them and tie them up again. Slip 'em off, slip 'em on. Maybe you couldn't beat the system, but at least you could try to keep up with it.

He was a businessman, obviously, and in his early forties or thereabouts. Keller guessed he'd played a minor sport in college—track, maybe—and had eaten well since then. He wasn't jowly yet, but he was on his way. And he had the florid complexion of someone who'd either spent a little too much time in the sun—unlikely, in Detroit—or whose blood pressure might bear watching.

"I'm from New York," he announced. "Yourself?"

"The same," Keller said.

"Live in the city itself? Manhattan?"

Keller nodded.

"Me too. Moved back after the divorce."

"I was never married," Keller said, "so I never left. Manhattan, I mean."

"Right. Name's Harrelson, Claude Harrelson."

"Pleased to know you," Keller said, and then realized it was now his turn to say who he was. "Eric Fischvogel," he said, supplying the name he was flying under, the name on the ID and credit cards he was carrying.

"Fischvogel," Harrelson said. "German?"

There was a lot to be said, Keller sometimes thought, for false ID with a name like Johnson or Brooks, something simple and unremarkable. "It means fish bird," he said.

"I figured out the fish part."

"I think it means like a fish hawk," Keller improvised. "In fact one branch of the family changed it to Osprey."

"Really. Well, Eric, it's a pleasure to meet you."

"Pleasure's mine."

The flight attendant came along with the cart, and Harrelson asked for a Bloody Mary. Keller thought about having a beer, but something made him ask for a Coke instead. She asked if Pepsi was all right, and he said it would be fine.

"I wonder," Harrelson said, "what would have happened if you told her no, Pepsi wasn't all right, and you had to have Coke. I mean, we're at what, thirty-five thousand feet? It's pretty much like it or lump it, wouldn't you say?"

"That's a point."

Harrelson took a moment to work on his drink, then looked at Keller over the brim. "Eric," he said, "mind a question?"

Which, Keller thought, was a little like asking him if Pepsi was all right, because how could he say no?

In any event, Harrelson didn't wait for an answer. "Eric," he said, "have you ever wanted to kill somebody?"

"**N**ow that's a hell of a question," Dot said. "I thought all men talked about was sports and the stock market."

"It shook me," he admitted, "coming out of the blue like that. What I said was I supposed everybody felt like that from time to time. When some clown cuts you off in traffic, say. But we learn to suppress those impulses, and they pass."

"That's what you said?"

"Something like that."

"Just who the hell did you think you were, Keller? Doctor Phil?"

"Well, I didn't know what to say. But he wasn't talking about getting cut off in traffic, or momentary impulses. He was serious."

"**M**y business partner," Harrelson was saying. "We've got this little company, merchandising generic pharmaceuticals. We were both in the field, and I was a born salesman,

171

and he's the kind of guy who makes the trains run on time. We were both itching to go on our own, and we figured the two of us would be a good fit, Mr. Inside and Mr. Outside."

"And you were wrong?"

"No, we were absolutely right. We showed a profit the first year, and both our sales and our net have gone up every year since."

"That's great."

"Yeah, it's just peachy."

Keller looked at him.

"We were never like buddy-buddy, see. But we got along. I was on the road most of the time, and he never left the city, so we didn't spend that much time looking at each other. Then he started nailing our secretary."

"A bad thing, eh?"

"I suppose it's never good policy," Harrelson said, "but I can't be too critical here, because I was shtupping her myself."

"Oh."

"I'm not really clear who started first," he said, "but she was having affairs with both of us. Overlapping affairs, except that's probably not a good word to use here. Or maybe it is. She was . . . nice."

"I see."

"And it was okay, Eric. I mean, if neither of us knew the other was boinking her, what difference did it make? I certainly didn't figure I was the only man in her life, and anyway I wouldn't have wanted to be. I mean, I was a married guy, I was on the road more often than not. I only had limited time for her, and what did I want with the responsibility?"

"It makes sense," Keller said.

"But then Chandra lost it."

"That was her name? Chandra?"

"That was her name," Harrelson said, "and she lost it big-time. The excrement made contact with the ventilation system."

"Hit the fan?"

"Hit it head-on. She went public, and by the time it was over my wife had left me and his wife had left him and we had two nasty divorces going on and Barry and I weren't speaking."

"Barry's your partner."

"My partner," Harrelson said heavily. "You can divorce your wife. You can't divorce your partner."

"They wound up stuck with each other," he told Dot. "By now they both hate each other, I mean really hate each other, and neither can buy the other out. And the company's all either of them has, and neither one of them can walk away from it."

"Couldn't they sell it?"

"I asked him that. I wasn't going to mention it just now because I figured you'd ask me who the hell I thought I was, Suze Orman? He explained why they couldn't, and the gist of it was that the business didn't have a lot of assets. It's only worth the profit it returns, and it only does that when they're running it. So it's worth far more to them than it would be to another buyer."

"I'll take your word for it," she said. "You know, Keller, I'm beginning to see where this is going."

CHAPTER TWENTY-THREE

"I swear I'd kill him," Harrelson said. "Except there's no way on earth I could get away with it. Who's got a motive here? Hell, you're looking at him."

"They'd certainly look long and hard at you."

"And they'd have me dead to rights. Besides, look at me. Am I a killer?"

"My guess would be that you're not."

"And your guess is a good one. I don't even like swatting flies. And spiders, my wife would get creeped out when she saw a spider and she'd want me to kill it. I'd take it outside and release it. I mean, what have I got against spiders?"

Keller, who had nothing against spiders himself, nodded encouragingly.

"Barry Blyden," Harrelson said, "is a different matter altogether. You know what I need?"

You need me, Keller thought.

"A sorceress," Harrelson said. "Like Whatshername, turned Odysseus's men into swine? Except she could turn Barry into a spider, or a fucking cockroach. And then I'd stomp him into the ground."

"Strangers on a plane," Dot said. "Like the Hitchcock movie, except at thirty-five thousand feet. You remember the setup? Two strangers, and each one commits the other one's murder."

"Well, they're supposed to. But then it gets complicated."

"It always does, Keller. Otherwise there's no movie. I don't suppose you gave him your card, told him you worked for a first-class removal service."

"No."

"He said he wanted his partner dead, if only someone could turn him into a cockroach first, and you left it at that."

"Right."

"The plane landed and you went your separate ways."

"Right."

She frowned. "So you're telling me this just to let me know that there are a lot of people out there who want other people dead? No, I don't think so. If that was all there was to it you wouldn't have bothered including the names. I'll be damned, Keller. You're trying to drum up a little business."

"I'm thinking about it," he admitted.

"You remember the time we ran an ad? And you wound up chasing out to the middle of nowhere?"

"Muscatine, Iowa."

"The town that time forgot," she said, "but you and I remember it well. What a mess that was."

"It turned out okay, Dot."

"The client was playing games with us."

"That's true."

"And then he tried to stiff us out of the final payment."

"We convinced him to change his mind."

"And taught him a lesson once the account was paid in full," she recalled. "Still, neither one of us was in a big rush to run the ad again."

"No."

"But you want to be proactive, don't you? You want this Harrelson to hire us."

"Well," he said.

She gave him a look. "He's met you," she said. "He knows who you are."

"He knows my name's Eric Fischvogel."

"He saw your face."

"He barely looked at it. All I was was somebody to talk to, and in a sense he was just talking to himself."

"He's in New York. He travels a lot, but his partner—Blyden?"

"Barry Blyden."

"Blyden's here in New York, right? And he's Mr. Inside, he stays put."

"That's right."

"Two things we try to avoid," she said, "are working for people who know who we are, and working close to home."

"Sometimes we don't have any choice."

"But in this case," she said, "we do." She looked long and hard at him. "You want to do this, don't you? In spite of everything."

"Well, I could use the work," he said. "And I could use the money. And here's the thing, Dot. When he asked me that question out of the blue, had I ever wanted to kill anybody, something just clicked."

"Opportunity knocked."

"Something like that. I want to take the next step, see where it goes."

Keller, wearing jeans and a Mets warm-up jacket, stood near a water fountain in Central Park. On the phone, he'd

176

designated a particular park bench, and he'd stationed himself where he could keep an eye on it. He'd set the meeting time for 10 p.m., and Claude Harrelson, wearing a suit and carrying a briefcase, was two minutes early.

Keller watched him walk right to the bench and sit down. The man didn't look around at all, but there was something furtive about him all the same. Keller circled around, came up behind Harrelson, and stood there for a moment.

I'm the man who sat next to you on the flight from Detroit, he'd said on the phone. *No names, all right? There was something you wished you could do. Suppose somebody could do it for you. Wouldn't that solve all your problems?*

And here was Harrelson, ready to have his problems solved.

"Don't turn around," Keller said quietly, and Harrelson started visibly, but didn't turn. "I don't want to see your face, and I don't want you to see mine. I'm going to touch you, though, because I need to make sure you're not wearing a wire." Harrelson offered no resistance, and Keller, who hadn't really expected to find a wire, made certain Harrelson wasn't wearing one.

Then he talked, explaining just what was on offer here. He had a friend, an associate, who would undertake to solve Harrelson's problem in return for a substantial fee, payable half in advance and half on completion of the work. "He won't know your name," Keller assured him, "and you won't know his, and you'll never meet him, so there'll be nothing to connect the two of you."

"I like that part," Harrelson said.

"So? Have you had enough time to think it over?"

"God knows I've been thinking about it," Harrelson

said. "I haven't been able to think of anything else. It's strange, you know? For all this time I've wanted him dead, I've had fantasies of killing him in dozens of different ways. Smashing his skull with a baseball bat, stabbing him, shooting him, running him over with a car. You can't imagine."

Keller, who had done all those things and more at one time or another, figured he could imagine well enough. But he didn't say anything.

"But it was never real," Harrelson went on. "It was safe to have fantasies like that because I knew that was all they were, just fantasies. Fantasies never got anybody killed."

Keller wasn't too sure about that, but he let it go.

"Now it's real," Harrelson said. "At least I think it's real. I mean, for all I know, *you* could be wearing a wire. How do I know I'm not being entrapped?"

How did you answer something like that? Keller decided a solemn approach was indicated. "You have my word," he said.

"Oh."

"I think you're probably a good judge of character, Claude. I think you know my word is good."

Harrelson, who still had not turned to look at him, considered the point and nodded. "Then it's real," he said. "I have a chance at getting what I've been wishing for all this time. Just because I was indiscreet enough to get on a plane and tell my troubles to the guy sitting next to me. I don't ordinarily do that."

"I don't ordinarily listen," Keller said, "and I certainly don't ordinarily try to drum up business for my friend. For one thing, he's got more business than he can handle."

"I can imagine."

"And it's dangerous, sticking your neck out that way.

But I'm a pretty good judge of character myself. I somehow sensed I could trust you."

"That's good of you to say that."

"You'll be out of town when it happens," Keller went on. "My friend's very good at making things look accidental, so the police may not even bother with you."

"The police," Harrelson said.

"If they ask you questions, you just say you don't know anything. Is that going to be a problem?"

"Actually," Harrelson said, "it's true. I won't know anything, will I?"

"Nothing concrete, no. You couldn't tell them anything if you wanted to. You sat next to a man on a plane? Somebody called you and you met him in the park and never even looked at his face? But you just say you don't know anything, and if they push it you refuse to answer any more questions without a lawyer."

"One thing I've learned, ever since my divorce, is I don't do anything without a lawyer."

Just don't bring him along to the park, Keller thought. He said, "The money. If you want to make the initial payment now, we can put this into play."

"Oh."

"Is there a problem?"

"Well, it's just that I didn't bring it," Harrelson said. "Carrying cash to the park at night, well, it sort of goes against the grain, if you know what I mean."

"I know what you mean. What's in the briefcase?"

"This?" Harrelson clutched the thing to his chest. "Nothing but papers," he said. "I don't know why I brought it. Force of habit, I guess."

*

179

"All I had to do was mention the briefcase," he said, "and he was hugging it like a long-lost brother. He had the money. He just didn't want to turn it over."

"Let's hope it was just money," Dot said, "and not a tape recorder. Don't look like that, Keller. You're not a deer and I'm not a headlight. I'm sure it was money. He brought it along and then he got second thoughts."

"That's what it felt like."

"You figure he's searching his soul, Keller?"

"Maybe."

"I have to say it's easier when the clients come to us. Whatever soul-searching they have to do, they've already done it by the time they get in touch. Now he's going out of town again?"

"For a couple of days. I'll call him when he gets back, and arrange another meeting, and either he'll bring the cash or he won't."

"Like eggplant ice cream," she said.

"Huh?"

"Either I'll have some for breakfast tomorrow," she said, "or I won't. I have to say the odds are pretty good I won't. Keller, you know what you could have done? You could have conked him over the head and walked off with the briefcase. We'd have half the money, and you wouldn't even have to kill anybody."

"I thought of that," he admitted, "but afterward, while I was walking home. And the first thought I had, and it's kind of silly, is that's not what I do, I'm not a mugger."

"You've got your code of honor."

"I don't know about codes, and I'm pretty sure honor hasn't got anything to do with it. But it's just not what I do. I told you it was silly."

"Maybe, but I can't argue with it. Next thing you know we'd be selling dope to schoolchildren and sucking tokens out of subway turnstiles. Except you can't do that anymore, what with MetroCards. What do you suppose the token-suckers are doing these days?"

"I'll have to think about that."

"God, why would you want to?" She heaved a sigh. "You said he wants to be able to contact you. I hope you told him that's not on."

"I told him I'd work on it."

"Well, don't work too hard."

"Don't worry," he said. "I think I've got it figured out."

By the time Harrelson showed up, at the same park bench they'd used the first time, Keller had been waiting almost forty-five minutes. Harrelson wasn't late, if anything he was a couple of minutes early, but Keller had wanted to make sure there weren't any surprises.

While he waited, trying to be unobtrusive without looking unobtrusive, a man and woman came along and sat down on the appointed bench. Keller couldn't hear what they were saying, but from what he could see they weren't picking out names for their unborn children. The woman looked on the brink of tears, and the man looked as though he wanted to give her something to cry about.

What if they were still there when Harrelson arrived? Would he have the sense to pick another bench? Or would he be spooked altogether, and head for home? It was moot, as it turned out, because after ten or twelve minutes of disagreement, the woman sprang to her feet, turned on her heel, and stalked off into the night. "Ignorant cunt," the man said—to himself, but just loud enough for Keller to hear it—and eventually stood up, yawned, stretched, and set off in the opposite direction.

Other park visitors passed the bench, but nobody else sat on it, until Harrelson appeared. He looked around carefully, reminding Keller of a dog turning around three times before lying down. Then he sat, and Keller moved to approach him from the rear.

"Claude," he said softly. "How was your trip?"

"Oh," Harrelson said. "You startled me. I wasn't expecting . . . well, that's not true, of course I was expecting you, but . . ."

"Right," Keller said. "Claude, let me ask you straight out. Do you want to go through with this?"

"Of course I do."

"Hold still." He frisked the man, wondering what he'd do if he actually found a wire. But he didn't, so what did it matter?

"What makes you think . . ."

"That you might have had second thoughts? Well, you didn't bring your briefcase."

"Oh," Harrelson said.

"So I'm taking a wild guess that you didn't bring the money, either."

"Last time," Harrelson said, "there wasn't any money in the briefcase."

"Whatever you say."

"The money's in an envelope," he said. "In my inside jacket pocket."

Harrelson made no move to get it, and Keller wondered if he was supposed to reach for it himself. He wasn't sure it was something he wanted to do. It was one thing to frisk a man, and another thing altogether to pick his pocket.

"The envelope," he prompted.

"Oh, right," Harrelson said, as if he hadn't thought of the envelope in days. He reached for it and paused with his hand inside his jacket. "When I give you the money," he said, "it's on, right?"

"Right."

"But it has to wait until I'm out of town."

"So tell me your schedule."

"Well, it varies," Harrelson said. "I'm back and forth all the time. That's why I need a way to get in touch with you."

He didn't really, as far as Keller could see, but he thought he did, and maybe that amounted to the same thing. He reached into his own pocket, extended his hand. "Here," he said. "No, don't turn around. And don't unwrap it now. It's a cell phone."

"I already have a cell phone."

No kidding, Keller thought. "This is untraceable," he said. "It's prepaid, and the only thing you can use it for is to call me at the number written on the wrapper. That's the number of my untraceable cell phone, which I'll only use to talk to you."

"Like a pair of walkie-talkies," Harrelson said.

"There you go. You call me when you need to, and I'll call you if I need to, and as soon as our business is done we can throw both phones down a storm drain and forget the whole thing. Don't lose the number."

"I won't. Incidentally, what's the number of my phone?"

"You don't need to know that. I mean, you're not going to call yourself, are you?"

"No, but—"

"And you're not going to give out the number, because the only person who's going to have it is me. Right?"

"Right."

"So all I need now," Keller reminded him, "is the envelope."

"It's right here," Harrelson said, drawing it at last from his pocket. "But, see, there's a slight problem."

CHAPTER TWENTY-FOUR

"He only had half," Dot said. "Well, that was the deal, right? Half in front?"

"He had half of half. Half of what he was supposed to have."

"In other words, twenty-five percent of the total price."

"Bingo."

"I hope you took it."

"If it was going to be in somebody's pocket," he said, "I figured it was better off in mine. But it's still only half of what it's supposed to be."

"Call it a good-faith deposit," Dot said. "When's he going to come up with the rest?"

"He was thinking maybe never."

"Huh?"

"Cash is evidently a problem for him these days," he said, "and he made the point that raising the money might leave a paper trail that could be suspicious. If the cops take a good look at him, and he's just liquidated assets and can't account for where the money went . . ."

"So you're supposed to do the job for a quarter of the price?"

"After it's all done," he said, "and Barry Blyden's out of the picture, he'll have access to all the company funds. At that point he'll pay everything he owes, plus a bonus if the death passes for accidental."

"What, like double indemnity?"

"Sort of. Not double, but a bonus. I didn't get into numbers, because it seemed to me the whole business was a little hypothetical."

"I'll say. Keller, tell me you didn't agree to do it for twenty-five percent down."

"Tell me you got a phone call from somebody in Seattle or Sioux Falls," he said, "and we got a real offer from a real client."

"I wish."

"So do I, but meanwhile I've got an envelope full of his cash, and I figure I can get started, you know? I can get a line on Blyden, track his movements, figure out his pattern, and make my plans."

"I suppose it can't hurt. What's that?"

"My phone," Keller said, and answered it. "Yes," he whispered into it. "Yes. Right." He rang off and told Dot that Harrelson was leaving town first thing in the morning. "Not that he has to be away for me to do a little reconnaissance."

"You whispered because voiceprints don't work with whispers."

"Right."

"So why are you still whispering, Keller?"

"Oh," he said aloud. "I didn't realize."

"I hate the idea of doing this for short money," she said, "but you're right about one thing. You need the work."

Five days later he was in White Plains again.

"It felt good to be working again," he told Dot. "Getting a look at the guy, tracking his movements, starting to put a plan together. He's not going to be easy."

"Oh?"

"He seems to lead a pretty regular life," he said, "which can make things easy or difficult, depending. It's easy because you know where he'll be, but it's not necessarily easy to get to him. He's always at his office or in his apartment, or on the way from one to the other. The office building has the kind of security procedures that used to be reserved for the Pentagon, and the apartment building is one of those Park Avenue fortresses with twenty-four-hour doormen and elevator attendants, and security cameras all over the place."

"How does he get from Point A to Point B?"

"He has a car service. The same driver every time, as far as I can see. Car pulls up in front of his apartment building in the morning, drops him at his office. Works the same way at night."

"What happens when he goes to a restaurant?"

"He eats lunch at his desk, orders in from somewhere or other. Same thing at night. Either he works late, which he does most of the time, or he goes home and orders dinner delivered."

"Workaholic, it sounds like."

"Assuming he's working. Maybe he goes to the office and puts his feet up, watches soap operas on a plasma TV."

"Maybe. Didn't he have an affair with somebody? Isn't that how all of this got started?"

"At the office. They were both having an affair with their secretary."

"My guess," she said, "is she doesn't work there anymore. He's got to be seeing someone, don't you think?"

"My guess is he orders in."

"Like lunch and dinner. Well, it's a tricky one, Keller. I'll grant you that. Have you doped out a way into either of the buildings?"

"Too risky."

"What does that leave?"

"Getting him between the door and the car. And that probably means in the morning, because the car seems to pick him up at the same time most mornings."

"Eight, eight-thirty?"

"Try a quarter to five."

"It's one thing to be a workaholic," Dot said, "but you don't have to be a nut about it. A quarter to five? And you were there to see this? It can't take long to get to the office, not at that hour."

"Call it fifteen minutes."

"So you'd do what, lurk outside his apartment building? Or lurk outside the office? Either way, that's a pretty conspicuous hour to be lurking."

"I'd have to time it so that I got there just in time. I'm not sure which is better, the apartment or the office. The apartment's on Park Avenue and Eighty-fourth, and there's nobody on the street at that hour, and you've got all those doormen keeping an eye on things. The office is on Madison Avenue and Thirty-seventh Street, and doormen aren't a factor, but there are more people on the street."

"You'd swoop in, catch him between the car and the door, and disappear before anybody can get a good look at you."

"Something like that."

"There's an awful lot that can go wrong, Keller."

"I know."

"And it's right here in New York. Thirty-seventh and Madison? That's what, half a mile from where you live?"

"Not even that."

"I can't say I like it. Maybe we should pull the plug on this one."

"Maybe we don't have to," he said. "Our client already did."

Dot's fingers drummed the tabletop. It was a gesture Keller had seen her make before, though not too often. From what he could tell, it did not indicate a feeling of peace and contentment and the sense that all was right with the world.

"He wants the money back," she said.

"He said it as if he really expected to get it," Keller told her, "but he's essentially a salesman, and that would make him an optimist, wouldn't it?"

"Evidently."

"He's probably read a lot of books about the value of a positive attitude."

"They've got seminars, Keller. He could have taken a seminar."

"I told him I didn't think it was possible. That I'd already passed the money on, and that it wasn't like a refundable deposit. This was over the phone, so I could only go by his voice, but he didn't seem surprised."

"I guess a positive attitude only goes so far. Why did he want to call it off? Money?"

"Cold feet."

"But while he was at it, he thought he'd ask for his money back."

"Worth a shot. And money's part of it, because he was

189

saying it might be a while before he had the balance."

"So it's off. It was interesting, everything you said a few minutes ago about how you'd make your move on Blyden, but why bother telling me? If it's all off."

"It's off until he tells me it's on again."

"Oh."

"Because he's going to call me in the next couple days and let me know. Cash flow is evidently a big consideration."

"It always is."

"He says he'll be in touch," he said, "and . . . Jesus, how's that for timing?"

"Timing?"

He drew the phone from his pocket, looked at the screen, frowned. "It's not him," he said, "but who else could it be?"

"It's not anybody," Dot said, "which seems obvious, given that it didn't ring."

He touched the phone to her forearm, let her feel the vibration. She nodded, and he squinted at the screen again, then answered it. He listened for a moment, then broke into the middle of a Harrelson sentence.

"I gave you a phone," he whispered. "Why aren't you using it? You lost it?"

Dot put her face in her hands.

"Hang up," Keller said. "I'll call you back." He broke the connection, got a dial tone, made a call. It rang a few times before Harrelson picked up.

"I didn't know there was such a thing as an angry whisper," Dot said. "You were whispering, and it sounded for all the world as if you were shouting."

"He called me from his hotel," he said. "Through the

hotel switchboard, or whatever it is when you dial direct from your room."

"Because he lost the phone you gave him?"

"Misplaced it, I guess you'd say. He knew it was somewhere in the room, but he couldn't find it."

"So you called him back, and when it rang he found it. It's good he didn't have it set to vibrate. I gather we're back on the case."

"More or less."

"And you told him he has to come up with another twenty-five percent in front."

"He'll be back the end of the week," he said, "and he'll have the money then."

"And the final payment? Is he going to be able to swing it?"

"He says it's no problem. I think that means he'll deal with it when the time comes."

"In other words, stall us."

He nodded. "He knows he'll have plenty of cash when his partner's dead and the situation with the company is settled. And I suppose he figures we can wait, because what else are we going to do?"

"Clients," Dot said.

"I know."

"If it weren't for the clients, this would be the perfect business, wouldn't it? Lucrative, challenging, and with enough variety built in that you'd never get bored."

"There's the moral aspect," Keller said.

"Well, that's true."

"But you get over that. And when you do one that bothers you, well, there are little mental exercises for getting over it."

"Making the image smaller in your mind and gradually fading it out."

"That's right. And the reaction, the bad feeling, it becomes familiar, you know? 'Oh, right, I've felt like this before, I know it'll go away.' And it does."

"So do the clients, sooner or later. The guy in Detroit, he went away before you could do the work."

"Don't remind me."

"Usually," she said, "we don't even know who the client is, because the job comes through somebody else. And that's ideal. And when we work directly, well, some clients are okay. But some of them are all wrong."

"Like this one," he said. "I'll tell you, the target's no bargain either."

They looked at each other.

"Keller," she said, "aren't you the naughty boy."

"Huh? I didn't say anything."

"It was the way you didn't say it," she said. "It spoke volumes."

CHAPTER TWENTY-FIVE

On balance, Keller would have liked to be going somewhere other than Detroit. Houston, St. Louis, Omaha, Cheyenne—almost anywhere, really. The flight was fine, he had to admit, but on his way out he kept looking around for a sign reading BOGART.

There was none, of course. He went to the Hertz desk and picked up the car he'd reserved as Eric Fischvogel. The Fischvogel ID was still good, but he'd used it on the previous flight to Detroit, and it was the name Harrelson knew for him, and he couldn't decide if that was good or bad.

The Hertz girl had given him a map, and he settled himself behind the wheel while he studied it. Then he dug out the phone and called the only number on his speed dial. Harrelson picked up halfway through the first ring. He spoke, and Keller whispered back, and by the end of the conversation Harrelson was whispering, too.

Keller rang off, checked the map again, and started the engine.

The mall, in Farmington Hills, was pretty much a straight shot north from the airport. It was huge, of course, but one of the anchor stores was a Sears, and that's where they'd arranged to meet. Harrelson would park his rented car nearby and walk to the store's main entrance, and Keller would swing by in his own rental and pick him up.

There was no one loitering in the appointed spot when Keller got there, and that was fine. He'd figured to be early. He parked near the rear entrance, spent five minutes in the store, then moved the car to a spot with a good view of the front door.

Harrelson was a few minutes late, and Keller watched him for two or three additional minutes, watched as he paced, glanced at his watch, looked here and there, and paced some more. If he was trying to look anxious, he was doing a good job of it.

Keller hit his speed dial.

Harrelson, looking startled now, patted his pockets until he found the phone. He said, "I'm here. Where are you?"

"Walk to your car," Keller whispered. "I'll meet you there."

"Oh. But I thought—"

Keller rang off. He got out of his car and watched while Harrelson gathered his resolve, such as it was, and headed for his car. Keller took a parallel aisle and had no trouble tracking the man.

"There you are," Harrelson said.

"Here I am."

"You know, I'd forgotten what your voice sounded like. All that whispering over the phone. Is that necessary, do you think?"

"Just a precaution. It's sort of automatic."

"For you, I guess. Me, I'm not cut out for this type of thing. I'll be glad when it's over."

Keller couldn't argue with that. He asked about the money.

"Oh, right," Harrelson said. "You know, it's a shame you had to come all this way just to pick up the money."

"You don't have it?"

"Oh, I've got it. But it would have saved you a trip to give it to you in New York."

"Security," Keller said. "Probably an unnecessary precaution, but the chance of our being seen together in the city was a risk they didn't want me to run."

"They," Harrelson said.

"Right."

"Well," he said, and drew an envelope from his breast pocket. Keller took it, and there was a comforting thickness to it.

"I'm going home Friday," Harrelson said. "I don't suppose you'll be staying that long."

"I won't be staying at all," Keller told him. "I'm going straight back to the airport."

"You fly in and you fly right back out again."

That was Detroit for you. He nodded, and Harrelson said, "The thing is, I go back on Friday. Now we agreed I shouldn't be in town when it happened, and—"

"You won't be. It'll be all taken care of before then."

"Oh."

"In fact," Keller said, improvising, "I'll make the call right now. I wouldn't be surprised if it's all wrapped up before the sun goes down."

"Wow."

Keller punched in a few numbers at random, then watched as the phone slipped from his fingers and tumbled to the pavement. "Hell," he said. "Just what I needed. Get that for me, will you?" And he reached for his hip pocket even as Harrelson bent obligingly to retrieve the phone.

CHAPTER TWENTY-SIX

"I guess the English would call it a spanner," he said.

"And what would we call it, Keller?"

"A wrench." He held his hand palm up, as if weighing the tool in his hand. "A monkey wrench, actually. Sears has this line, Craftsman tools. Quality at a price. Guaranteed for life, if you can believe that."

"Whose life?"

"Well," he said.

He'd drawn the heavy wrench from his hip pocket and swung it in an arc at Harrelson, who never saw it coming and consequently never knew what hit him. The first blow probably killed the man, but Keller made sure with two more, then scanned the area for bystanders before stooping to go through the dead man's pockets. He dug out Harrelson's calfskin wallet, took the cash and the credit cards, and tucked the near-empty wallet under the dead man's extended right arm. He found a cell phone and pocketed it but kept searching until he turned up a second phone, this the one he'd given Harrelson. He loaded his pockets with everything he'd taken from Harrelson, used Harrelson's pocket handkerchief to wipe anything he might have touched, and was in his car and on his way out of the lot before anyone walked down that aisle and spotted the body.

"There's a bridge over the Detroit River," he said, "but on the other side of it you've got Windsor, Ontario. It's strange, because you actually drive south across the bridge, so you're going south to get from the United States to Canada."

"And then I'll bet you drove north to get back."

"I would have," he said, "but I decided not to take the bridge in the first place, because who knows what kind of records they keep of people crossing into Canada, or back into the States. The Canadian border used to be like crossing a state line, but that's different these days."

"Like everything else. So you settled for a storm drain?"

"I liked the idea of the river. And it turned out there's a bridge a little ways south of the city that runs to Grosse Ile, which is an island in the Detroit River between the U.S. and Canada."

"What's so gross about it?"

"It means big. And it's got some size to it. I mean, it has its own airport."

"For people who don't like to drive over bridges?"

"The bridge is free," he said. "No toll, nobody checking license plates. And not much traffic. I drove across it, turned around, and halfway back I stopped the car and threw three cell phones and a Craftsman wrench over the rail."

"Why three cell phones? Oh, two from him and the one you used for calling him."

He nodded. "It bothered me a little, tossing the wrench. Lifetime guarantee and all."

"We've got a Sears right here in White Plains, Keller. You can always pick up a replacement."

"What for?"

"I don't know. Maybe it would come in handy when

197

you're playing with your stamps. What's the matter, aren't you going to correct me?"

"Correct you?"

"Tell me you don't play with your stamps, you work with them."

He shrugged.

"Something the matter, Keller? You in a mood?"

"I don't know. Maybe."

"What's wrong? The job's done, the loose ends are tied off, and we got paid. Got paid time and a half, since Barry Blyden paid the whole amount, and Harrelson's in no position to request a refund of his deposit." She sipped her iced tea and grinned over the brim of the glass. "Like I always say, Keller, now you can buy yourself some stamps."

"I guess."

"I'd say you're definitely in a mood."

"I think you're right."

She thought about it. "You met the guy, you got to know him, and then you had to do him. There was a personal element to it, and that's what bothers you."

He thought about it, shook his head. "No," he said. "I don't think so. Yes, I met him, and yes, I got to know him, but the more I got to know him the less I liked him. I wouldn't say it was a pleasure to kill him, but it was satisfying, and not just in the sense of the satisfaction of a job well done."

"He was a pain in the neck."

"He was."

"But?"

"I solicited him, Dot. He ran his mouth on the plane, but he wasn't really looking to kill his partner. I put the idea into his head. That's why he kept dragging his feet, and being a pain. He never would have been a client if I hadn't pitched him."

"You went proactive."

"And then, when he became difficult to deal with—"

"Try impossible, Keller."

"—I went to his partner, and Harrelson stopped being the client and became the target. It seems . . ."

"Strange?"

"Strange," he agreed. "And, I don't know. Inappropriate."

"I'll give you strange," she said. "But I'm not signing on for inappropriate."

"No?"

"No. He was the target from the beginning. It just took us a while to realize it."

"I don't follow you."

"You sat next to him on the plane," she said, "and he appointed you his designated psychotherapist and poured his heart out to you, and you saw an opportunity."

"I was looking for one, after the turnaround I'd just gone through."

"You were looking for one, and you recognized this one when you saw it. Here are two partners who hate each other and can't get out from under each other. You came home, and you got the idea of turning proactive, and you approached Harrelson."

"Right."

"And that was your mistake."

"Turning proactive."

"No," she said. "Actually that was brilliant, because we needed the money and you were going stale for lack of work. The mistake was you approached the wrong man.

You should have gone straight to Blyden."

"It never occurred to me."

"Of course it didn't. But when you think about it, it becomes obvious. Harrelson met you, he sat next to you on the plane, he heard your voice and saw your face. He's got a name to go with the face, even if it's not yours. It's a risk, working for somebody who knows that much about you."

"I know."

"Besides," she went on, "Blyden's tough to kill. He's in New York all the time, which means violating the don't-crap-where-you-eat rule. And he's got this routine that makes him very hard to get at."

"I'd have found a way."

"But it wouldn't have been easy. Whereas Harrelson—"

"Was in a different city every week."

"Exactly. And Blyden has never seen your face, or heard your voice, and never will. He's heard *my* voice, but he doesn't know who I am or how to reach me, and he doesn't seem to care. All he had to know was that the partner he hated was planning to have him killed, and he was happy to spend a few dollars to turn the tables."

"And he's not going to talk about it," Keller said, "because he's Mr. Inside. He won't spill the beans to the guy sitting next to him on the plane, because he's not going to be on the plane in the first place."

"There you go."

"And you're right," he said. "Going proactive was fine, but my mistake was I didn't see the whole picture. I should have gone straight to Blyden."

"No."

"No?"

"You should have come straight to me," she said, "and *I* should have gone straight to Blyden."

"You're right."

"But it came out all right," she said, "and they tell me that's all that matters. You feel better about it now?"

"I think so," he said. "I guess I'll go buy some stamps."

"Keller," she said, "you took the words right out of my mouth."

KELLER
THE
DOGKILLER

CHAPTER TWENTY-SEVEN

Keller, trying not to feel foolish, hoisted his flight bag and stepped to the curb. Two cabs darted his way, and he got into the winner, even as the runner-up filled the air with curses. "JFK," he said, and settled back in his seat.

"Which airline?"

He had to think about it. "American."

"International or domestic?"

"Domestic."

"What time's your flight?"

Usually they just took you there. Today, when he didn't have a plane to catch, he got a full-scale inquiry.

"Not to worry," he told the driver. "We've got plenty of time."

Which was just as well, because it took longer than usual to get through the tunnel, and the traffic on the Long Island Expressway was heavier than usual for that hour. He'd picked this time—early afternoon—because the traffic tended to be light, but today for some reason it wasn't. Fortunately, he reminded himself, it didn't matter. Time, for a change, was not of the essence. ·

"Where you headed?" the driver asked while Keller's mind was wandering.

"Panama," he said, without thinking.

"Then you want International, don't you?"

Why on earth had he said Panama? He'd been wondering if he should buy a straw hat, that was why. "Panama

City," he corrected himself. "That's in Florida, you change planes in Miami."

"You got to fly all the way down to Miami and then back up again to Panama City? Ought to be a better way to do it."

Thousands of cabdrivers in New York, and for once he had to draw one who could speak English. "Air miles," he said, in a tone that brooked no argument, and they left it at that.

At the designated terminal, Keller paid and tipped the guy, then carried his flight bag past the curbside check-in. He followed the signs down to baggage claim and walked around until he found a woman holding a hand-lettered sign that read NIEBAUER.

She hadn't noticed him, so he took a moment to notice her, and to determine that no one else was paying any attention to either of them. She was around forty, a trimly built woman wearing a skirt and blouse and glasses. Her brown hair was medium length, attractive if not stylish, her sharp nose contrasted with her generous mouth, and on balance he'd have to say she had a kind face. This, he knew, was no guarantee of anything. You didn't have to be kind to have a kind face.

He approached her from the side, and got within a few feet of her before she sensed his presence, turned, and stepped back, looking a little startled. "I'm Mr. Niebauer," he said.

"Oh," she said. "Oh, of course. I . . . you surprised me."

"I'm sorry."

"I had noticed you, but I didn't think . . ." She swallowed, started over. "I guess you don't look the way I expected you to look."

"Well, I'm older than I was a few hours ago."

"No, I don't mean . . . I don't know what I mean. I'm sorry. How was your flight?"

"Routine."

"I guess we have to collect your luggage."

"I just have this," he said, holding up the flight bag. "So we can go to your car."

"We can't," she said. She managed a smile. "I don't have one, and couldn't drive it if I did. I'm a city girl, Mr. Niebauer. I never learned to drive. We'll have to take a cab."

There was a moment, of course, when Keller was sure he'd get the same cab, and he could see himself trying to field the driver's questions without alarming the woman. Instead they got into a cab driven by a jittery little man who talked on his cell phone in a language Keller couldn't recognize while his radio was tuned to a talk program in what may or may not have been the same unrecognizable language.

Keller, once again trying not to feel foolish, settled in for the drive back to Manhattan.

Two days earlier, on the wraparound porch of the big old house in White Plains, Keller hadn't felt foolish. What he'd felt was confused.

"It's in New York," he said, starting with the job's least objectionable aspect. "I live in New York. I don't work there."

"You drummed up a job on your own, remember? And it was right here in New York."

"And it was a mistake, and we wound up spinning it, and by the time it ended it wasn't in New York after all. It was in Detroit."

"So it was," she said, "but you've worked other jobs in New York."

"A couple of times," he allowed, "and it worked out all right, all things considered, but that doesn't make it a good idea."

"I know," Dot said, "and I almost turned it down without consulting you. And not just because it's local."

"That's the least of it."

"Right."

"It's short money," he said. "It's ten thousand dollars. It's not exactly chump change, but it's a fraction of what I usually get."

"The danger of working for short money," she said, "is word gets around. But one thing we'd make sure of is nobody knows you're the one who took this job. So it's not a question of ten thousand dollars versus your usual fee, because your usual fee doesn't come into the picture. It's ten thousand dollars for two or three days' work, and I know you can use the work."

"And the money."

"Right. And, of course, there's no travel. Which was a minus the first time we looked at it, but in terms of time and money and all of that—"

"Suddenly it's a plus." He took a sip of his iced tea. "Look, this is stupid. We're not talking about the most important thing."

"I know."

"The, uh, subject is generally a man. Sometimes it's a woman."

"You're an equal-opportunity kind of guy, Keller."

"One time," he said, "somebody wanted me to do a kid. You remember?"

"Vividly."

"We turned them down."

"You're damn right we did."

"Grown-ups," he said. "Adults only. That's where we draw the line."

"Well," she said, "if it matters, the subject this time around is an adult."

"How old is he?"

"Five."

"A five-year-old adult," he said heavily.

"Do the math, Keller. He's thirty-five in dog years."

"Somebody wants to pay me ten thousand dollars to kill a dog," he said. "Why me, Dot? Why can't they call the SPCA?"

"I wondered that myself," she said. "Same token, every time we get a client who wants a spouse killed, I wonder if a divorce wouldn't be a better way to go. Why call us? Has Raoul Felder got an unlisted phone number?"

"But a dog, Dot."

She took a long look at him. "You're thinking about Nelson," she said. "Am I right or am I right?"

"You're right."

"Keller," she said, "I met Nelson, and I liked Nelson. Nelson was a friend of mine. Keller, this dog is no Nelson."

"If you say so."

"In fact," she said, "if Nelson saw this dog and trotted over to give him a friendly sniff, that would be the end of Nelson. This dog's a pit bull, Keller, and he's enough to give the breed a bad name."

"The breed already has a bad name."

"And I can see why. If this dog was a movie actor, Keller, he'd be like Jack Elam."

"I always liked Jack Elam."

"You didn't let me finish. He'd be like Jack Elam, but nasty."

"What does he do, Dot? Eat children?"

She shook her head. "If he ever bit a kid," she said, "or even snarled good and hard at one, that'd be the end of him. The law's set up to protect people from dogs. What with due process and everything, he might rip the throats out of a few tykes before the law caught up with him, but once it did he'd be out of the game and on his way to Doggie Heaven."

"Would he go to heaven? I mean, if he killed a kid—"

"All dogs go to heaven, Keller, even the bad ones. Where was I?"

"He doesn't bite children."

"Never has. Loves people, wants to make nice to everyone. If he sees another dog, however, or a cat or a ferret or a hamster, it's another story. He kills it."

"Oh."

"He lives with his owner in the middle of Manhattan," she said, "and she takes him to Central Park and lets him off his leash, and whenever he gets the chance he kills something. You're going to ask why somebody doesn't do something."

"Well, why don't they?"

"Because about all you can do, it turns out, is sue the owner, and about all you can collect is the replacement value of your pet, and you've got to go through the legal system to get that much. You can't have the dog put down for killing other dogs, and you can't press criminal charges against the owner. Meanwhile, you've still got the dog out there, a menace to other dogs."

"That doesn't make sense."

"Hardly anything does, Keller. Anyway, a couple of women lost their pets and they don't want to take it anymore. One had a twelve-year-old Yorkie and the other had a frisky Weimaraner pup, and neither of them had a snowball's chance against Fluffy, and—"

"Fluffy?"

"I know."

"This killer pit bull is named Fluffy?"

"That's his call name. He's registered as Percy Bysshe Shelley, Keller, whom you'll recall as the author of 'Ozymandias.' I suppose they could call him Percy, or Bysshe, or even Shelley, but instead they went for Fluffy."

And Fluffy went for the Yorkie and the Weimaraner, with tragic results. As Dot explained it, this did seem like a time when one had to go outside the law to get results. But did they have to turn to a high-priced hit man? Couldn't they just do it themselves?

"You'd think so," Dot said. "But this is New York, Keller, and these are a couple of respectable middle-class women. They don't own guns. They could probably get their hands on a bread knife, but I can't see them trying to stab Fluffy, and evidently neither can they."

"Even so," he said, "how did they find their way to us?"

"Somebody knew somebody who knew somebody."

"Who knew us?"

"Not exactly. Someone's ex-husband's brother-in-law is in the garment trade, and he knows a fellow in Chicago who can get things taken care of. And this fellow in Chicago picked up the phone, and next thing you know my phone was ringing."

"And he said, 'Have you got anybody who'd like to kill a dog?'"

"I'm not sure he knows it's a dog. He gave me a number to call, and I drove twenty miles and picked up a pay phone and called it."

"And somebody answered?"

"The woman who's going to meet you at the airport."

"A woman's going to meet me? At an airport?"

"She had somebody call Chicago," Dot said, "so I told her *I* was calling from Chicago, and she thinks you're flying in from Chicago. So she'll go to JFK to meet a flight from Chicago, and you'll show up, looking like you just walked off a plane, and she'll never guess that you're local."

"I don't have a Chicago accent."

"You don't have any kind of an accent, Keller. You could be a radio announcer."

"I could?"

"Well, it's probably a little late in life for a career change, but you could have. Look, here's the thing. Unless Fluffy gets his teeth in you, your risk here is minimal. If they catch you for killing a dog, about the worst that can happen to you is a fine. But they won't catch you, because they won't look for you, because catching a dog killer doesn't get top priority at the NYPD. But what we don't want is for the client to suspect that you're local."

"Because it could blow my cover sooner or later."

"I suppose it could," she said, "but that's the least of it. The last thing we want is people thinking a top New York hit man will kill dogs for chump change."

CHAPTER TWENTY-EIGHT

"**T**he person I spoke to said there was no need for us to meet. She told me all I had to do was supply the name and address of the dog's owner, and you could take it from there. But that just didn't seem right to me. Suppose you got the wrong dog by mistake? I'd never forgive myself."

That seemed extreme to Keller. There had been a time in St. Louis when he'd gotten the wrong man, through no fault of his own, and it hadn't taken him terribly long to forgive himself. On the other hand, forgiving himself came easy to him. His, he'd come to realize, was a forgiving nature.

"Is the coffee all right, Mr. Niebauer? It feels strange calling you Mr. Niebauer, but I don't know your first name. Though come to think of it I probably don't know your last name either, because I don't suppose it's Niebauer, is it?"

"The coffee's fine," he said. "And no, my name's not Niebauer. It's not Paul, either, but you could call me that."

"Paul," she said. "I always liked that name."

Her name was Evelyn, and he'd never had strong feelings about it one way or another, but he'd have preferred not to know it, just as he'd have preferred not to be sitting in the kitchen of her West End Avenue apartment, and not to know that her husband was an attorney named George Augenblick, that they had no children, and that their eight-month-old Weimaraner had answered to the name of Rilke.

"I suppose we could have called him Rainer," she said, "but we called him Rilke." He must have looked blank, because she explained that they'd named him for Rainer Maria Rilke. "He had the nature of a German Romantic poet," she added, "and of course the breed is German in origin. From Weimar, as in Weimar Republic. You must think I'm silly, saying a young dog had the nature of a poet."

"Not at all."

"George thinks I'm silly. He humors me, which is good, I suppose, except he's careful to make it clear to me and everyone else that that's what he's doing. Humoring me. And I in turn pretend I don't know about his girl-friends."

"Uh," Keller said.

They'd come to her apartment because they had to talk somewhere. They'd shared long silences in the cab, interrupted briefly by observations about the weather, and her kitchen seemed a better bet than a coffee shop, or any other public place. Still, Keller wasn't crazy about the idea. If you were dealing with pros, a certain amount of client contact was just barely acceptable. With amateurs, you really wanted to keep your distance.

"If he knew about you," Evelyn said, "he'd have a fit. It's just a dog, he said. Let it go, he said. You want another dog, I'll buy you another dog. Maybe I am being silly, I don't know, but George, George just doesn't get the point."

She'd taken her glasses off while she was talking, and now she turned her eyes on him. They were a deep blue, and luminous.

"More coffee, Paul? No? Then maybe we should go look for that woman and her dog. If we can't find her, at least I can show you where they live."

Rilke," he told Dot. "How do you like that for a coincidence? A Weimaraner and a pit bull, and they're both named after poets."

"What about the Yorkie?"

"Evelyn thinks his name was Buster. Of course that could just be his call name, and he could have been registered as John Greenleaf Whittier."

"Evelyn," Dot said thoughtfully.

"Don't start."

"Now how do you like that for a coincidence? Because that's just what I was about to say to you."

His name aside, there was nothing remotely fluffy about Percy Bysshe Shelley. Nor did his appearance suggest an evil nature. He looked capable and confident, and so did the woman who held on to the end of his leash.

Her name, Keller had learned, was Aida Cuppering, and she was at least as striking in looks as her dog, with strong features and deeply set dark eyes and an athletic stride. She wore tight black jeans and black lace-up boots and a leather motorcycle jacket with a lot of metal on it, chains and studs and zippers, and she lived alone on West Eighty-seventh Street half a block from Central Park, and, according to Evelyn Augenblick, she had no visible means of support.

Keller wasn't so sure about that. It seemed to him that she had a means of support, and that it was all too visible. If she wasn't making a living as a dominatrix, she ought to make an appointment right away for vocational counseling.

There was no way to lurk outside her brownstone without looking as though he was doing precisely that, but Keller had learned that lurking wasn't required. Whenever Cuppering took Fluffy for a walk, they headed straight for the park. Keller, stationed on a park bench, could lurk to his heart's content without attracting attention.

And when the two of them appeared, it was easy enough to get up from the bench and tag along in their wake. Cuppering, with a powerful dog for a companion, was not likely to worry that someone might be following her.

The dog seemed perfectly well behaved. Keller, walking along behind the two of them, was impressed with the way Fluffy walked perfectly at heel, never straining at his leash, never lagging behind. As Evelyn had told him, the dog was unmuzzled. A muzzle would prevent Fluffy from biting anyone, human or animal, and Aida Cuppering had been advised to muzzle her dog, but it was evidently advice she was prepared to ignore. Still, three times a day she walked the animal, and three times a day Keller was there to watch them, and he didn't see Fluffy so much as glower at anyone.

Suppose the dog was innocent? Suppose there was a larger picture here? Suppose, say, Evelyn Augenblick had found out that her husband had been dillydallying with Aida Cuppering. Suppose the high-powered attorney liked to lick Cuppering's boots, suppose he let her lead him around on a leash, muzzled or not. And suppose Evelyn's way of getting even was to . . .

To spend ten thousand dollars having the woman's dog killed?

Keller shook his head. This was something that needed more thought.

"Excuse me," the woman said. "Is this seat taken?"

Keller had read all he wanted to read in the *New York Times*, and now he was taking a shot at the crossword puzzle. It was a Thursday, so that made it a fairly difficult puzzle, though nowhere near as hard as the Saturday one would be. For some reason—Keller didn't know what it might be—the *Times* puzzle started out each Monday at a grade-school level, and by Saturday became damn near impossible to finish.

Keller looked up, abandoning the search for a seven-letter word for "Diana's nemesis," to see a slender woman in her late thirties, wearing faded jeans and a Leggs Mini-Marathon T-shirt. Beyond her, he noted a pair of unoccupied benches, and a glance to either side indicated similarly empty benches on either side of him.

"No," he said, carefully. "No, make yourself comfortable."

She sat down to his right, and he waited for her to say something, and when she didn't he returned to his crossword puzzle. Diana's nemesis. Which Diana? he wondered. The English princess? The Roman goddess of the hunt?

The woman cleared her throat, and Keller figured the puzzle was a lost cause. He kept his eyes on it, but his attention was on his companion, and he waited for her to say something. What she said, hesitantly, was that she didn't know where to begin.

"Anywhere," Keller suggested.

"All right. My name is Myra Tannen. I followed you from Evelyn's."

"You followed me . . ."

"From Evelyn's. The other day. I wanted to come along to the airport, but Evelyn insisted on going alone. I'm paying half the fee, I ought to have as much right to meet you as she has, but, well, that's Evelyn for you."

Well, Dot had said there were two women, and this one, Myra, was evidently the owner of the twelve-year-old Yorkie of whom Fluffy had made short work. It wasn't bad enough that he'd met one of his employers, but now he'd met the other. And she'd followed him from Evelyn's—followed him!—and this morning she'd come to the park and found him.

"When you followed me . . ."

"I live on the same block as Evelyn," she said. "Just two doors down, actually. I saw the two of you get out of the taxi, and I was watching when you left. And I, well, followed you."

"I see."

"I got a nice long walk out of it. I don't walk that much now that I don't have a dog to walk. But you know about that."

"Yes."

"She was the sweetest thing, my little dog. Well, never mind about that. I followed you all the way through the park and down to First Avenue and wherever it was. Forty-ninth Street? You went into a building there, and I was going to wait for you, and then I told myself I was being silly. So I got in a cab and came home."

For God's sake, he thought. This amateur, this little housewife, had followed him home. She knew where he lived.

He hesitated, looking for the right words. Would it be

enough to tell her that this was no way to proceed, that contact with his clients compromised his mission? Was it in fact time to abort the whole business? If they had to give back the money, well, that was one good thing about working for chump change: a refund wasn't all that expensive.

He said, "Look, what you have to understand—"

"Not now. There she is."

And there she was, all right. Aida Cuppering, dressed rather like a Doberman pinscher, all black leather and metal studs and high black lace-up boots, striding along imperiously with Fluffy, leashed, stepping along at her side. As she drew abreast of Keller and his companion, the woman stopped long enough to unclip the dog's lead from his collar. She straightened up, and for a moment her gaze swept the bench where Keller and Myra Tannen sat, dismissing them even as she took note of them. Then she walked on, and Fluffy walked along at heel, both of them looking perfectly lethal.

"She's not supposed to do that," Myra said. "In the first place he's supposed to be muzzled, and every dog's supposed to be kept on a leash."

"Well," Keller said.

"She wants him to kill other dogs. I saw her face when my Millicent was killed. It was quick, you know. He picked her up in his jaws and shook her and snapped her spine."

"Oh."

"And I saw her face. That's not where I was looking, I was watching what was happening, I was trying to do something, but my eyes went to her face, and she was . . . excited."

"Oh."

"That dog's a danger. Something has to be done about it. Are you going to—"

"Yes," he said, "but, you know, I can't have an audience when it happens. I'm not used to working under supervision."

"Oh, I know," she said, "and believe me, I won't do anything like this again. I won't approach you or follow you, nothing like that."

"Good."

"But, you see, I want to . . . well, amend the agreement."

"I beg your pardon?"

"Besides the dog."

"Oh?"

"Of course I want you to take care of the dog, but there's something else I'd like to have you do, and I'm prepared to pay extra for it. I mean, considerably extra."

The owner too, he thought. Well, that was appropriate, wasn't it? The dog couldn't help its behavior, while the owner actively encouraged it.

She was carrying a tote bag bearing the logo of a bank, and she started to draw a large brown envelope from it, then changed her mind. "Take the whole thing," she said, handing him the tote bag. "There's nothing else in it, just the money, and it'll be easier to carry this way. Here, take it."

Not at all the professional way to do things, he thought. But he took the tote bag.

"This is irregular," he said carefully. "I'll have to talk to my people in Chicago, and—"

"Why?"

He looked at her.

"They don't have to know about this," she said, avoiding his eyes. "This is just between you and me. It's all cash, and it's a lot more than the two of us gave you for the dog, and if you don't say anything about it to your people, well, you won't have to split with them, will you?"

He wasn't sure what to say to that, so he didn't say anything.

"I want you to kill her," she said, and there was no lack of conviction in her tone. "You can make it look like an accident, or like a mugging gone wrong, or, I don't know, a sex crime? Anything you want, it doesn't matter, just as long as she dies. And if it's painful, well, that's fine with me."

Was she wearing a wire? Were there plainclothes cops stationed behind the trees? And wouldn't that be a cute way to entrap a hit man. Bring him in to kill a dog, then raise the stakes, and—

"Let me make sure I've got this straight. You're paying me this money yourself, and it's in cash, and nobody else is going to know about it."

"That's right."

"And in return you want me to take care of Aida Cuppering."

She stared at him. "Aida Cuppering? What do I care about Aida Cuppering?"

"I thought—"

"I don't care about her," Myra Tannen said. "I don't even care about her damn dog, not really. What I want you to do is kill Evelyn."

221

CHAPTER TWENTY-NINE

"What a mess," Dot said.

"No kidding."

"All I can say is I'm sorry I got you into this. Two women hired you to put a dog down, and you've met each of them face-to-face, and one of them knows where you live."

"She doesn't know that I live there," he said. "She thinks I flew in from Chicago. But she knows the address, and probably thinks I'm staying there for the time being."

"You never noticed you were being followed?"

"It never occurred to me to check. I walk home all the time, Dot. I never feel the need to look over my shoulder."

"And you'd never have to, if I'd borne in mind the old rule about not crapping where we eat. You know what it was, Keller? There were two reasons to turn the job down, because it was in New York and because it was a dog, and what I did, I let the two of them cancel each other out. My apologies. Still, a question arises."

"Oh?"

"How much was in the bag?"

"Twenty-five."

"I hope that's twenty-five thousand."

"It is."

"Because the way things have been going, it could have been twenty-five hundred."

"Or just plain twenty-five."

"That'd be a stretch. So the whole package is thirty-five. It's still a hard way to get rich. What's she got against Evelyn, anyway? It can't be that she's pissed she didn't get to go to the airport."

"Her husband's been having an affair with Evelyn."

"Oh. I thought it was Evelyn's husband that was fooling around."

"I thought so, too. I guess the Upper West Side's a hotbed of adultery."

"And here I always figured it was all concerts and dairy restaurants. What are you going to do, Keller?"

"I've been wondering that myself."

"I bet you have. A certain amount of damage control would seem to be indicated. I mean, two of them have seen your face."

"I know."

"And one of them followed you home. Which doesn't mean you can keep her, in case you were wondering."

"I wasn't."

"I hope not. I gather both of them are reasonably attractive."

"So?"

"And they're probably attracted to you. A dangerous man, a mysterious character—how can they resist you?"

"I don't think they're interested," he said, "and I know I'm not."

"How about the dog owner? The one who looks like a dominatrix."

"I'm not interested in her, either."

"Well, I'm relieved to hear it. You think you can find a way to make all of this go away?"

"I was ready to give back the money," he said, "but we're past that point. I'll think of something, Dot."

Just as Keller reached to knock on the door, it opened. Evelyn Augenblick, wearing a pants suit and a white blouse and a flowing bow tie, stood there beaming at him. "It's you," she said. "Thank God. Quick, so I can shut the door."

She did so, and turned to him, and he saw something he had somehow failed to notice before. She had a gun in her hand, a short-barreled revolver.

Keller didn't know what to make of it. She'd seemed relieved to see him, so what was the gun for? To shoot him? Or was she expecting somebody else, against whom she felt the need to defend herself?

And should he take a step toward her and swat the gun out of her hand? That would probably work, but if it didn't . . .

"I guess you saw the ad," she said.

The ad? What ad?

" 'Paul Niebauer, Please Get in Touch.' On the front page of the *New York Times,* one of those tiny ads at the very bottom of the page. I always wondered if anybody read those ads. But you didn't, I can see by the look on your face. How did you know to come here?"

How indeed? "I just had a feeling," he said.

"Well, I'm glad you did. I didn't know how else to reach you, because I didn't want to go through the usual channels. And it was important that I see you."

"The gun," he said.

She looked at him.

"You're holding a gun," he said.

"Oh," she said, and looked at her hand, as if surprised to discover a gun in it. "That's for you," she said, and before he could react she handed the thing to him. He didn't

224

want it, but neither did he want her to have it. So he took it, noting that it was a .38, and a loaded one at that.

"What's this for?" he asked.

She didn't exactly answer. "It belongs to my husband," she said. "It's registered. He has a permit to keep it on the premises, and that's what he does. He keeps it in the drawer of his bedside table. For burglars, he says."

"I don't really think it would be useful to me," he said. "Since it's registered to your husband, it would lead right back to you, which is the last thing we'd want, and—"

"You don't understand."

"Oh."

"This isn't for Fluffy."

"It's not?"

"No," she said. "I don't really care about Fluffy. Killing Fluffy won't bring Rilke back. And it's not so bad with Rilke gone, anyway. He was a beautiful dog, but he was really pretty stupid, and it was a pain in the ass having to walk him twice a day."

"Oh."

"So the gun has nothing to do with Fluffy," she explained. "The gun's for you to use when you kill my husband."

"Damnedest thing I ever heard of," Dot said. "And that covers a lot of ground. Well, she'd said her husband was running around on her. So she wants you to kill him?"

"With his own gun."

"Suicide?"

"Murder-suicide."

"Where does the murder come in?"

"I'm supposed to stage it," he said, "so that it looks as

225

though he shot the woman he was having an affair with, then turned the gun on himself."

"The woman he's having the affair with."

"Right."

"Don't tell me, Keller."

"Okay."

"Keller, that's an expression. It doesn't mean I don't want to know. But I have a feeling I know already. Am I right, Keller?"

"Uh-huh."

"It's her, isn't it? Myra Tannenbaum."

"Just Tannen."

"Whatever. They both fly you in from the Windy City to kill a dog, and now neither one really gives a hoot in hell about the dog, and each one wants you to kill the other. How much did this one give you?"

"Forty-two thousand dollars."

"Forty-two thousand dollars? How did she happen to arrive at that particular number, do you happen to know?"

"It's what she got for her jewelry."

"She sold her jewelry so she could get her husband killed? I suppose it's jewelry her husband gave her in the first place, don't you think? Keller, this is beginning to have a definite 'Gift of the Magi' quality to it."

"She was going to give me the jewelry," he said, "since it was actually worth quite a bit more than she got for it, but she figured I'd rather have the cash."

"Amazing. She actually got something right. Didn't you tell me Myra Tannen's husband was having the affair with Evelyn?"

"That's what she told me, but it may have been a lie."

"Oh."

226

"Or maybe each of them is having an affair with the other's husband. It's hard to say for sure."

"Oh."

"I didn't know what to do, Dot."

"Keller, neither of us has known what to do from the jump. I assume you took the money."

"And the gun."

"And now you still don't know what to do."

"As far as I can see, there's only one thing I can do."

"Oh," she said. "Well, in that case, I guess you'll just have to go ahead and do it."

Myra Tannen lived in a brownstone, which meant there was no doorman to deal with. There was a lock, but Evelyn had provided a key, and at two-thirty the following afternoon, Keller tried it in the lock. It turned easily, and he walked in and climbed four flights of stairs. There were two apartments on the top floor, and he found the right door and rang the bell.

He waited, and rang a second time, and followed it up with a knock. Finally he heard footsteps, and then the sound of the cover of the peephole being drawn back. "I can't see anything," Myra Tannen said.

He wasn't surprised; he'd covered the peephole with his palm. "It's me," he said. "The man you sat next to in the park."

"Oh?"

"I'd better come in."

There was a pause. "I'm not alone," she said at length.

"I know."

"But . . ."

"We've got a real problem here," he said, "and it's going to get a lot worse if you don't open the door."

CHAPTER THIRTY

It was almost three when he picked up the phone. He wasn't sure how good an idea it was to use the Tannen telephone. The police, checking the phone records, would know the precise time the call was made. Of course it would in all likelihood be just one of many calls made from the Tannen apartment to the Augenblick household across the street, and in any event all it could do was tie the two sets of people together, and what difference could that make to him?

Evelyn Augenblick answered on the first ring.

"Paul," he said. "Across the street."

"Oh, God."

"I think you should come over here."

"Are you sure?"

"It's all taken care of," he said, "but there are some things I really need your input on."

"Oh."

"You don't have to look at anything, if you don't want to."

"It's done?"

"It's done."

"And they're both . . ."

"Yes, both of them."

"Oh, good," she said. "I'll be right over. But you've got the key."

"Ring the bell," he said. "I'll buzz you in."

It didn't take her long. Time passed slowly in the Tannen apartment, but it was only ten minutes before the bell sounded. He poked the buzzer to unlock the door downstairs, and waited for her in the hallway while she climbed four flights of stairs. She was breathing hard from the effort, and the sight of her husband and her friend did nothing to calm her down.

"Oh, this is perfect," she said. "Myra's in her nightgown, sprawled on her back, with two bulletholes in her chest. And George—he's barefoot, and wearing his pants but no shirt. The gun's still in his hand. What did you do, stick the gun in his mouth and pull the trigger? That's wonderful, it blew the whole back of his head off."

"Well, not quite, but—"

"But close enough. God, you really did it. They're both gone, I'll never have to look at either one of them again. And this is the way I get to remember them, and that's just perfect. You're a genius for thinking of this, getting me to see them like this. But . . ."

"But what?"

"Well, I'm not complaining, but why did you want me to come over here?"

"I thought it might be exciting."

"It is, but—"

"I thought maybe you could take off all your clothes."

Her jaw dropped. "My God," she said, "and here I thought *I* was kinky. Paul, I never even thought you were interested."

"Well, I am now."

"So it's exciting for you, too. And you want me to take my clothes off? Well, why not?"

She made a rather elaborate striptease of it, which was a

waste of time as far as he was concerned, but it didn't take her too long. When she was naked he picked up her husband's gun, muffled it with the same throw pillow he'd used earlier, and shot her twice in the chest. Then he put the gun back in her husband's hand and got out of there.

It was hard to believe that they charged two dollars for a Good Humor. Keller wasn't positive, but it seemed to him he could remember paying fifteen or twenty cents for one. Of course that had been many years ago, and everything had been cheaper way back when, and cost more nowadays.

But you really noticed it when it involved something you hadn't bought in years, and a Good Humor, ice cream on a stick, was not something he'd often felt a longing for. Now, though, walking in the park, he'd seen a vendor, and the urge for a chocolate-coated ice cream bar, with a firm chocolate center and assorted gook embedded in the chocolate coating, was well nigh irresistible. He'd paid the two dollars—he probably would have paid ten dollars just then, if he'd had to—and went over to sit on a bench and enjoy his Good Humor.

If only.

Because he couldn't really characterize his own humor as particularly good, or even neutral. He was, in fact, in a fairly dismal mood, and he wasn't sure what to do about it. There were things he liked about his work, but its immediate aftermath had never been one of them; whatever feeling of satisfaction came from a job well done was mitigated by the bad feeling brought about by the job's nature. He'd just killed three people, and two of them had been his clients. That wasn't the way things were supposed to go.

But what choice had he had? Both of the women had met him and seen his face, and one of them had tracked him to his apartment. He could leave them alive, but then he'd have to relocate to Chicago; it just wouldn't be safe to stay in New York, where there'd be all too great a chance of running into one or the other of them.

Even if he didn't, sooner or later one or the other would talk. They were amateurs, and if he did just what he was supposed to do originally—send Fluffy to that great dog run in the sky—either Evelyn or Myra would have an extra drink one night and delight in telling her friends how she'd managed to solve a problem in a sensible Sopranos-style way.

And of course if he executed the extra commission from one of them by killing the other, well, sooner or later the cops would talk to the survivor, who would hold out for about five minutes before spilling everything she knew. He'd have to kill Myra, because she'd followed him home and thus knew more than Evelyn, and that's what he'd done, thinking he might be able to leave it at that, but with George dead the cops would go straight to Evelyn, and . . .

He had to do all three of them. Period, end of story.

And the way he left things, the cops wouldn't really have any reason to look much further. A domestic triangle, all three participants dead, all shot with the same gun, with nitrate particles in the shooter's hand and the last bullet fired through the roof of his mouth and into his brain. (And, as Evelyn had observed with delight, out the back of his skull.) It'd make tabloid headlines, but there was no reason for anyone to go looking for a mystery man from Chicago or anywhere else.

Usually, after he'd finished a piece of work, the next order of business was for him to go home. Whether he drove or flew or took a train, he'd thus be putting some substantial physical distance between himself and what he'd just done. That, plus the mental tricks he used to distance himself from the job, made it easier to turn the page and get on with his life.

Walking across the park wasn't quite the same thing.

He centered his attention on his Good Humor. The sweetness helped, no question about it. Took the sourness right out of his system. The sweetness, the creaminess, the tang of the chocolate center that remained after the last of the ice cream was gone—it was all just right, and he couldn't believe he'd resented paying two dollars for it. It would have been a bargain at five dollars, he decided, and an acceptable luxury at ten. It was gone now, but . . .

Well, couldn't he have another?

The only reason not to, he decided, was that it wasn't the sort of thing a person did. You didn't buy one ice cream bar and follow it with another. But why not? He wouldn't miss the two dollars, and weight had never been a problem for him, nor was there any particular reason for him to watch his intake of fat or sugar or chocolate. So?

He found the vendor, handed him a pair of singles. "Think I'll have another," he said, and the vendor, who may or may not have spoken English, took his money and gave him his ice cream bar.

He was just finishing the second Good Humor when the woman showed up. Aida Cuppering walked briskly along the path, wearing her usual outfit and flanked by her usual companion. She stopped a few yards from Keller's bench, but Fluffy strained at his leash, making a sound that was sort of an angry whimper. Keller looked in the direction the dog was pointing, and fifty yards or so up the path he saw what Fluffy saw, a Jack Russell terrier who was lifting a leg at the base of a tree.

"Oh, you good boy," Aida Cuppering said, even as she stooped to unclip the lead from Fluffy's collar.

"Go!" she said, and Fluffy went, tearing down the path at the little terrier.

Keller couldn't watch the dogs. Instead he looked at the woman, and that was bad enough, as she glowed with the thrill of the kill. After the little dog's yelping had ceased, after Cuppering's body had shuddered with whatever sort of climax the spectacle had afforded her, she looked over and realized that Keller was watching her.

"He needs his exercise," she said, smiling benignly, and turned to clap her hands to urge the dog to return.

Keller never planned what happened next. He didn't have time, didn't even think about it. He got to his feet, reached her in three quick strides, cupped her jaw with one hand and fastened the other on her shoulder, and broke her neck every bit as efficiently as her dog had broken the neck of the little terrier.

CHAPTER THIRTY-ONE

"**S**o you saw Fluffy make a kill."

He was in White Plains, drinking a glass of iced tea and watching Dot's television. It was tuned to the Game Show Channel, and the sound was off. Game shows, he thought, were dopey enough when you could hear what the people were saying.

"No," he said. "I couldn't watch. The animal's a killing machine, Dot."

"Now that's funny," she said, "because I was just about to say the same thing about you. I don't get it, Keller. We take a job for short money because all you have to do is kill a dog. The next thing I know, four people are dead, and two of them used to be clients of ours. I don't know how we can expect them to recommend us to their friends, let alone give us some repeat business."

"I didn't have any choice, Dot."

"I realize that. They already knew too much when it was just going to be a dog that got killed, but as soon as human beings entered the equation, it became very dangerous to leave them alive."

"That's what I thought."

"And when you come right down to it, all you did was what each of them hired you to do. A says to kill B and C, you kill B and C. And then you kill A, because that's what B hired you to do. I have to say I think D came out of left field."

"D? Oh, Aida Cuppering."

"Nobody wanted her killed," she said, "and at last report nobody paid to have her killed. Was that what you call pro bono?"

"It was an impulse."

"No kidding."

"That dog of hers, killing other dogs is his nature, but there's no question she did everything she could to encourage it. Just because she liked to watch. I was supposed to kill the dog, but he was just a dog, you know?"

"So you broke her neck. If anyone was watching . . ."

"Nobody was."

"A good thing, or you'd have had more necks to break. The police certainly seem puzzled. They seem to think the killing might have been the work of one of her clients. It turns out she really was a dominatrix after all."

"She would sort of have to have been."

"And one of her clients lived in the apartment where the love triangle murder-suicide took place earlier that afternoon."

"George was her client?"

"Not George," she said. "George lived across the street with Evelyn, remember? No, her client was a man named Edmund Tannen."

"Myra's husband. I thought he was supposed to be having an affair with Evelyn."

"I don't suppose it matters who was doing what to whom," she said, "since they're all conveniently dead now. Or inconveniently, but one way or another they've all been wiped off the board. I don't know about you, but I can't say I'm going to miss any of them."

"No."

"And from a financial standpoint, well, it's not the best payday we ever had, but it's not the worst, either. Ten for the dog and twenty-five for Evelyn and forty-two for Myra and George. You know what that means, Keller."

"I can buy some stamps."

"You sure can. You know the real irony here? Everybody else in the picture is dead, except for the Good Humor man. You didn't do anything to him, did you?"

"No, for God's sake. Why would I?"

"Who knows why anybody would do anything. But except for him, they're all dead. Except for the one creature you were supposed to kill in the first place."

"Fluffy."

"Uh-huh. What is it, professional courtesy? One killing machine can't bear to kill another?"

"He'll get sent to the YMCA," he said, "and when nobody adopts him, which they won't because of his history, he'll be put to sleep."

"Is that what they do at the YMCA?"

"Is that what I said? I meant the SPCA."

"That's what I figured."

"The animal shelter, whatever you want to call it. She lived alone, so there's nobody else to take the dog."

"In the paper," Dot said, "it says they found him standing over her body, crying plaintively. But I don't suppose you stuck around to watch that part."

"No, I went straight home," he said. "And this time nobody followed me."

CHAPTER THIRTY-TWO

The following Thursday afternoon, the phone was ringing when he got back to his apartment. "Stay," he said. "Good boy." And he went and picked up the phone.

"There you are," Dot said. "I tried you earlier, but I guess you were out."

"I was."

"But now you're back," she said. "Keller, is everything all right? You seemed a little out of it when you left here the other day."

"No, I'm okay."

"That's really all I called to ask, because I just . . . Keller, what's that sound?"

"It's nothing."

"It's a dog."

"Well," he said.

"This whole dog business, it made you miss Nelson, so you went out and got yourself a dog. Right?"

"Not exactly."

" 'Not exactly.' What's that supposed to mean? Oh, no. Keller, tell me it's not what I think it is."

"Well."

"You went out and adopted that goddam killing machine. Didn't you? You decided putting him to sleep would be a crime against nature, and you just couldn't bear for that to happen, softhearted creature that you are, and now you've saddled yourself with a crazed bloodthirsty beast that's going to make your life a living hell. Does that pretty much sum it up, Keller?"

"No."

"No?"

"No," he said. "Dot, they sent the dog to a shelter, just the way I said they would."

"Well, there's a big surprise. I thought for sure they'd run him for the Senate on the Republican ticket."

"But it wasn't the SPCA."

"Or the YMCA either, I'll bet."

"They sent him to IBARF."

"I beg your pardon?"

"The Inter-Boro Animal Rescue Foundation, IBARF for short."

"Whatever you say."

"And the thing about IBARF," he said, "is they never euthanize an animal. If it's not adoptable, they just keep it there and keep feeding it until it dies of old age."

"How old is Fluffy?"

"Not that old. And, you know, it's not like a maximum-security institution there. Sooner or later somebody would leave a cage open, and Fluffy would get a chance to kill a dog or two."

"I think I see where this is going."

"Well, what choice did I have, Dot?"

"That's the thing with you these days, Keller. You never seem to have any choice, and you wind up doing the damnedest things. I'm surprised they let you adopt him."

"They didn't want to. I explained how I needed a vicious dog to guard a used-car lot after hours."

"One that would keep other dogs from breaking in and

driving off in a late-model Honda. I hope you gave them a decent donation."

"I gave them a hundred dollars."

"Well, that'll pay for fifty Good Humors, won't it? How does it feel, having a born killer in your apartment?"

"He's very sweet and gentle," he said. "Jumps up on me, licks my face."

"Oh, God."

"Don't worry, Dot. I know what I have to do."

"What you have to do," she said, "is go straight to the SPCA, or even the YMCA, as long as it's not some chickenhearted outfit like IBARF. Some organization that you can count on to put Fluffy down in a humane manner, and to do it as soon as possible. Right?"

"Well," he said, "not exactly."

"**W**hat a nice dog," the young woman said.

The animal, Keller had come to realize, was an absolute babe magnet. In the mile or so he'd walked from his apartment to the park, this was the third woman to make a fuss over Fluffy. This one said the same thing the others had said: that the dog certainly looked tough and capable, but that he really was just a big baby, wasn't he? Wasn't he?

Keller wanted to urge her to get down on all fours and bark. Then she'd find out just what kind of a big old softie Fluffy was.

He'd waited until twilight, hoping to avoid as many dogs and dog walkers as possible, but there were still some to be found, and Fluffy was remarkably good at spotting them. Whenever he caught sight of one, or caught the scent, his ears perked up and he strained at the leash. But

Keller kept a good tight hold on it and kept leading the dog to the park's less-traveled paths.

It would have been easy to follow Dot's advice, to pay another hundred dollars and palm the dog off on the SPCA or some similar institution. But suppose they got their signals crossed and let someone adopt Fluffy, the way the damned fools at IBARF had let him? Suppose, one way or another, something went wrong and Fluffy got a chance to kill more dogs?

This wasn't something to delegate. This was something he had to do for himself. That was the only way to be sure it got done, and got done properly. Besides, it was something he'd hired on to do long ago. He'd been paid, and it was time to do the work.

He thought about Nelson. It was impossible, walking in the park with a dog on a leash, not to think about Nelson. But Nelson was gone. In all the time since Nelson's departure, it had never seriously occurred to him to get another dog. And, if it ever did, this wasn't the dog he'd get.

He patted his pocket. There was a small-caliber gun in it, an automatic, unregistered, and never fired since it came into his possession several years ago. He'd kept it, because you never knew when you might need a gun, and now he had a use for it.

"This way, Fluffy," he said. "That's a good boy."

KELLER'S
DOUBLE
DRIBBLE

KELLER'S
DOUBLE
DRIBBLE

CHAPTER THIRTY-THREE

Keller, his hands in his pockets, watched a dark-skinned black man with his shirt off drive for the basket. His shaved head gleamed, and the muscles of his upper back, the traps and lats, bulged as if steroidally enhanced. Another man, wearing a T-shirt but otherwise of the same shade and physique, leapt to block the shot, and the two bodies met in midair. It was a little like ballet, Keller thought, and a little like combat, and the ball kissed off the backboard and dropped through the hoop.

There was no net, just a bare hoop. The playground was at the corner of Sixth Avenue and West Third Street, in Greenwich Village, and Keller was one of a handful of spectators standing outside the high chain-link fence, watching idly as ten men, half wearing T-shirts, half bare-chested, played a fiercely competitive game of half-court basketball.

If this were a game at the Garden, the last play would have sent someone to the free-throw line. But there was no ref here to call fouls, and order was maintained in a simpler fashion; anyone who fouled too frequently was thrown out of the game. It was, Keller felt, an interesting libertarian solution, and he thought it might be worth a try outside the basketball court, but had a feeling it would be tough to make it work.

Keller watched a few more plays, feeling his spirits sink as he did, yet finding it oddly difficult to tear himself away.

He'd had a tooth drilled and filled a few blocks away, by a dentist who had himself played varsity basketball years ago at the University of Kentucky, and had been walking around waiting for the Novocain to wear off so he could grab some lunch, and the basketball game had caught his eye, and here he was. Watching, and being brought down in the process, because basketball always depressed him.

His mouth wasn't numb anymore. He crossed the street, walked two blocks east, turned right on Sullivan Street, left on Bleecker. He considered and rejected restaurants as he walked, knowing he wanted something spicy. If basketball depressed him, highly seasoned food put him right again. He thought it odd, didn't understand it, but knew it worked.

The restaurant he found was Indian, and Keller made sure the waiter got the message. "You tone things down for Westerners," he told the man. "I only look like an American of European ancestry. Inside, I am a man from Sri Lanka."

"You want spicy," the waiter said.

"I want very spicy," Keller said. "And then some."

The little man beamed. "You wish to sweat."

"I wish to suffer."

"Leave it to me," the little man said.

The meal was almost too hot to eat. Nominally a lamb curry, its ingredients might have been anything. Lamb, beef, dog, duck. Tofu, shoe leather, balsa wood. Papier-mâché? Plaster of Paris? The searing heat of the cayenne obscured everything else. Keller, forcing himself to finish every bite, loved and hated every minute of it. By the time he was done he was drenched in perspiration, and felt as if he'd just gone ten rounds with a worthy opponent. He felt, too, a sense of accomplishment, and an abiding sense of peace with the world.

Something made him call home to check his answering machine. Two hours later he was on the front porch of the big old house on Taunton Place, sipping a glass of iced tea. Three days after that he was in Indiana.

At the Avis desk at Indy International, Keller turned in the Chevy he'd driven from New York. At the Hertz counter, he picked up the keys to the Ford he'd reserved. He carried his bag to the car, left it in short-term parking, and went back into the airport, remembering to take his bag with him. There was a fellow waiting at baggage claim, wearing the green and gold John Deere cap they'd said he'd be wearing.

"Oh, there you are," the fellow said, when Keller approached him. "The bags are just starting to come down."

Keller brandished his carry-on, said he hadn't checked anything.

"Then I guess you didn't bring a nail clipper," the man said, "or a Swiss Army knife. Never mind a bazooka."

Keller had a Swiss Army knife in his carry-on and a nail clipper in his pocket, attached to his key ring. Since he hadn't flown anywhere, he'd had no problem. As for the other, well, he had never minded a bazooka in his life, and saw no reason to start now.

"Now let's get you squared away," the man said. He was around forty, and lean, except for an incongruous potbelly, as if he'd swallowed a small watermelon. "Quick orientation, drive you around, show you where he lives.

We'll take my car, and when we're done you can drop me off and keep it."

The airport was at the southwest corner of Indianapolis, and the man (who'd flipped the John Deere cap into the backseat of his Hyundai squareback, alongside Keller's carry-on) drove to Carmel, an upscale suburb north of the I-465 beltway. He made a few efforts at conversation, which Keller let wither on the vine, whereupon he gave up and switched on the radio. He kept it tuned to an all-talk station, and right now two opinionated fellows were arguing about the outsourcing of jobs.

Keller thought about turning it off. You're a hit man, brought in at great expense from out of town, and some gofer picks you up and plays the radio, and you turn it off, what's he gonna do? Be impressed and a little intimidated, he thought, but decided it wasn't worth the trouble.

The driver killed the radio himself when they left the interstate and drove through the tree-lined streets of Carmel. Keller paid close attention now, noting street names and landmarks, and taking a good look at the house that was pointed out to him. It was a Dutch Colonial with a mansard roof, he noted, and it reminded him of a house in Roseburg, Oregon.

Funny what you remembered.

When they were done the man asked him if there was anything else he wanted to see, and Keller said there wasn't. "Then I'll drive you to my house," the man said, "and you can drop me off."

Keller shook his head. "Drop me at the airport," he said.

"Oh, Jesus," the man said. "Is something wrong? Did I say the wrong thing?"

246

Keller looked at him.

" 'Cause if you're backing out, I'm gonna get blamed for it. They'll have a goddam fit. Is it the location? Because, you know, it doesn't have to be at his house. It could be anywhere."

Oh. Keller explained that he didn't want to use the Hyundai, that he'd pick up a car at the airport. He preferred it that way, he said.

Driving back to the airport, the man obviously wanted to ask why Keller wanted his own car, and just as obviously was afraid to say a word. Nor did he play the radio. The silence was a heavy one, but that was okay with Keller.

When they got there the fellow said he supposed Keller wanted to rent a car. Keller shook his head and directed him to the lot where he'd already stowed the Ford. "Keep going," he said. "Maybe that one . . . no, that's the one I want. Stop here."

"What are you gonna do?"

"Borrow a car," Keller said.

He'd added the key to his key ring, and now he stood alongside the car and made a show of flipping through keys, finally selecting the one they'd given him. He tried it in the door and, unsurprisingly, it worked. He tried it in the ignition, and it worked there, too. He switched off the ignition and went back to the Hyundai for his carry-on, where the driver, wide-eyed, asked him if he was really going to steal that car.

"I'm just borrowing it," he said.

"But if the owner reports it—"

"I'll be done with it by then." He smiled. "Relax. I do this all the time."

The fellow started to say something, then changed his

mind. "Well," he said instead. "Look, do you want a piece?"

Was the man offering him a woman? Or, God forbid, offering to supply sexual favors personally? Keller frowned, and then realized the piece in question was a gun. Keller, relieved, shook his head, and said he had everything he needed in his carry-on. Amazing the damage you could inflict with a Swiss Army knife and a nail clipper.

"Well," the man said again. "Well, here's something." He reached into his breast pocket and came out with a pair of tickets. "To the Pacers game," he said. "They're playing the Knicks, so you'll probably get to see the home team win. Tonight, eight sharp. They're not courtside, but they're damn good seats. You want, I could dig up somebody to go with you, keep you company."

Keller said he'd take care of that himself, and the man didn't seem surprised to hear it.

CHAPTER THIRTY-FOUR

"**H**e's a witness," Dot had said, "but apparently nobody's thought of sticking him in the Federal Witness Protection Program, but maybe that's because the situation's not federal. Do you have to be involved in a federal case in order to be protected by the federal government?"

Keller wasn't sure, and Dot said it didn't really matter. What mattered was that the witness wasn't in the program, and wasn't hidden at all, and that made it a job for Keller, because the client really didn't want the witness to stand up and testify.

"Or sit down and testify," she said, "which is what they usually do, at least on the television programs I watch. The lawyers stand up, and even walk around some, but the witnesses just sit there."

"What did he witness, do you happen to know?"

"You know," she said, "they were pretty vague on that point. The guy I talked to wasn't a principal. He was more like a booking agent. I've worked with him before, when his clients were OC guys."

"Huh?"

"Organized crime. So he's connected, but this isn't OC, and my sense is it's not violent."

"But it's going to get that way."

"Well, you're not going all the way to Indiana to talk sense into him, are you? What he witnessed, I think it was like corporate shenanigans. What's the matter?"

"Shenanigans," he said.

"It's a perfectly good word. What's the matter with *shenanigans*?"

"I just didn't think anybody said it anymore," he said. "That's all."

"Well, maybe they should. God knows they've got occasion to."

"If it's corporate fiddle-faddle," he began, and stopped when she held up a hand.

"*Fiddle-faddle*? This from a man who has a problem with *shenanigans*?"

"If it's that sort of thing," he said, "then it actually could be federal, couldn't it?"

"I suppose so."

"But he's not in the witness program because they don't think he's in danger."

She nodded. "Stands to reason."

"So they probably haven't assigned people to guard him," he said, "and he's probably not taking precautions."

"Probably not."

"Should be easy."

"It should," she agreed. "So why are you disappointed?"

"Disappointed?"

"That's the vibe I'm getting. Are you picking up on something? Like it's really going to be a lot more complicated than it sounds?"

He shook his head. "I think it's going to be easy," he said, "and I hope it is, and I'm not picking up any vibe. And I certainly didn't mean to sound disappointed, because I don't feel disappointed. I can use the money, and besides that I can use the work. I don't want to go stale."

"So there's no problem."

"No. As far as your vibe is concerned, well, I spent the morning at the dentist."

"Say no more. That's enough to depress anybody."

"It wasn't, really. But then I was watching some guys play basketball. The Indian food helped, but the mood lingered."

"You're just one big non sequitur, aren't you, Keller?" She held up a hand. "No, don't explain. You'll go to Indianapolis, you lucky man, and your actions will get to speak for themselves."

Keller's motel was a Rodeway Inn at the junction of Interstates 465 and 69, close enough to Carmel but not too close. He signed in with a name that matched his credit card and made up a license plate number for the registration card. In his room, he ran the channels on the TV, then switched off the set. He took a shower, got dressed, turned the TV on, turned it off again.

Then he went to the car and found his way to the Conseco Fieldhouse, where the Indiana Pacers were playing host to the New York Knicks.

The stadium was in the center of the city, but the signage made it easy to get there. A man in a porkpie hat asked him in an undertone if he had any extra tickets, and Keller realized that he did. He took a good look at his tickets for the first time, and saw that he had a pair of $96 seats in Section 214, wherever that was. He could sell one, but wouldn't that be awkward, if the man he sold it to then sat beside him? He'd probably be a talker, and Keller didn't want that.

But a moment's observation clarified the situation. The

man in the porkpie hat—who had, Keller noted, a face straight out of an OTB parlor, a woulda-coulda-shoulda gambler's face—was doing a little business, buying tickets from people who had too many, selling them to people who had too few. So he wouldn't be sitting next to Keller. Someone else would, but it would be someone he hadn't met, so it would be easy to keep an intimacy barrier in place.

Keller went up to the man in the hat, showed him one of the tickets. The man said "Fifty bucks," and Keller pointed out that it was a $96 ticket. The man gave him a look, and Keller took the ticket back.

"Jesus," the man said. "What do you want for it, anyway?"

"Eighty-five," Keller said, picking the number out of the air.

"That's crazy."

"The Pacers and the Knicks? Section two-fourteen? I bet I can find somebody who wants it eighty-five dollars' worth."

They settled on $75, and Keller pocketed the money and used his other ticket to enter the arena. Then it struck him that he could have unloaded both tickets and had $150 to show for it, and gone straight home, spared the ordeal of a basketball game. But he was already through the turnstile when the thought came to him, and by that point he no longer had a ticket to sell.

He found his seat and sat down to watch the game.

CHAPTER THIRTY-FIVE

Keller, an only child, was raised by his mother, whom he had come to realize in later years was probably mentally ill. He never suspected this at the time, although he was aware that she was different from other people.

She kept a picture of Keller's father in a frame in the living room. The photograph showed a young man in a military uniform, and Keller grew up knowing his father had been a soldier, a casualty of the war. As a teenager, he'd been employed cleaning out a stockroom, and one of the boxes of obsolete merchandise he'd hauled out had contained picture frames, half of them containing the familiar photograph of his putative father.

It occurred to him that he ought to mention this to his mother. On further thought, he decided not to say anything. He went home and looked at the photo and wondered who his father was. A soldier, he decided, though not this one. Someone passing through, who'd fathered a son and never knew it.

And died in battle? Well, a lot of soldiers did. His father might very well have been one of them.

Growing up, in a fatherless home with a mother who didn't seem to have any friends or acquaintances, was something Keller had been on the point of addressing in therapy, until a problem with his therapist put an end to that experiment. He'd had trouble deciding just how he felt about his mother but had ultimately come to the conclusion that she was a good woman who'd done a good job of raising him, given her limitations. She was a serviceable cook if not an imaginative one, and he had a hot breakfast every morning and a hot dinner every night. She kept their house clean and taught Keller to be clean about his person. She was detached, and talked more to herself than to him—and, in the afternoons, talked to the characters in her TV soap operas.

She bought him presents at Christmas and on his birthday, usually clothing to replace garments he'd outgrown, but occasionally something more interesting. One year she bought him an Erector set, and he'd proved quite hopeless at following the diagrams in an effort to produce a flatbed railcar, or, indeed, anything else. Another year's present was a beginner's stamp collecting kit—a stamp album, a packet of stamps, a pair of tongs to pick them up with, and a supply of hinges for mounting them in the album. The Erector set wound up in the closet, gathering dust, but the stamp album turned out to be the foundation of a lifelong hobby. He'd abandoned it after high school, of course, and the original album was long gone, but Keller had taken up the hobby again as an adult and cheerfully poured much of his spare time and extra cash into it.

Would he have become a stamp collector if not for his mother's gift? Possibly, he thought, but probably not. It was one more reason to thank her.

The Erector set was a good thought that failed, the stamp album an inspiration. The biggest surprise, though, of all the gifts she gave him, was neither of these.

That would have to be the basketball backboard.

Keller hadn't bothered to note the seat number of the ticket he sold to the man in the porkpie hat. His own seat was number 117, situated unsurprisingly enough between seats 116 and 118, both of them unoccupied when he sat down between them. Then two men came along and sat down in 115 and 116. One was substantially older than the other, and Keller found himself wondering if they were father and son, boss and employee, uncle and nephew, or gay lovers. He didn't really care, but he couldn't keep from wondering, and he kept changing his mind.

The game had already started by the time a man turned up and sat down in 118. He was wearing a dark suit with a subtle pinstripe and looked as though he'd come straight from the office, an office where he spent his days doing something no one, least of all the man himself, would describe as interesting.

The man in the porkpie hat had paid Keller $75 for that seat, which suggested that the man in the suit must have paid at least $100 for it, and perhaps as much as $125. But of course the fellow had no idea that Keller was the source of his ticket, and in fact paid no attention to Keller, devoting the full measure of his attention to the action on the court, where the Pacers had jumped off to an early lead.

Keller, with some reluctance, turned his attention to the game.

Across the street and two doors up from Keller's house, a family named Breitbart filled a large frame house to overflowing. Mr. Breitbart owned and ran a furniture store on Euclid Avenue, and Mrs. Breitbart stayed home and, for a while at least, had a baby every year. The year Keller was born she had two—twin sons, Andrew and Randall, the names no doubt selected so that their nicknames could rhyme. The twins were the family's only boys; the other five little Breitbarts, some older than the twins, the rest younger, were all girls.

Every afternoon, weather permitting, boys gathered in the Breitbart backyard to play basketball. Sometimes they divided into teams, and one side took off their shirts, and they played the sort of half-court game you could play with a single garage-mounted backboard. Other times, when fewer boys showed up or for some other reason, they found other ways to compete—playing Horse, say, where each player had to duplicate the particular shot of the first player. There were other games as well, but Keller, watching idly from across the street, was less clear on their rules and objectives.

One night at dinner, Keller's mother told him he should go across the street and join the game. "You watch all the time," she said—inaccurately, as he only occasionally let himself loll on the sidewalk watching the action in the Breitbart yard. "I bet they'd love it if you joined in. I bet you'd be good at it."

As it turned out, she lost both bets.

Keller, a quiet boy, always felt more at ease with grown-ups than with his contemporaries. On his own, he moved with an easy grace; in group sports, self-consciousness turned him awkward and made him ill at ease. Nonetheless, later that week he crossed the street and presented himself in the Breitbart backyard. "It's Keller," Andy or Randy said. "From across the street." Someone tossed him the ball, and he bounced it twice and tossed it unsuccessfully at the basket.

They chose up sides, and he, the unknown quantity, was

picked last, which struck him as reasonable enough. He was on the Skins team, and shucked his shirt, which made him feel a little self-conscious, but that was nothing compared to the self-consciousness that ensued when the game began.

Because he didn't know how to play. He was ineffectual at guarding, and more obviously inept when someone tossed him the ball and he didn't know what to do with it. "Shoot," someone yelled, and he shot and missed. "Here, here!" someone called out, and his pass was intercepted. He just didn't know what he was doing, and before long his teammates figured out as much and stopped passing him the ball.

After fifteen or twenty minutes the Shirts were a little more than halfway to the number of points that would end the game, when a boy a grade ahead of Keller showed up. "Hey, it's Lassman," Randy or Andy said. "Lassman, take over for Keller."

And just like that, Lassman, suddenly shirtless, was in, and Keller was out. This, too, struck him as reasonable enough. He went to the sidelines and put his shirt on, relief and disappointment settling over him in equal parts. For a few minutes he stood there watching the others play, and relief faded while disappointment swelled. Well, I better be getting home now, he planned to say, and he rehearsed the line, rephrasing it in his mind, giving it different inflections. But nobody was paying any attention to him, so why say anything? He turned around and went home.

When his mother asked him about it, he said it had turned out okay, but he wouldn't be going over there anymore. They had regular teams, he said, and he didn't really fit in. She looked at him for a moment, then let it go.

A few days later he came home from school to see two workmen mounting a backboard and basket on the Keller garage. At dinner he wanted to ask her about it but didn't know how to start. She didn't say anything either at first, and years later, when he heard the expression "the elephant in the living room that nobody talks about," he thought of that basketball backboard.

But then she did talk about it. "I thought it would be good to have," she said. "You can go out there and practice anytime you want, and the other boys will see you there, and come over and play."

She was half right. He practiced, dribbling, driving toward the basket, trying set shots and jump shots and hook shots from different angles. He paced off a foul line and practiced foul shots. If practice didn't make perfect, it certainly didn't hurt. He got better.

And the other boys saw him there, she was right about that, too. But nobody ever came over to play, and before long he stopped going out there himself. Then he got an afterschool job, and he put the basketball in the garage and forgot about it.

The backboard stayed where it was, securely mounted on the garage. It was the elephant in the driveway that nobody talked about.

CHAPTER THIRTY-SIX

The Pacers won in overtime, in what Keller supposed was an exciting game, although it didn't excite him much. He didn't care who won, and found his attention drifting throughout, even at the game's most crucial moments. The fact that the visiting team was the New York Knicks didn't make any difference to him. He didn't follow basketball, and his devotion to the city of New York didn't make him a partisan follower of the city's sports teams.

Except for the Yankees. He liked the Yankees, and enjoyed it when they won. But he didn't eat his heart out when, on rare occasions, they lost. As far as he was concerned, getting upset over the outcome of a sports event was like getting depressed when a movie had a sad ending. I mean, get a grip, man. It's only a movie, it's only a ball game.

He walked to his car, which was where he'd parked it, and drove to his motel, which was where he'd left it. He was seventy-five dollars richer than he'd been a few hours ago, and his only regret was that he hadn't thought to sell both tickets. And skip the game.

Grondahl had a backboard in his driveway.

That was the target's name, Meredith Grondahl, and when Keller had first seen it, before Dot showed him the photograph, he'd supposed it was a woman. He'd even said, "A woman?" and Dot had asked him if he'd become a sexist overnight. "You've done women before," she reminded him. "You've always been an equal-opportunity kind of guy. But all that's beside the point, because this particular Meredith is a man."

What, he'd wondered, did Meredith's friends call him for short? Merry? Probably not, Keller decided. If he had a nickname, it was probably Bud or Mac or Bubba.

Grondahl, he figured, meant "green valley" in whatever Scandinavian language Meredith's forebears had spoken. So maybe the guy's friends called him Greenie.

Or maybe not.

The backboard, which Keller saw on a drive-by the morning after the basketball game, was freestanding, mounted on a post a couple of feet in front of the garage. It was a two-car garage, and the post was positioned so that it didn't block access to either side.

The garage door was closed, so Keller couldn't tell how many cars it held at the moment. Nor was anybody shooting baskets in the driveway. Keller drove off, picturing Grondahl playing a solitary game, dribbling, shooting, all the while considering how his testimony might expose corporate shenanigans, making of basketball a meditative experience.

You could get a lot of thinking done that way. Provided you were alone, and didn't have to break your concentration by interacting with somebody else.

South and east of downtown Indianapolis, tucked into a shopping mall, Keller found a stamp dealer named Hubert Haas. He'd done business with the man in the past, when he'd managed to outbid other collectors for lots Haas offered on eBay. So the name rang a bell when he came across it in the Yellow Pages.

He'd brought his Scott catalog, which he used as a checklist, so he could be sure he wasn't buying stamps he already owned. Haas, a plump and owlish young man who looked as though his chief exercise consisted of driving past a health club, was happy to show Keller his stock. He did almost all of his business online, he confided, and hardly ever had a real customer in the shop, so this was a treat for him.

So why pay rent? Why not work out of his house?

"Buying," Haas said. "I've got a presence in a high-traffic mall. That keeps the noncollectors aware of me. Uncle Fred dies, they inherit his stamp collection, who do they bring it to? Somebody they heard of, and they not only heard of Hubert Haas, they know he's for real, because he's got a store in the Glendale Mall to prove it. And then there's the walk-in who buys a starter album for his kid, the collector who runs out of hinges or Showgard mounts or needs to replace a lost pair of tongs. Helps with the rent, but buying's the real reason."

Keller found a comforting quantity of stamps to buy from Haas, including an inexpensive but curiously elusive set of Venezuelan airmails. He walked out imbued with a sense of accomplishment, and took a few minutes to walk around the mall, to see what further accomplishments might be there for the taking.

The mall had the sort of stores malls usually had, and he found it easy enough to scan their window displays and walk on by. Until he came to the library.

Who had ever heard of a public library in a shopping mall? But that's what this was, occupying substantial space on the second and third levels, and complete with a turnstile and, yes, a metals detector, its purpose unapparent to Keller. Was there a problem of folks toting guns in hollowed-out books?

No matter. Keller wasn't carrying a gun, or anything metallic but a handful of coins and his car keys. He entered without raising any alarms, and ten minutes later he was scanning back issues of the Indianapolis *Star*, learning all manner of things about Meredith Grondahl.

"It's pretty interesting," he told Dot. "There's this company called Central Indiana Finance. They buy and sell mortgages, and do a lot of refinancing. The stock's traded on the NASDAQ. The symbol is CIFI, but when people talk about it they refer to it as Indy Fi."

"If that's interesting," she said, "I'd hate to hear your idea of a real yawner."

"That's not the interesting part."

"No kidding."

"The stock's very volatile," he said. "It pays a high dividend, which makes it attractive to investors, but it could be vulnerable to changes in the interest rates, which makes it speculative, I guess. And a couple of hedge funds have shorted the stock heavily, along with a lot of private traders."

"Let me know when we get to the interesting part, will you, Keller?"

"Well, it's all kind of interesting," he said. "You walk around in a shopping mall, you don't expect to find out this stuff."

"Here I am, finding it out without even leaving the house."

"There's this class action suit," he said. "Brought on behalf of the Indy Fi stockholders, though probably ninety-nine percent of them are opposed to the whole idea of the suit. The suit charges the company's management with irregularities and cover-ups, that sort of thing. It's the people who shorted the stock who are behind the suit, the hedge fund guys, and their whole reason for bringing it seems to be to destroy confidence in the company, and further depress the price of the stock."

"Can they do that?"

"Anybody can sue anybody. All they risk, really, is their legal expenses, and having the suit get tossed out of court. Meanwhile the company has to defend the suit, and the controversy keeps the stock price depressed, and even if the suit gets settled in the company's favor, the short interests will have had a chance to make money."

"I don't really care about any of this," Dot said, "but I have to admit you're starting to get me interested, although I couldn't tell you why. And our quarry's going to testify for the people bringing the suit?"

"No."

"No?"

"They subpoenaed him," he said. "Meredith Grondahl. He's an assistant to the chief financial officer, and he's supposed to testify about irregularities in their accounting procedures, but he's no whistle-blower. He's more of a cheerleader. As far as he's concerned, Indy Fi's a great company, and his personal 401-K is full of the company's stock. He can't really damage either side in the suit."

"Then why would somebody decide to summon you to Indianapolis?"

"That's what I've been wondering."

He thought the connection might have broken, but she was just taking her time thinking it over. "Well," she said at length, "even though this gets us interested, Keller, we're also disinterested, if you get my drift."

"It doesn't change things."

"That's my drift, all right. We've got an assignment, and the fee's half paid already, so the whys and wherefores don't make any difference. Somebody doesn't want the guy to testify about something, and as soon as you nail that down, you can come on home and play with your stamps. You bought some today, didn't you tell me that earlier? So come on home and you can paste them in your book. And we'll get paid, and you can buy some more."

CHAPTER THIRTY-SEVEN

The next morning, Keller got up early and drove straight to Grondahl's house in Carmel. He parked across the street and sat behind the wheel of his rented Ford, a newspaper propped on the steering wheel. He read the national and international news, then the sports. The Pacers, he noted, had won last night, in double overtime. The local sports-writer described the game as thrilling, and said the shot from half court that fell in just as the second overtime period ran out demonstrated "the moral integrity and indomitable spirit of our guys." Keller wished he'd taken it a small step further, claiming the ball's unerring flight to the basket as proof of the Almighty's clear preference for the local heroes.

Reading, he kept an eye on Grondahl's front door, waiting for Greenie to appear. He still hadn't done so by the time Keller was done with the sports pages. Well, it was early, he told himself, and turned to the business section. The Dow was up, he learned, in heavy volume.

He knew what this meant, he wasn't an idiot, but it was something he never followed because it didn't concern him, or hold interest for him. Keller earned good money when he worked, and didn't live high, and for years he had saved a substantial portion of the money that came into his hands. But he'd never bought stocks or mutual funds with it. He tucked some of it into a safe-deposit box and the rest in savings accounts. The money grew slowly if it grew at all, but it didn't shrink, and there was something to be said for that.

Eventually he reached a point where retirement was an option, and he realized that he'd need a hobby to fill the golden years. He took up stamp collecting again, but in a far more serious fashion this time around. He started spending serious money on stamps, and his retirement savings waned as his collection grew.

So he'd never managed to get interested in the world of stocks and bonds. This morning, for some reason, he found the business section interesting, not least because of an article on Central Indiana Finance. CIFI, which opened the day at $43.27 a share, had fluctuated wildly, up five points at its high for the day, down as much as seven, and finishing the day at $40.35. On the one hand, he learned, the shorts were scrambling to cover before the ex-dividend date, when they would be liable for the company's substantial dividend. On the other, players were continuing to short the stock and drive the price down, encouraged by the pending class action lawsuit.

He was thinking about the article when the door opened and Meredith Grondahl emerged.

Grondahl was dressed for the office, wearing a dark gray suit and a white shirt and a striped tie and carrying a briefcase. That was to be expected, it being a Thursday, but Keller realized he'd unconsciously been waiting for the man to show himself in shorts and a singlet, dribbling a basketball.

In the driveway, Grondahl paid no attention to the basketball backboard but triggered a button to raise the garage door. There was, Keller noted, only one car in the garage, and a slew of objects (he made out a barbecue grill and some lawn furniture) took up the space where a second car might otherwise have been parked.

Grondahl, given his position in the corporate world, could clearly have afforded a second car for his wife. Which suggested to Keller that he didn't have a wife. The fine suburban house, on the other hand, suggested that he'd had one once upon a time, and Keller suspected she'd chosen to go away, and taken her car with her.

Poor bastard.

Keller, comfortable behind the wheel, stayed where he was while Grondahl backed his Grand Cherokee out of the driveway and drove off somewhere. He thought about following the man, but why? For that matter, why had he come here to watch him leave the house?

Of course there were more basic questions than that. Why wasn't he getting down to business and fulfilling his contract? Why was he watching Meredith Grondahl instead of punching the man's ticket?

And a question that was, strictly speaking, none of his business, but no less compelling for it: Why did somebody want Meredith Grondahl dead?

Thinking, he reminded himself, was one thing. Acting was another. His mind could go where it wanted, as long as his body did what it was supposed to.

Drive back to the motel, he told himself, and find a way to use up the day. And tonight, when Meredith Grondahl comes home, be here waiting for him. Then return this car to Hertz, pick up a fresh one from somebody else, and go home.

He nodded, affirming the wisdom of that course of action. Then he started the engine, backed up a few yards, and swung the car into the Grondahl driveway. He got out, found the button Grondahl had used to raise the garage door, pressed it, got back in the car, and pulled into the spot recently vacated by the Grand Cherokee.

There was a small boulder the size of a bowling ball standing just to the right of Grondahl's front door. It might have been residue from a local avalanche, but Keller thought that unlikely. It looked to him like something to hide a spare house key under, and he was right about that. He picked up the key, opened the door, and let himself in.

CHAPTER THIRTY-EIGHT

There was a chance, of course, that there was still a Mrs. Grondahl, and that she was home. Maybe she didn't drive, maybe she was an agoraphobe who never left the house. Keller thought this was unlikely, and it didn't take him long to rule it out. The house was antiseptically clean, but that didn't necessarily signal a woman's presence; Grondahl might be neat by nature, or he might have someone who cleaned for him once or twice a week.

There were no women's clothes in the closets or dressers, and that was a tip-off. And there were two dressers, a highboy and a low triple dresser with a vanity mirror, and the low dresser's drawers were empty, except for one that Grondahl had begun to use for suspenders and cuff links and such. So there had indeed been a Mrs. Grondahl, and now there wasn't.

Keller, having established this much, wandered around the two-story house, trying to see what else he could learn. Except he wasn't trying very hard, because he wasn't really looking for anything, or if he was he didn't know what it might be. It was more as if he was trying to get the feel of the man, and that didn't make any sense, but then what sense was there in letting yourself into the house of the man you were planning to kill?

Maybe the best course of action was to settle in and wait. Sooner or later Grondahl would return to the house, and he'd probably be alone when he did, since he was beginning to strike Keller as your typical lonely guy.

Your typical lonely guy. The phrase resonated oddly for Keller, because he couldn't help identifying with it. He was, face it, a lonely guy himself, although he didn't suppose you could call him typical. Did this resonance get in the way of what he was supposed to do? He thought it over and decided it did and it didn't. It made him sympathize with Meredith Grondahl, and thus disinclined to kill him; other hand, wouldn't he be doing the poor bastard a favor?

He frowned, found a chair to sit in. When Grondahl came home, he'd be alone. And he'd be relieved to return to the safe harbor of his empty house. So he'd be unguarded, and getting taken from behind by a man with a club or a knife or a garrote—Keller hadn't decided yet—was the last thing he'd worry about.

It'd be the last thing, all right.

The problem, of course, was to figure out what to do with the day. If he just holed up here, it looked to be a minimum of eight hours before Grondahl returned, and the wait might well stretch to twelve or more. He could read, if he could find something he felt like reading, or watch TV with the sound off, or—

Hell. His car was parked in Grondahl's garage. That assured that the neighbors wouldn't see it and grow suspicious, but what happened when Grondahl came home and found his parking spot taken?

No good at all. Keller would have to move the car, and the sooner the better, because for all he knew Grondahl might feel the need to come home for lunch. So what should he do? Drive it around the block, leave it in front of some stranger's house? And then he'd have to return on foot, hoping no one noticed him, because nobody walked anywhere in the suburbs and a pedestrian was suspicious by definition.

Maybe waiting for Grondahl was a bad idea altogether. Maybe he should just get the hell out and go back to his motel.

He was on his way to the door when he heard a key in the lock.

Funny how decisions had a way of making themselves. Grondahl, who had returned for something he'd forgotten, was insisting on being put out of his misery. Keller backed out of the entrance hall and waited around the corner in the dining room.

The door opened, and Keller heard steps, a lot of them. And a voice called out, "Hello? Anybody home?"

Keller's first thought was that it was an odd thing for Grondahl to do. Then another voice, pitched lower, said, "You better hope you don't get an answer to that one."

Had Grondahl brought a friend? No, of course not, he realized. It wasn't Grondahl, who was almost certainly doing something corporate at his office. It was someone else, it was a pair of somebody elses, and they'd let themselves in with a key and wanted the house to be empty.

If they came into the dining room, he'd have to do something about it. If they took a different tack, he'd have to slip out of the door as soon as the opportunity presented itself. And hide in the garage, waiting for them to emerge from the house and drive away, so that *he* could drive away, too.

"I think the den," one voice said. "House like this, guy living alone, he's gotta have a den, don't you think?"

"Or a home office," the other voice offered.

"A den, a home office, what the hell's the difference?"

"One's deductible."

"But it's the same room, isn't it? No matter what you call it?"

"I suppose, but for tax purposes—"

"Jesus," the first voice said. It was, Keller noted, vaguely familiar, but maybe that was just because the speaker had a Hoosier accent. "I'm not planning to audit his fucking tax returns," the man said. "I just want to plant an envelope in his desk."

Out the door, Keller told himself. Let them plant whatever they wanted in whatever they decided to call the room with the desk in it. He'd be gone, and they'd never know he'd been there in the first place.

But when he left the dining room, something led him not to the door but away from it. He tagged along after the two men, and caught a glimpse of them as he rounded a corner into the living room. He saw them from the back, and only for a moment, but that was time enough to note that they were both of average height and medium build, and that one was bald as an egg. The other might or might not have hair; you couldn't tell at a glance, because he was wearing a cap.

A green cap, with gold piping, and when had Keller seen a cap like that? Oh, right. Same place he'd heard that voice.

It was a John Deere cap, and the man wearing it had met him at the airport and given him tickets to that goddamn basketball game. Depressed the hell out of him, ruined his first evening in Indianapolis, and thanks a lot for that, you son of a bitch.

Keller, oddly irritated, padded silently after the two of them, and lurked around a corner while they stationed themselves at Meredith Grondahl's desk. "Definitely a home office," the bald man said. "You got your filing cabinets, you got your desk and your computer, you got your Canon desktop copier, you got your printer and your fax machine—"

"You also got a big-screen TV and a La-Z-Boy recliner, which shouts den to me," the man in the Deere cap said. "Look at this, will you? The drawer's locked."

"This one ain't. Neither's this one. You got seven drawers, for Chrissake, who cares if one of 'em's locked?"

"This is incriminating evidence, right? Dangerous stuff?"

"So?"

"You got a desk with a locked drawer, don't you think that's the drawer you're gonna keep the shit in?"

"The cops in this town," the bald man said, "they find a locked drawer, they might just decide it's too much trouble to open it."

"Point."

Keller, out of sight in the adjoining room, heard a drawer open and close.

"There," Deere Cap said. "Right where they'll find it."

"And if Grondahl finds it first?"

"I figure that's in the next day or two, because he's not gonna wait that long."

"The shooter."

"A real piece of work."

"You told me."

"I tell you how he walks up to a car in the airport lot and drives off with it? Has a master key on his ring, pops the lock like it was made for it. 'I'll just borrow it,' he tells me."

"Casual son of a bitch."

"But how long is he gonna drive around in a stolen vehicle? I'm surprised he hasn't made his move already."

"Maybe he has. Maybe we go to the bedroom, we find Grondahl sleeping with the fishes."

"That'd be in the river, wouldn't it? You don't find fishes sleeping in beds."

Oysters, Keller thought. In oyster beds. He retreated a few steps, because there was no longer any reason to stick around. These two worked for the client, and they were just planting evidence to support the same end as Grondahl's removal. They could have let him plant the stuff himself, all part of the service, but they hadn't thought of that, or hadn't trusted him, so—

The bald guy said, "It's not really finished until he's dead, you know."

"Grondahl."

"Well, that, obviously. No, I mean the shooter. He's killed, and he's the one took out Grondahl, and he's tied to Indy Fi's management. Then you got them good."

CHAPTER THIRTY-NINE

Jesus, Keller thought. And he'd almost walked away from this. They were moving, the two of them, and he moved as well, so that he could wind up behind them when they headed for the door.

"All part of the plan," Deere Cap said.

"But if he just goes and steals another car and flies back to wherever he came from—"

"Portland, I think somebody said."

"Which Portland?"

"Who cares? He ain't making it back. What I did, I stuck a bug on the underside of his back bumper while he was showing me how slick his key worked. He went to that basketball game, incidentally. Guy loves basketball."

"Who won the game?"

"You'd have to ask him. That Global Positioning shit is wonderful. He's at the Rodeway Inn near the I-69 exit. That's our next stop. What we'll do, I got a pair of tickets for tomorrow night's game, and we'll leave 'em at the motel desk for him. What I figure—"

It might have been interesting to learn how the basketball tickets were part of the man's plan, but they were almost at the door at this point, and that was as far as Keller could let them get. Following them, he'd paused long enough to snatch a brass candlestick off a tabletop, and he closed the distance between him and them and swung the candlestick in a sweeping arc that ended at a patch of gold braid on the green John Deere cap. It caught the man in midstride and midsentence, and he never finished either. He dropped in his tracks, and the bald man was just beginning to take it in, just beginning to react, when Keller backhanded him with the candlestick, striking him right across his endless forehead. The scalp split and blood spurted, and the man let out a cry and clapped a hand to the spot, and Keller swung the candlestick a third time, like a woodsman with an ax, and brought it down authoritatively on the back of the bald man's neck.

Jack be nimble, he thought.

It took Keller a moment to catch his breath, but only a moment. He stood there, still holding on to the candlestick, and looked down at the two men lying a couple of feet apart on the patterned area rug. They both looked dead. He checked, and the bald man was every bit as dead as he looked, but the guy in the cap still had a pulse.

Keller, waiting for him to regain consciousness, did what he could to clean up. He washed and wiped the candlestick and put it back where he'd found it. He wasn't going to be able to do anything about the blood on the rug, and couldn't even make an attempt while the two of them were lying on it.

He stationed himself alongside them and waited. Eventually the Deere cap guy came to, and Keller asked him a couple of questions. The man didn't want to answer them, but eventually he did, and then there was no need to keep him alive anymore.

The hardest part, really, was getting the two bodies out of the house and into their car, which turned out to be the same Hyundai squareback that had picked him up at the airport. It was parked in the driveway, and the keys were in the Deere cap guy's pocket.

He could see how it was all going to work out.

"Like we don't have enough to contend with," Dot said. "You do everything right and then you get killed by the client. This business isn't the bed of roses people think it is."

"Is that what people think?"

"Who knows what people think, Keller? I know what I think. I think you better come home."

"Not just yet."

"Oh?"

"One of the fellows gave me a name."

"Probably his very last words."

"Just about."

"And you want to get together with this fellow?"

"I probably won't be able to," he said. "My guess is he'll be overcome by fear or remorse."

"And he'll take his own life?"

"It wouldn't surprise me."

"And it wouldn't start me crying, I have to tell you that. All right, sure, why not? We can't let people get away with that crap. Do what you have to do and then come home. We got half in front, and I don't suppose there's any way to collect the back half, so—"

"Don't be too sure of that," Keller said. "I've been thinking, and why don't you see how this sounds to you?"

CHAPTER FORTY

When Meredith Grondahl pulled into his driveway around five-thirty, Keller was parked halfway down the block at the curb. He got out of the car and stood where he could watch the Grondahl driveway, and after five minutes Grondahl emerged from the house. He'd changed from a suit and tie to sneakers and sweats, and he was dribbling a basketball. He took a shot, missed, took the ball as it came off the backboard, and drove for a layup.

Keller headed up the driveway. Grondahl turned, saw him, and tossed him the ball. Keller shot, missed.

They played for a few minutes, just taking turns trying shots, most of which failed to make it through the hoop. Then Keller sank a fadeaway jump shot, surprising both of them, and Grondahl said, "Nice."

"Luck," Keller said. "Listen, we should talk."

"Huh?"

"You had a couple of visitors earlier today. They got into an argument, and they bled all over your rug."

"My rug."

"That area rug with the geometric pattern, right when you come into the house."

"*That's* what was different," Grondahl said. "The rug wasn't there. I knew there was something, but I couldn't put my finger on it."

"Or your foot."

"You said there was blood on it?"

"Their blood, and you don't want that. Anyway, you get a lot of blood on a rug and it's never the same. So the rug's not there anymore."

"And the two men?"

"They're not there anymore either."

Grondahl had been holding the basketball, and now he turned and flipped it at the basket. It hit the rim and bounced away, and neither man made any move toward it.

Grondahl said, "These men. They came into my house?"

"Right through the door over there. They had a key—not the one you keep under the fake rock, either."

"And then, inside my house, they got into an argument and . . . killed each other?"

"That's close enough," Keller said.

Grondahl thought about it. "I think I get the picture," he said.

"You probably get as much of the picture as you need to get."

"That's what it sounds like. Why did they come here in the first place?"

"They were going to leave an envelope."

"An envelope."

"In a desk drawer."

"And the envelope contained . . ."

"A motive for a murder."

"My murder?"

Keller nodded.

"They were going to kill me?"

"Their employer," Keller said, "had already hired someone else for that job."

"Who?"

"Some stranger," Keller said. "Some faceless assassin flown in from out of town."

Grondahl looked thoughtfully at him, the way one might look at a putative faceless assassin. "But he's not going to do it," he said. "At least I don't think he is."

"He's not."

"Why?"

"Because he happened to learn that once his job was done, they were planning to kill him."

"And pin everything on the Indy Fi management," Grondahl said. "Making it look like I was killed to keep me from giving testimony I never had any thought of giving in the first place. Jesus, it might have worked. I can imagine what must have been in the envelope. Is it still around? The envelope? Or did it disappear along with the two men?"

"The men will turn up eventually," Keller said. "The envelope is gone forever."

Grondahl nodded, retrieved the basketball, bounced it a few times. Keller could almost see the wheels turning in the man's head. He was bright, Keller was pleased to note. You didn't have to spell things out for him, you gave him the first paragraph and he got the rest of the page on his own.

"I owe you," Grondahl said.

Keller shrugged.

"I mean it. You saved my life."

"I was saving my own at the time," Keller pointed out.

"When the two of them, uh, had their accident, I'll concede that was in your own self-interest. But you could have just walked away. And you certainly didn't have to show up here and fill me in. Which leads to a question."

"Why am I here?"

"If you don't mind my asking."

"I don't mind," Keller said. "As a matter of fact, I've got a couple of questions of my own."

CHAPTER FORTY-ONE

"**I** think I get it," Dot said. "This is a new thing for me, Keller. I wrote it down, and I'm going to read it back to you, to make sure I've got it all straight."

She did, and he told her she had it right.

"That's a miracle," she said, "because it was a little like taking dictation in a foreign language. I'll take care of it tomorrow. Can I do it all in a day?"

"Probably."

"Then I will. And you'll be . . ."

"Biding my time in Indianapolis. I switched motels, by the way."

"Good."

"And found the bug they put on my bumper, and switched it to the bumper of another Ford the same color as mine."

"That should muddy the waters nicely."

"I thought so. So I'll do what I have to do, and then I'll be a couple of days driving home."

"Not to worry," she said. "I'll leave the porch light on for you."

It was a full week later when Keller drove his rented Toyota through the Lincoln Tunnel and found his way to the National garage, where he turned it in. He went home, unpacked his bag, and spent two full hours working on his stamp collection before he picked up the phone and called

White Plains.

"Come right on up," Dot said, "so I can turn the light off. It's attracting moths."

In the kitchen of the house on Taunton Place, Dot poured him a big glass of iced tea and told him they'd done very well indeed. "I was wondering at first," she said, "because I bought a big chunk of Indy Fi, and the first thing it did was go down a couple of points. But then it turned around and went back up again, and the last I checked it's up better than ten points from when I bought it. I bought options, too, for increased leverage. I don't understand how they work exactly, but I was able to buy them, and this morning I sold them, and do you want to know exactly how much we made on them?"

"It doesn't have to be exact."

She told him, down to the last decimal point, and it was a satisfying number.

"We're about that much ahead on the actual stock we bought," she said, "but I haven't sold that yet, because I kind of like owning it, especially the way it's going up. Maybe we can sell half and let the rest ride, something like that, but I figured I'd wait and see what you want to do."

"We'll work it out."

"My thought exactly." She sat forward, rubbed her hands together. "What really kick-started things," she said, "was when Clocker killed himself. His hedge fund had been shorting Indy Fi's stock all along, and he was behind the lawsuit they were going through, and when he was out of the picture, and in a way that put the cloud right over his own head, well, the price of Indy Fi's stock could go back where it belonged. And the price of his hedge fund . . ."

"Sank?"

"Like a stone," she said. "And we sold it short, and covered our shorts very cheaply, and made a killing. It's nice to make a killing without having to drive anywhere. How did you know how to do all this?"

"I had advice," he said. "From a fellow who couldn't do any of this himself, because it would be insider trading. But you and I aren't insiders, so there's no problem."

"Well, I've got no problem with it myself, Keller. That's for sure. You know, this isn't the first time you've wound up killing a client of ours."

"I know."

"This one brought it on himself, no question. But usually it costs us money, and this time we came out way ahead. You're going to be able to buy a veritable shitload of stamps."

"I was thinking about that."

"And we're a giant stride closer to being able to retire, when the time comes."

"I was thinking about that, too."

"And you bonded with What's-his-name."

"Meredith Grondahl."

"What do his friends call him, did you happen to find out?"

"It never came up. I'm not sure he's got any friends."

"Oh."

"I was thinking I ought to send him something, Dot. I had an idea of how to make money in the market, but he spelled the whole thing out for me. I didn't know a thing about options, and I never would have thought of shorting the hedge fund."

"How big a share do you want to send him?"

"Not a share. He's pretty straight-arrow, and even if he

284

weren't, the last thing he wants is cash he can't explain. No, I was thinking more of a present. A token, really, but something he'd like to have and probably wouldn't ever buy for himself."

"Like?"

"Season tickets to the Pacers' home games. He loves basketball, and a pair of courtside season tickets should really do it for the guy."

"What's it cost?" Before he could answer she waved the question away. "Not enough to matter, not the way we just made out. That's a great idea, Keller. And who knows? Next time you're in Indianapolis, maybe the two of you can take in a game."

He shook his head. "No," he said. "Leave me out of it. I hate basketball."

QUOTIDIAN
KELLER

CHAPTER FORTY-TWO

"**W**ill you look at that?" Dot said.

Keller looked, but all he could see was a chart of the price of some stock and, across the bottom of the screen, a crawl of stock symbols and numbers. The sound was off, as usual. Dot seemed to prefer TV with the sound off. Keller figured that worked okay with Animal Planet or the National Geographic channel, but it seemed less effective with CNBC. What good was a talking head if you couldn't tell what it was talking about?

"We're doing okay," she said.

"We are?"

"I seem to have a knack for this," she said, "or else I've been lucky, which is probably just as good. Don't you think?"

"I suppose so. I didn't know you were in the stock market."

"I'm not," she said. "I'm right here in my kitchen, sipping iced tea and talking to my partner."

"We're partners?"

She nodded. "Remember Indianapolis?"

"Basketball," he said.

"Basketball and stock manipulation. We made out very nicely, and it was you who came up with the idea. We did some buying and selling, and no special prosecutor turned up to charge us with insider trading."

"And you're still in the market?"

"We both are, Keller. I never gave you your share."

"You didn't?"

She rolled her eyes. "And after the dust settled on that deal," she said, "well, I looked around and found some other things to buy. It's real easy, you just get online and click your mouse and there you are. You never have to have a conversation with a human being who might ask you what the hell you think you're doing. We've been making money."

"That's great, Dot."

"You want your half? Or should I keep doing what I've been doing?"

"If you're making money for us," he said, "I'd be crazy to tell you to stop."

"That's assuming we'll continue to do well. I could lose it all, too."

"What have we got at this point?"

She named a number, and it was higher than he would have guessed, considerably higher.

"That's what our account's worth," she said, "so half of that is yours. I'm inclined to keep playing, because I'd have to put the money somewhere, and it might as well be where it's making more money. But if you have a use for it, or want to add it to your retirement fund—"

"No," he said. "You hang on to it, and keep on doing what you've been doing. I didn't even know I had it, and if I drew the money I know what would happen to it."

"Stamps."

"Stamps," he agreed. "It's a good thing you didn't give me my share of the original stock profits, because it'd probably be gone by now. Well, not gone, but—"

"But pasted in an album."

"Mounted."

"I stand corrected. Look at that, will you?"

He glanced at the screen, with no idea what he was supposed to be looking at. "Fascinating," he said.

"Isn't it? Who would have guessed?"

The stock crawl went on during the commercials until they finally cut to some sort of mega-commercial that filled the screen. He seized the opportunity to ask her if that was why she'd asked him to come out to White Plains.

"No," she said, "it's something else. I got so caught up in this that I almost forgot. It's wonderful to develop an interest late in life, you know?"

"I know."

"You with your stamps, me with my stocks. Our stocks. Keller, when I say Detroit, what comes to mind?"

"Cars."

"That's right, they still make a few cars there, don't they? What else?"

"Detroit," he said, and thought about it. "Well, the Tigers, of course. The Lions, the Pistons. There's a hockey team, too, but I can't remember the name of it."

"Could it be the Horvaths?"

"The Horvaths?"

"As in Len Horvath."

"Len Horvath."

"That ring a muted bell for you, Keller?"

"Quotidian," Keller said.

"Huh?"

"Putative."

She held up her hands. "I give up," she said. "Are you just throwing words at me, or did you pick up some charms from Harry Potter?"

"They were words he used," he told her. "Len Horvath, in Detroit. 'I read books,' he said. He had a stamp collection when he was a kid. At least he said he did."

"It'd be a strange thing to lie about. He liked you, Keller."

"He liked me?"

"Not enough to ask you to the prom, but enough to call me on the phone and tell me who he was and what he wanted. And what he wants is you."

"I thought he was going to kill me," he remembered. "He had me picked up at the airport, and I thought he was going to have me killed, but all he did was use some big words and send me back."

"And you haven't been back to Detroit since."

He started to nod, then remembered. "Just once," he said, and thought of a shopping mall in Farmington Hills. "That fellow I met on the plane."

"You didn't run into Len Horvath on that trip, did you? Because he remembers you fondly. He wants you to do some work for him."

"I can use the work."

"Just what I was thinking, although I didn't come right out and say as much to Horvath. I told him I'd have to make sure the time worked for you. Because this is one of those where time is of the essence. You don't get to spend a whole season following a baseball player around the country. It all has to be done next weekend."

"By next weekend? That's not much time."

"Not by next weekend. During next weekend. Today's what, Tuesday?"

"Wednesday."

"Really? So it is. I wonder what happened to Tuesday.

Then again, I wonder what happened to the last five years." She glanced at the screen, frowned, then triggered the remote. "I don't want to get distracted," she said, "and the damn thing's distracting, sound or no sound. Today's Wednesday, and the window of opportunity here is Friday through Sunday. Not this Friday through Sunday but next Friday through Sunday. What's the matter?"

"Nothing."

"Nothing?"

"Well, nothing I can't change. I had a trip planned, I even had my plane tickets bought."

"Maybe you can get a refund."

"Or maybe I can just change the flight to Detroit, if the airline goes there."

She shook her head. "Forget Detroit," she said. "After we got off the phone, your friend Horvath sent us something, and it wasn't his boyhood stamp collection."

"Money?"

"Uh-huh. Plus a photograph. It's from a newspaper, but he cut it out so neatly there's no caption." She passed it to Keller. "Guy looks like he's getting ready to accept an award."

The man in the photo had a broad forehead, a strong jawline, and a full head of iron gray hair. And his facial expression—well, Keller could see what Dot meant. "He probably is," he agreed.

"Oh? Anyway, his name is—"

"Sheridan Bingham," Keller said. "People call him Sherry."

Dot stared at him.

"He lives in Bloomfield Village," he told her. "That's a suburb of Detroit."

"He called you himself, did he?"

"Bingham?"

"No, Horvath. He called me and worked it out, and then he called you directly. He didn't? Then how in the hell . . . no, don't tell me. It'll come to me in a minute. He never said one word to me about Bloomfield Village, or even about Bingham being in the Detroit area. He just said where Bingham would be next weekend."

"San Francisco."

"So you talked to him after all. You just said you didn't."

"I didn't."

"But—"

"It took me a minute to recognize his name, remember?"

She nodded. "And then you said those words. Quo something."

"*Quotidian*. It means 'everyday, ordinary.' "

"Then why not just say that? Never mind. What was the other word?"

"*Putative.*"

"What's that mean?"

"I don't know," he admitted. "I looked it up, but I forget what it means."

"So the hell with it," she said. "Okay, I give up. How do you know about San Francisco? How'd you know the guy's name, and where he lives?"

"I recognized the picture," he said. "Bingham's a stamp collector."

CHAPTER FORTY-THREE

Keller changed his mind several times over the next week, but in the end he flew to San Francisco as originally scheduled, on a nonstop American Airlines flight that got him there early Thursday afternoon. He flew under his own name, used his own driver's license as ID, and charged the ticket to his own credit card.

All this resulted from the fact that the weekend had started out as a pleasure trip. If it had been a business trip from the outset, he'd probably be in the front of the plane, but he'd decided to economize so he'd have more money to spend on stamps. The plane was half empty, and American gave you adequate legroom in coach, so he was comfortable enough. But he felt oddly exposed, and somehow conspicuous. He was wearing a suit and tie, he looked for all the world like any other business traveler, but he felt as though the nature of his real business was somehow evident, and that anyone who glanced in his direction would know all about him.

They used to feed you a full meal on a transcontinental flight, even though it was never very good, but this time all he got was a cup of weak coffee and a bag of pretzels. No peanuts, the flight attendant told him, because some people were allergic. He must have made a face, because the fellow nodded in sympathy. "I know," he said. "Some people are allergic to coffee, too, and probably to pretzels, but the peanut people have a good lobby. But don't get me started."

Keller ate the pretzels and drank the coffee, and when the plane landed he got a cab to his hotel. He was staying at the Cumberford, where the stamp show was being held, and his room was on a high floor with a good view. He'd checked a bag, because he'd brought his Scott catalog and a few other reference books, along with a couple of changes of clothing, and he had a pair of tongs and a magnifier, and you never knew what some security person might decide was a deadly weapon. According to a sign he'd seen at the airport, you couldn't go through security with a cigarette lighter or a book of matches, nor could you transport either in your checked luggage. Keller, who had never smoked, wondered what a smoker could do these days. You couldn't smoke on the plane, or anywhere in the airport, and now you couldn't even light up after you got off, unless you managed to find somebody with a match.

He unpacked, took a shower, stretched out on the bed. And studied the newspaper photo of Sheridan Bingham.

"I'll call Horvath," Dot had said. "I'll tell him it's a scheduling problem, that we have to turn it down. I hate to give back money, especially once I've actually got it in my hand, but I don't see what choice we've got."

"I'll go to San Francisco," he said, "and do the job."

"I thought you just said you knew the guy."

"I know who he is."

"You're not friends?"

"I don't think we've ever spoken," he said, "and if we did, it would have been about the weather. I know I've been in the same room with him a couple of times. But I've seen his photo more than I've seen him in person."

"On *America's Most Wanted*?"

"In *Linn's Stamp News*. He's an exhibitor, he enters frames from his collection in stamp shows and wins prizes, or tries to. His specialty is German states."

"You mean like Wisconsin and Pennsylvania?"

"Like Hanover and Lubeck," he said. "And the Mecklenburgs."

"The Mecklenburgs? Would that be Ralph and Sheila Mecklenburg?"

"Mecklenburg-Schwerin," he said, "and Mecklenburg-Strelitz. There were all these different states and provinces during the nineteenth century, before they united to form modern Germany."

"And they all had stamps."

"Well, a lot of them did. Thurn and Taxis, that was one of the first postal systems."

"There's nothing certain except Thurn and Taxis. Isn't that what they say?"

"I never thought of that," he said, "and now I'll never be able to get it out of my head. Anyway, that's his specialty, German states. Plus Germany, and the German colonies, but—"

"Germany has colonies?"

"Nobody has colonies," he said. "Not anymore. Germany had colonies up until the end of the First World War. There was German East Africa, which the British wound up with, and German Southwest Africa, which is Namibia now, and Togo and Cameroon, which the French took, and . . ."

He told her more than she may have needed to know about Germany's long-lost empire, and when he stopped she looked at him and shook her head. "It's really educational," she said. "Stamp collecting."

"Well, that's not the point, but you do wind up picking up a lot of stuff. Useless information, I guess."

"All information's useless," she said. "You collect German states yourself?"

"It's not a major interest of mine."

"So the two of you haven't bumped heads when some particularly desirable stamp comes up."

"No."

"And you haven't sat up together drinking mai tais and telling old stamp stories."

"I'd be surprised if I'm even a familiar face to him."

"And the fact that you're both stamp collectors wouldn't keep you from punching his ticket?"

"Do you think it should?"

"Well, I don't know, Keller. Horvath used to be a stamp collector, and it's not stopping him from putting out the contract. It all comes down to how you feel about it."

He thought it over. "It's not as though he was a friend," he said, "or even an acquaintance. It's something in common, but so's wearing the same brand of sneakers. You know how you'll be riding the subway, and you're wearing New Balance sneakers, and the guy across from you is wearing New Balance, too, and you feel a sort of kinship?"

"I never ride the subway," she pointed out, "because it doesn't reach all the way to White Plains. And I never wear sneakers. But I guess I know what you mean."

"Well," he said, "just because some guy happens to be wearing the same brand of sneakers, I don't see why that should give him a free pass."

Keller had attended stamp shows at the Javits Center that had it all over this one in terms of size. The dealers' bourse fit neatly into the main ballroom at the Cumberford, and the exhibits were housed in a smaller room on the mezzanine. It was quality that had drawn him here, the quality of the material in the exhibits, the quality of the dealers in the bourse room, and especially the quality of the lots offered at the three-day auction, which was run by the white-shoe firm of Halliday & Okun.

Of course you didn't have to show up at an auction in order to bid. You could bid by mail, and the auction house would bid on your behalf, going no higher than your maximum figure for each lot. Or you could bid over the phone, saying yea or nay in real time and having the option of getting carried away and spending more than you'd intended, just as if you were there in person.

But it was more exciting to be there, no question. And, sitting on your folding chair, waiting for your lot to come up, you were able to find out just how much you really wanted a particular stamp. Sometimes you wound up sitting there, never even raising your numbered bidder's paddle, letting the lot go to somebody else for far less than you'd been willing to pay for it. Other times you sailed recklessly past your maximum bid, discovering that you wanted the material more than you'd anticipated.

Another advantage to being there was you got to see the auction lots up close and personal. The auction catalog featured photos of the more important items, but you couldn't pick up a photo with your stamp tongs and determine just how much you liked the looks of it. Keller, taking advantage of his early arrival, went to the auction room as soon as he'd unpacked, signed in and got his bidder's number—304—and sat down with his catalog. He went through it and called for the lots he was sufficiently interested in to examine, and one of the Halliday & Okun minions brought them to him for his inspection.

Stamp collecting, except for a few moments now and then in a heated auction, was not an exciting hobby. It didn't provide much in the way of edge-of-the-chair suspense, and that was fine with Keller. That really wasn't what he wanted from it. He got enough of that in his work, or in what Len Horvath might categorize as his quotidian life.

What it did offer, and what Keller appreciated, was total absorption. Seated at his table with his albums and a selection of approvals, or sprawled on his couch with the latest issue of *Linn's*, Keller's attention was entirely occupied by something which was, all things considered, essentially trivial. Trimming a mount with his guillotine-style mount cutter, dipping a British colonial issue in watermark detection fluid, checking another with his perforation gauge, Keller was completely caught up in the moment. Hours could fly by, with Keller quite unaware of their passage.

Over the past month, he'd spent quite a few hours with the Halliday & Okun catalog, putting a little check mark next to those lots in which he had any interest. There were half a dozen items that interested him enough to bring him to San Francisco, high-ticket stamps, five of them from various French colonies, one an early stamp from Great Britain. He could afford to buy two or three of the six, depending on how the bidding went, and by careful examination he managed to reduce his list from six to four. (He didn't care for the color of the stamp from Gabon, which seemed to him to have faded as a result of exposure to sunlight, and the British issue, nicely centered and with a wing margin, had a couple of raggedy perforations. He was partial to wing margins, but he decided the perfs bothered him.)

Besides those six stamps, though, there were thirty or forty other lots, ranging in estimated value from ten to two hundred dollars. They would fill spaces in his collection, and he might or might not bid on them, depending on how they looked on close inspection and how the bidding proceeded. So he had all of those lots to look at as well, and notes to make in his catalog, and he gave himself up completely to the task at hand.

He was not the only prospective bidder in the room. There were eight chairs positioned at the bank of tables, and at no time was his the only one occupied. Others came and went, with Keller never more than marginally aware of their coming and going. The conversation in the room was subdued, and largely limited to men (and at least one woman) calling the lots they wanted to examine. But occasionally some small talk crept into the conversation, most of it dealing with sports or the weather, or an inquiry about a mutual acquaintance. One man talked about airport security and what a nuisance it was, and Keller expressed his agreement without looking up or having any idea whose opinion he was seconding. Or caring, because his concentration remained centered upon the stamp he was holding to the light, to determine if the paper had thinned where a previous collector's hinge had been removed. It hadn't, and he made a note to that effect in his catalog.

"Thurn and Taxis," someone said. There'd been words preceding those, but Keller hadn't noted them. His mind registered the phrase, Thurn and Taxis, and Dot's wordplay popped into his head, and out of his mouth.

"The only certainties," he said.

He spoke almost without realizing he'd done so, but the words echoed in the room, and an attention-getting silence followed them.

"Say again?"

"Oh," Keller said. "Well, you know what they say. Nothing's inevitable in this life besides Thurn and Taxis."

"Well, I'm damned," a man said. He had a shock of iron gray hair, and wore a well-tailored suit. A wafer-thin watch contrasted with a surprisingly gaudy ring. "All the years I've been collecting the damned stamps, and there's a connection I never made. Do I know you? You're not a German states guy, are you?"

Keller shook his head. "Worldwide before 1940," he said. "Well, through '49, actually. British Empire through '52."

"To include all of George the Sixth."

"Right."

"Never had the urge to specialize?"

"Not really. Although there are some areas I'm more interested in than others."

"Like?"

"Well, French colonies."

"Pretty interesting," the fellow acknowledged. "And you don't go crazy with watermarks and perf varieties. Of course you've got to watch out for counterfeit overprints."

"I know."

"Tons of counterfeits in the German states issues. And then there are all the stamps that are worth more used than mint, so you've got fake cancellations to worry about. It's almost as bad as early Italy, where something like ninety-five percent of the used stamps have fake cancels."

"I'd rather have mint anyway," Keller said.

"If you can find them, what with all the counterfeiters buying up the mint stamps and hitting 'em with fake cancellations. But, see, I want mint *and* used. And cancellation varieties. And multiples, mint and used, and covers. That's what happens when you specialize. You want everything, and there's just no end to it."

Keller just nodded. He should never have piped up in the first place, he thought, and now if he just let the conversation die maybe he could get out of this.

No such luck.

"Say, can I buy you a drink? Seems like the least I can do, since you were kind enough to point out the inevitability of Thurn and Taxis."

And that wasn't all that was inevitable, Keller thought, and raised his eyes to meet those of the man in the newspaper photograph.

CHAPTER FORTY-FOUR

At least the hotel bar was dimly lit, and the table he shared with Bingham was off to the side. Even so, it was a terrible idea for the two of them to be sitting together. Anything that connected them would give the authorities a reason to talk to Keller after Bingham's death, and the last thing Keller wanted was to draw the attention of the police. His edge professionally lay in his professionalism. When his job was done, there was nothing to tie him to the deceased.

If that was the last thing Keller wanted, getting to know the man he had come to kill was a close runner-up. When he got to know somebody, the person became a human being instead of an impersonal target, and that made for complications. There was a time when Keller had worried that he might be a sociopath, and now it struck him that there were certain advantages to sociopathy. A true sociopath could befriend a potential victim without being conflicted. He could enjoy the man's company and then enjoy killing him; he wouldn't have to perform mental gymnastics in order to depersonalize the man.

What Keller hoped, raising his glass in acknowledgment of Bingham's toast—"To philately, the king of hobbies and the hobby of kings!"—was that the man would turn out to be loutish and obnoxious. A passion for postage stamps, he knew, was no guarantee of a noble character or a congenial personality, and with any luck at all Sheridan

Bingham would turn out to be a greedy and purse-proud type, gobbling up German states issues like a glutton gorging himself at a buffet.

"You ever exhibit at these clambakes, Jackie?"

Call me Sherry, Bingham had urged, which more or less compelled Keller to invite Bingham to call him by name. His name was John, but nobody ever called him that. Virtually everyone called him Keller, but *Call me Keller* seemed an inadequate response to *Call me Sherry*.

His name was John, he'd told Bingham, and started to say what everybody called him, and veered in midsentence, claiming that everybody called him Jack. As far as Keller could recall, no one had ever called him Jack. Nor did Sheridan Bingham, who immediately converted Jack to Jackie.

He shook his head. "Never even considered it," he said. "When you're a general collector, you don't wind up with anything exhibit-worthy. Except . . ."

"Except what?"

"Well, my collection of Martinique is complete, and I've been adding minor varieties when I run across them."

"Sounds as though you're specializing in spite of yourself."

"Well . . ."

"And aren't there a couple of high-ticket items from Martinique? One or two genuine rarities? My friend, you could exhibit if you wanted to."

"I suppose I could. I never thought of it."

"And now that you think of it?"

"I don't think it's my style," he said. "Not that I don't like to look at what other collectors exhibit."

"You been to the exhibit room yet?"

"No, I went straight to the auction room."

"Well, when you get there, you'll see a couple of frames of my stuff." Keller said he looked forward to it, and Bingham made a dismissing gesture. "Nothing to make a special trip for," he said. "Decent material, and well displayed, if I say so myself. And why shouldn't I? It's not as though I had anything to do with it."

"How's that?"

"There's a fellow who prepares my exhibits for me. Does the layout and lettering, decides what should or shouldn't go on display. You ever raise show dogs, Jackie?"

Dogs? How did dogs get into this?

"Never," he said.

"Well, neither have I, but a cousin of mine wins prizes more often than not at the Westminster Kennel Club show. Got a wall full of blue ribbons. He's got a guy who tells him what dogs to buy, and a woman who grooms the animals and gets them in peak condition for each show, and a handler who parades around the ring with the dog and makes sure the judges are properly impressed. My cousin's involvement is pretty much limited to writing a bunch of checks every month, which is something he does reasonably well. And in return he gets the ribbons and the trophies, and he's so proud of them you'd think he was the one who taught the dog to raise his leg when he needs to pee."

"I thought it was instinctive."

"You'd think so, wouldn't you? Anyway, I do pretty much the same thing as my cousin, with stamps instead of dogs. I write the checks and I take home the ribbons. I don't know why the hell I bother."

"It's a contribution to the hobby."

"You think so? I think it's a contribution to my own ego and that's about all. My glass is empty, Jackie, and my throat's still dry. You've hardly touched yours."

"You go ahead," Keller said. "One's my limit, this early in the day."

Bingham caught the waiter's eye, motioned for another round. "Easier this way," he told Keller. "Just leave it on the table if you don't want to drink it. You know what I'm beginning to do? I'm beginning to relax."

"Well, that's what the drinks are for."

"That's what stamps are for," Bingham said. "They take you out of where you are and put you in a nice peaceful place. Lately it hasn't been working."

"You're losing interest in your collection?"

"No, but it's harder to get away from what's on my mind." He fell silent while the waiter brought the drinks, then picked up his glass and stared into it. "I didn't begin to relax," he said, "until I got on the plane this morning. I had a shorter flight than you, flew nonstop on Northwest from Detroit, and I started to unwind when we pulled away from the gate." He took a sip from the new drink. "And this helps the process along. If your limit's one, well, my limit's going to be two, because I don't want to get sloshed. I just want to reach that state where I know everything's going to be okay." He managed a twisted smile. "Because," he said, "it's not."

Don't tell me about it, Keller thought. Stick to stamps, will you? Tell me all about the pressing problem of fake cancellations.

And, mercifully, the man did just that.

Keller ordered dinner from room service.

Which was ridiculous, in a city with such a wealth of restaurants. All he had to do was walk a block in any direction and he'd stumble on a restaurant with food that was better, cheaper, and more interesting than he could expect to get from the hotel kitchen. But for some reason he didn't want to leave his room, and after the waiter wheeled in the cart and lifted the metal lids off the various dishes, he realized what the reason was. He was afraid of running into Sheridan Bingham again.

Silly.

Still, after he'd eaten, he stayed in the room and watched television until it was time to go to bed.

"**W**ell, good morning yourself," Dot said. "Although it's afternoon here. What time does the auction start?"

"It started almost an hour ago," he said. "But there's nothing in today's session that I'm interested in. It's all U.S."

"As in America the Beautiful? What's the matter with the United States, Keller?"

"I collect worldwide."

"Oh? And what's America, stuck on some other planet?"

"No, but—"

"I thought you were a patriot, Keller. Dishing out quiche to the rescue workers at the Trade Center. And now you don't even think enough of your country to collect its stamps?"

"I could explain," he said, "but I don't think that's what either of us wants."

"Well, you're not going to get an argument from me on

that score. Did you, uh, establish that our friend made the trip?"

"Oh, he's here, all right."

"That sounds ominous somehow."

"We had drinks yesterday afternoon," he said, and told her briefly what had happened.

"Not great," she said.

"I know."

"Are you going to be able to do what you're supposed to do?"

"I think so. In one respect it's easier this way."

"Because he won't be suspicious of his new best friend."

"Something like that."

"But in another respect," she said, "it's got to be harder."

"Remember when you called me a sociopath?"

"How could I forget? I also remember how upset you got."

"There are times," he said, "when being a sociopath would make things a lot easier."

"What you need to do," she said, "is meditate."

"Meditate?"

"Get into a place of quiet stillness and peace," she said, "and try to get in touch with your inner sociopath."

He thought about that while he checked out the exhibits. They were more interesting than usual, and, while the overall quality was high, he didn't think that explained it. He had a different perspective on exhibits as a result of the conversation he'd had with Bingham.

The exhibits were anonymous, presumably to avoid prejudicing the judges, but Keller was sure those worthies were well aware of the identities of most of the exhibitors. He himself could put names on several of the displays, having seen the material before, and of course he had no trouble spotting Bingham's entry, which he'd already had described to him by the man himself. Three frames showed material from the three German island colonies in the Pacific—the Marshalls, the Marianas, and the Carolines. There were mint and used specimens of all the stamps, including minor varieties, and there were envelopes—covers, collectors called them—and blocks of four and six, and, well, a wealth of material, all artistically arranged and professionally written up. You could see the work of the pro who'd prepared the exhibit, but you could also see the hand of the collector, Sheridan Bingham, who'd tracked down the material in the first place and paid what he'd needed to for it.

Would he want to do anything like this himself? He thought about it and decided he wouldn't. His hobby was private, and he wanted to keep it that way.

But what he might do, he thought, was expand his interest in Martinique to include covers and multiples. They'd look good, even if no one else ever saw them.

And no one ever would. He was no artist, and layout and lettering were way beyond him. Like Bingham, he'd have to hire someone.

No thanks. He'd had a dog once, and he'd hired a young woman to walk the animal in his absence, and before he knew it he had a live-in girlfriend. And the next thing he knew, she disappeared, walking herself and his dog clear out of his life.

You didn't have to take a stamp collection for a walk. You had to feed it—it ate money, and its appetite was bottomless—but it could go as long as it had to between meals. And if you had to go somewhere, you just locked the door on it and the albums sat on their shelves without complaining.

He took another tour around the exhibit room, admiring what he saw, weighing the relative merits of the different displays. Very nice, he decided, but it was like the way he'd come to feel about dogs and girlfriends. He liked to look at them, but he wouldn't want to own one.

CHAPTER FORTY-FIVE

"Thought I might find you here."

A hand fastened on the edge of the table where Keller was seated, and the overhead light of the bourse room glinted off the blue stone of the high school class ring.

Keller was in the dealers' bourse room, where he'd sifted through several shoe boxes full of covers without finding anything he had any reason to buy. It was interesting, though, because he'd never bothered with covers, and looking at them gave him some sense of his own response to them.

"I was looking at covers," he told Bingham.

"From Martinique?"

"From all over. I didn't see anything from Martinique. I'm trying to decide how I feel about covers."

"It's a Pandora's box," Bingham said. "No two covers are identical, so you never know when to stop buying them. Or what's a good price. So you wind up buying everything, even though you're not sure you want it, and when you pass something up you wind up thinking about it for years, wishing you hadn't missed your chance."

"Maybe I shouldn't get started."

Bingham looked at him, then shook his head. "My guess," he said, "is you're not going to be able to resist. But go ahead and hold out as long as you can. Meanwhile, what do you say we get some lunch?"

It was a long, leisurely lunch, in a restaurant that was all red leather and hand-rubbed wood and well-polished brass. The clientele was mostly male, and they were all wearing suits and ties, with the occasional blue blazer for Casual Friday. Lawyers and stockbrokers, Keller guessed, starting with martinis and finishing up with brandy, and pausing en route to take on a load of prime beef and fresh seafood.

"My party," Bingham had announced when they ordered their drinks, and waved away Keller's insistence that they split the check. "You can grab the dinner check tonight, if you want. But this is gonna be on me. You've never been here before, Jackie? Well, outside of a place I know in Dallas, they serve the best steak I ever had."

Keller hadn't been sure he wanted a steak that early in the day, but the first bite he took convinced him. Conversation during the meal was light—the food demanded their full attention—and when they did talk it was about stamps.

The coffee was what you'd expect—dark, rich, and perfectly brewed—and when Bingham ordered an elderly Armagnac to keep it company, Keller went along with him. He was no big fan of brandy, it usually gave him heartburn, but he went along anyway.

What the hell, he thought. What the hell.

And he found himself wondering if a mistake might have been made. Suppose someone back in Detroit had clipped the wrong photo. Suppose it wasn't Sheridan Bingham but some other resident of the Motor City who had incurred Len Horvath's displeasure. Because, really, how could anyone want this perfectly pleasant gentleman killed?

But somebody did.

". . . Glad we ran into each other," Bingham was saying. "Except I have a confession to make. I was looking for you."

"Oh?"

"I didn't want to have lunch alone. Didn't want to *be* alone, to tell you the truth."

"You must know a lot of other collectors."

"In a casual way," Bingham said. "The other exhibitors, there's a competitive element that keeps you at arm's length. The other German specialists, well, we can't get too close because we're competing for the same material. And I'll tell you something. It's not my nature to get close to another person. I'm sort of a standoffish guy."

"You could have fooled me, Sherry."

"Well, we seem to have hit it off, Jackie." He pursed his lips, let out a toneless whistle. "Monday morning I fly back to Detroit. I'm not looking forward to it."

"Today's only Friday."

"Monday'll be here soon enough. Tomorrow's the auction, or at least the part of it I'm interested in, and I've got lots coming up in Sunday's section as well."

"So do I."

"So that'll fill some time, and give me something to think about. And then there's the judging of the exhibits, and maybe I'll win something and maybe I won't. But whatever happens, Monday I go back home."

"And you don't want to?"

"My life's very different back there."

"Oh?"

Bingham lowered his eyes. "In Detroit," he said, "I don't go anywhere without bodyguards, and even with them I rarely leave the house. I've got a safe room—you know what that is?"

"Sort of like a vault with food and water?"

"And air-conditioning," Bingham said, "and a sofa, so that a rich man can hide in there in the event of a home invasion. I pretty much live in my safe room, Jackie. I moved my stamp collection in there months ago."

"You're afraid somebody'll steal your stamps?"

"The hell with the stamps," Bingham said. "They're my chief interest, but I'm not the kind of fool who'll tell you that stamps are his life. My *life* is my life, and that's what I'm in fear of. There are people back home who want me dead, Jackie, and sooner or later they're going to get their wish."

"Isn't there anything you can do?"

"I've got a safe room and a team of bodyguards. That's about as much as I can think of. But if somebody really wants to kill you, how can you stop them? They could buy the house across the street, dig a tunnel into my basement, plant explosives, and blow the safe room to hell and me along with it."

"You really think—"

"What I really think," he said, "is that they could come up with something simpler and more efficient than that, and sooner or later they will. No, there's nothing I can do, Jackie. I wish there were."

"I don't mean for protection," he said. "I mean to change their minds, to get them to call it off."

"Not a chance." Bingham picked up his glass of brandy, put it down untasted, and took a sip of coffee instead. "I did something that some people are never going to for-give. I can't buy their forgiveness, and there's no other way

I can get it, either. They're not about to let me off the hook."

"You seem awfully calm about it."

"It's like having a terminal illness," Bingham said, and this time he drank the brandy. "Once you accept it, well, you learn to live with it. And for the next few days it's in remission. I'm safe here."

They had dinner that evening at a Thai place, mostly empty, with prints in bamboo frames on the walls and a lot of paper lanterns. The food was fiery hot, and they ate a lot of it and washed it down with Mexican beer. They began by talking stamps, almost ritualistically, and then the conversation shifted.

"I won't ask how it happened," Keller said, "but I have to say you don't seem like the kind of guy who'd make anybody that mad at him."

"From where you sit, Jackie, I'm a stamp collector. That's the great thing about a hobby. You get to be a nice guy. My life in Detroit is a little different."

"I guess it would have to be."

"All you and I really know about each other is what we collect. For all you know, I could be an ax murderer or a predatory pedophile. I'm not, I'd be safer if I were, but the point is I could be. And you could be, hmm, I don't know. Nothing violent, you're too gentle for that, but you could be a stock swindler or a confidence man, something like that."

"I could?"

"Well, no, I don't really think you could, but you see what I mean. When we're collecting stamps, we're none of those other things, no matter what we are in real life."

316

Keller nodded, and asked a question that had occupied him much of the afternoon. "Did you bring bodyguards with you? I guess it's not the sort of thing I would notice, but—"

"I don't need them here, Jackie. They're back in Detroit, guarding an empty house."

"I would think you'd bring one or two along just as a precaution."

The man shook his head. "I'm safer without them. See, nobody knows I'm here."

"Oh?"

"I've got a friend with access to his company's Gulf-stream. I hitched a ride out here, and I'll fly back the same way on Monday. My bodyguards think I'm holed up in the safe room."

"You don't trust them?"

"Up to a point, but they can't tell what they don't know, can they? I'm registered at the hotel under a false name, so that's not going to set off any bells and whistles. And if my exhibit pulls in the top prize, even if they put my picture on the front page of *Linn's*, well, somehow I don't think the boys in Detroit are subscribers. If they are, it won't do them any good, because I'll be home before the story runs."

So there wouldn't be any bodyguards to worry about. Keller, who'd been looking, hadn't spotted anyone suspicious, but he figured he'd ask. You couldn't be too careful.

It was difficult to decide what he thought of Sheridan Bingham.

Because he kept flipping back and forth. On the one hand, the man was very close to being a friend, and Keller had warm feelings toward him. At the same time, Bingham was a job that had to be done, a problem that had to be solved, and Keller couldn't help resenting him. Some people in his line of work, he knew, worked up a genuine hatred for their targets, in order to make the work easier to stomach. Keller had never felt the need to do that, but he was beginning to understand why other men did.

In the auction room Saturday morning, he sat halfway back on the center aisle with his auction catalog and his numbered paddle and his pen, waiting for his lots to come up. He tried to concentrate on the auction, and he managed reasonably well, but he still found his mind wandering now and then.

You could be a stock swindler, Bingham had said. *Or a confidence man.* And he thought about con men, and how their victims were often less wounded by the financial loss they'd sustained than by the betrayal itself. *I thought he was my friend,* they'd say, *and he betrayed me.*

Even as he would be betraying Bingham.

"And now the New Britain issues," the auctioneer said. "Lot 402. I have sixty, will you go sixty-five? I have sixty-five, will you go seventy? I have seventy in the back of the room, will you go seventy-five? I have seventy once, I have seventy twice, sold to bidder number 214."

The same bidder bought all of the New Britain issues, and Keller didn't have to turn around to know who it was. New Britain, he knew, was an island in the Bismarck Archipelago, named New Pomerania by the Germans, who discovered it back in 1700, and administered as part of German New Guinea. When it changed hands during the war, the British changed the island's name to New Britain and applied the name to all of the occupied territory in the immediate region, overprinting some German colonial stamps while they were at it.

Keller had a few of the New Britain issues, but not that many. He might have bid on one or two of the lots in the sale, but he couldn't go against his new friend. He could plan on killing him, but he couldn't compete with him at a stamp auction.

But it wasn't really betrayal, was it? It would be different, he thought, if he and Bingham had been friends before Horvath gave him the contract. If that had been the case he'd have turned it down, and even found a way to warn his friend.

That wasn't the way it had happened. The contract came first, and he would never have gotten to know Bingham if he hadn't already accepted the job of killing him.

Still, there was something about the whole business . . .

It would be a lot easier if you were a sociopath. A shame there wasn't a school you could go to. Earn a degree, become a licensed sociopathic personality. Job placement guaranteed.

"Lot 721. I have twenty dollars, will you go twenty-two? I have twenty-two, will you go twenty-four? I have twenty-two on the aisle, will you go twenty-four? Are you all through at twenty-four? I have twenty-four once, I have twenty-four twice, sold to bidder number 304."

Keller lowered his paddle, circled the lot number, noted the price, and looked to see what was coming up next.

That night they went back to the steakhouse. "Quiet on Saturdays," Bingham observed. "The businessmen are either home with their wives or in bed with their girl-friends. Not that it's ever noisy here, but we've practically got the place to ourselves tonight. You make out okay this afternoon? Seems to me I saw a few lots hammered down to you."

"I picked up a couple of bargains," Keller said. "The lots I'm really interested in come up tomorrow."

"I bought quite a bit today, and I'll do the same tomorrow. Though sometimes I wonder why I bother."

"Well, a stamp collection's like a shark," Keller said.

"Huh?"

"A shark has to keep swimming forward all the time," he explained, "or it dies. At least that's what I heard somewhere."

"It does sound like the sort of thing a person would hear somewhere."

"Well, whether it's true or not for sharks, it works that way with a stamp collection. If you're not adding to it, there's not much pleasure in having it."

"Absolutely true," Bingham said. "I was always interested in Germany, but when I started out I collected Vatican City. Don't ask me why. I'm not Catholic, but then I'm not German, either. It didn't take me long to complete the collection, varieties and all, and it sat there in an album, and I never looked at it. I haven't sold it, though I probably should, for all the pleasure I get out of it. Like a shark, eh? I never thought of it quite that way, but I like it, because I can picture a collection swimming along, devouring everything in its path."

A little later he said, "You have a family, Jackie? No? Well, I've got a few stray cousins myself, but nobody I've had any contact with in years. Way my will's drawn, I'm leaving everything to Wayne State University."

"Is that where you went to college?"

"No, but they gave me an honorary degree a few years ago. You could call me Dr. Bingham, but don't you dare. That degree's going to turn out to be bread upon the waters, and they might as well have the money as anyone else. God knows what they'll do with the stamps."

"You could require that they keep the collection and display it."

"What the hell for? Let 'em auction it off, so some other collectors can grab up chunks of it and have some fun with it."

"Well," Keller said, "that's not going to happen anytime soon."

Bingham just looked at him.

CHAPTER FORTY-SIX

"I was thinking natural causes," he told Dot the following day.

"And why not? One of your subspecialties, Keller. You're about as natural a cause of death as I've ever known."

"Cyanide's always good," he said, "and I don't think it would be hard to get my hands on some. It looks like a heart attack."

"And it's every bit as funny, too."

"But you find it," he said, "if you look for it. In a tox screen. And they'd look for it. The local cops might not know who he is, but they'd find out, and when the full story came back from Detroit they'd order a full workup, and they'd find it. Or anything else I can think of."

"And if they look at it, they're looking at you."

"Whatever happens to him," he said, "they're going to be looking at me. We've been hanging out all over the place. I made sure I paid cash for our dinner last night, but I might as well have used a credit card, because what difference does it make?"

"You want to come home, Keller?"

"I've thought about it."

"We can give back the money. You're out the cost of your flight, but you were going there anyway, weren't you? So we'll just write it off and let somebody else figure out how to kill the son of a bitch."

"He's actually a pretty nice guy."

"Oh, terrific. Just what I wanted to hear."

"Out here, that is. He may not be such a nice guy in Detroit."

"So do you want to follow him to Detroit and kill him there? Along with all his bodyguards?"

"I don't think so."

"Well, I'm glad to hear it. What do you think, Keller? Should I make a phone call, and you can just write off the airfare?"

"It's not just the airfare."

"And the hotel, I suppose. But you were in for the airfare and the hotel anyway, weren't you? You already had the room and the flight booked, if I remember correctly."

"Besides the hotel."

"What, a couple of meals? I don't see how . . . oh, I get it, Keller. Stamps. But weren't you going to buy stamps anyway?"

"Up to a point," he said.

"And you sailed right past that point, didn't you? Because you had the money from Detroit, burning a hole in your pocket."

"I didn't lose control," he assured her. "I spent pretty much what I intended to spend. I had all this money coming in, so I figured I could afford for some of it to go out. But if I have to give it back . . ."

"There's a reason why giving money back goes against the grain. Once I've got it in my hand, it's my money. And giving it back is like spending it, and what am I getting for it?" She sighed. "Other hand, anything happens to him and somebody with a badge is going to want to talk to you. And you've made a very good career out of so arranging your life that you never have to talk to anybody with a badge."

"There ought to be a way."

"How old is the guy, Keller? Sixty, sixty-five?"

"Sixty-seven."

"Even better. Maybe you'll catch a break. He's up there in years, he's under a lot of stress and strain. Maybe nature'll help you out. It wouldn't be the first time."

"He seems pretty healthy, Dot."

"Never sick a day in his life, and then pow! The old ticker blows out, and next thing you know he's approaching room temperature. Who's to say it couldn't happen?"

"It would have to happen within the next twenty-four hours."

"Makes it a little less likely, doesn't it? Suppose he wins one of those blue ribbons? Maybe the excitement'll do it."

"He's got a whole wall full of them back home. I don't think it would be all that exciting."

"Well, maybe he'll lose, and he'll be so disappointed he'll kill himself . . . Keller? Where'd you go?"

"I'm here," he said. "But I'd better get back to the auction room. I've got a couple of lots coming up."

The last lot he bid on was from St. Pierre & Miquelon, a couple of French islands off the coast of Newfoundland. He had strong competition from a determined telephone bidder, and went higher than he'd planned, but that was all right. He had cash to pay for it, and he wasn't going to have to give it back.

He went to his room, picked up the phone, then changed his mind and went downstairs to use the house phone in the lobby.

"It's Jackie," he said, the name sounding strange to him. But it evidently sounded fine to Bingham, who said he'd just gotten out of the shower, and had he lost track of the time? Because he didn't think they were meeting for dinner for another hour and a half.

"No, this is something else," he said. "Are you alone? Can I come to your room?"

"I'm always alone. And yes, give me five minutes to put some clothes on, then come on up."

Bingham supplied the room number, and seven or eight minutes later Keller was knocking on the door of 617. Which was fine, he'd decided. Room 1217 would have been better, but 617 would have to do.

And it was certainly spacious enough. Keller's room three floors down was comfortable enough, if a little on the small side, but Bingham had a suite. "More space than I've got any use for," he told Keller, "but when you spend a little more you get treated a little better. And if I fart in one room I can go in the other until the air clears. You want a drink?"

He didn't, but said he did. Because that way Bingham would take a drink—although his breath already held the bouquet of good whiskey.

Bingham poured, and they touched glasses, and Keller wet his lips while Bingham drank deeply. "Just as well you came up here," he said. "I've got something for you, and I was going to bring it along to dinner, but who's to say I wouldn't forget? I'll give it to you now and you can leave it in your room before we go out."

The clear plastic sheet held a cover, postmarked 1891 in Martinique's capital city of Fort-de-France, and backstamped in Paris and surcharged here and there, bearing several different stamps from the island colony's first issue.

"It's a beauty," Keller said. "What do I owe you for it?"

"It's a present."

"Oh, come on," he said. "You've got to let me pay for it."

"Nope. You can't buy it, Jackie. It's not for sale. It's a gift."

"But—"

"It'll cost you plenty in the long run," Bingham told him, and paused to top up his own drink. "All the covers you'll buy. But you've got to feed the shark, don't you?"

"Well, I'm very happy to have it. I wish I had something for you in return. And maybe I do."

"Oh?"

"The reason I came up here," Keller said. "You really expect to be killed, don't you?"

"Sooner or later. When someone with money and power is determined to kill you, you don't stand much of a chance."

"Sherry, I think I know a way to get you off the hook."

"I don't think there is any such way. But I'd be a fool not to hear you out."

"Well," Keller said. "You know, the other day you were talking about how people don't know that much about each other. And you said for all you knew I could be a stock swindler, or a confidence man."

"It wasn't meant as an insult."

"I know that, but it hit a little close to the bone. I'm neither of those things, not exactly, but I haven't lived my whole life inside the law, either."

"You know, I had the sense you were a man of the world, Jackie."

"I wouldn't have the collection I do," he said, "if it weren't for insurance fraud."

"Reporting your own stamps as stolen? I wouldn't think—"

"When it comes to stamps, I've always been completely on the up-and-up."

"Same here. That's the thing about hobbies."

"I'm talking about life insurance fraud. A couple of times over the years I've faked my own death. So I know a little about the mechanics of it. Sherry, you've got somebody back home who wants to kill you. You can't buy him off or scare him off, and he won't let up as long as you're alive. But if he doesn't think you're alive . . ."

Bingham had a ton of questions. Where would you get a body? What about DNA? Dental forensics?

"Have another drink," Keller suggested, "and I'll explain what I have in mind."

"It just might work," Bingham said. "You want to know something? It's scarier than dying. I was pretty much used to the idea of that, but this . . ."

"I know what you mean."

"And at the same time it's exciting as hell. Because it's a whole new life. I'd be starting over with next to nothing. Wayne State'll get my stamps and everything else I own. I've got a little cash tucked away in secret accounts, and I can get that, so I'll never have to wonder where my next meal is coming from. But where will I live, and how'll I keep from running into somebody who can recognize me?" He ran a hand through his hair. "I suppose I could dye this. Or cut it real short. Or shave it off, but then people start wondering how you'd look with hair."

"There are a lot of tricks," Keller said, figuring there would have to be. "And I can help you come up with them."

"And you can find a body that'll pass for mine. Jackie, I'm not going to ask how."

"Nobody's going to get killed," he assured Bingham, and talked vaguely about cooperative funeral parlors. Even as he spoke, the whole prospect sounded dubious to him, and he was glad Bingham's intake of whiskey was increasing its credibility.

"Now here's what's crucial," he said. "First of all, it has to happen here, in San Francisco. Where nobody knows you, and where the police will have every reason to wrap it up in a hurry and ship the body back to Detroit. Where nobody will bother with an autopsy, because San Francisco already held one."

"Stands to reason."

"Number one," he said, "is that ring of yours. It's distinctive."

"My high school ring. I'm not even sure I can get it off. Let me try some soap."

He returned from the bathroom with the ring in hand. "There," he said, presenting it to Keller. "And number two?"

"Your suicide note. You'll want a sheet of Cumberford letterhead."

"In the desk drawer."

"Could you get it? We'll want to have your fingerprints on it, and nobody else's."

"Good thinking. Now what should I write?"

Keller frowned in thought. "Let's see," he said. " 'To Whom It May Concern. I suppose I'm taking the easy way out, but I have no choice.'" He went on, and Bingham said he had the sense of it, and how would it be if he phrased it more in his own words? Keller told him it would be ideal.

By the time he'd finished, he'd filled the whole sheet of hotel stationery. "'I would advise my heirs at Wayne State University to sell my entire collection of stamps,'" he read aloud, "'and recommend the San Francisco firm of Halliday & Okun for this purpose.' You know, I spent close to fifty thousand this weekend. I might not have bothered if I'd had any idea I was only going to own the stamps for a matter of hours."

"You could take them along."

"You think so? No, it's got to be more convincing to leave them behind. And it's not as though I'm going to resume collecting German states in my new life, or anything else in the world of stamps. Handwriting's a little shaky."

"Well, you're about to kill yourself. That might make a man the least bit unsteady."

"I think the scotch may have had something to do with it. Just let me sign this. Signature looks okay, doesn't it?"

"It looks fine."

"So. What happens next?"

CHAPTER FORTY-SEVEN

"**P**retty slick," Dot said. "Got him to write a note, got him to take off his ring, and then gave him a helping hand out the window. I know people who drown themselves tend to leave their clothes all folded up on the beach, but do many jumpers do it naked?"

"It happens," he said. "What never happens is that somebody undresses a guy before shoving him out a window."

"Until now."

"Well," he said.

"But you said he was dressed when you went upstairs. So you had to undress him."

"When I phoned him," he recalled, "he said he'd just got out of the shower. I should have told him to just put on a robe."

"I think he did enough, Keller. How'd you get him unconscious?"

"Rabbit punch."

"Always a popular favorite."

"At first I thought I'd killed him. I figured it was better to hit him too hard than not hard enough. Because I didn't want him to know what was happening."

"But the blow didn't kill him."

"No, he was alive when he went out the window."

"But not for long. Six stories?"

"Six stories."

"With no overhangs or canopies to break his fall."

"That was the pavement's job," he said.

"And the cops? Were you in town long enough for them to get around to you?"

"I went to them myself," he said.

"Jesus, that's a first."

"As soon as I heard about Bingham's death, and that didn't take long. I told them how I'd spent some time with him over the weekend, and that it'd be my guess that he'd received bad news from his doctor, because he would say things like why was he buying these stamps when he couldn't look forward to owning them for very long. And he'd sort of hinted at suicide, talking about meeting fate head-on instead of waiting for it to come up on him from behind."

"How'd this go over?"

"Well, the detective I talked to wrote everything down, but it just seemed to be confirming what he'd already decided. It was pretty much open and shut, Dot."

"The window was open," she said, "and the door was shut."

"That's about it. A very candid suicide note in his own hand, signed and dated, and weighted down with his watch and his class ring. And, alongside it, all the stamps he'd bought over the weekend, plus a wallet full of cash."

"That's enough to fool just about anybody," she allowed. "Except for Len Horvath, who thinks you're the greatest thing since Google. He said he can't wait until somebody pisses him off so he can use you again."

"He actually said that?"

"No, of course not. But he's a happy man, and he sent us the cash to prove it. I have to say he's not the only one you managed to impress, Keller. Getting him to write the note, that's kind of rich."

"You gave me the idea."

"How do you figure that?"

"You said maybe he'd kill himself. Out of disappointment at losing the blue ribbon."

"I said that? I don't even remember, but I'll take your word for it. Did he lose the blue ribbon?"

"No, he won."

"But he found something else to be disappointed about. That's what gave you the idea? My idle remark?"

"Plus an idle remark of Bingham's, saying I could be a confidence man or a stock swindler. And I realized that I felt like a con man, pretending to be his friend while I was getting ready to take him out, and then I thought, well, what would a con man do?" He frowned. "It was interesting, manipulating things, making it all work out, but I wouldn't want to be a con man full-time. I really did like him, you know."

"But you didn't let that stop you."

"Well, no. And if I did, then what? It only meant Horvath would bite the bullet and find a way to do the job in Detroit. Tunnel under Bingham's house and blow him up, like Bingham suggested. Or send in a private army to overwhelm the bodyguards. Bingham knew it was all over. He didn't want to go back to Detroit."

"And you fixed it so he didn't have to."

"Well," he said.

"I've got a bundle of cash for you. Horvath was quick, and so was FedEx. I'd tell you to buy some stamps, but you already did that." She pointed at an envelope. "So you can put this toward your retirement fund."

He glanced at the soundless television set, where stock symbols and prices crawled across the screen beneath two men holding a furious silent argument. "How're we doing?" he asked.

"In the market? We have good days and we have bad days, but lately the good days are running ahead of the bad ones."

"What are you going to do with your share?"

"I might just stick it in the market," she said, "and see if I can fatten it up a little."

He pushed the envelope across the table. "Do the same with mine," he said. "Otherwise I'll spend it."

"If you're sure. I was thinking we should diversify into some overseas companies. India and Korea are booming."

"Whatever you say."

She put a hand on the envelope, drew it closer to her. She said, "Keller? Those stamps he bought at auction, that you just left on the table with the suicide note. Weren't you tempted?"

"No, not at all."

"Because it's your hobby."

"That's right."

"I guess I get it," she said. "There was an envelope he gave you, except you called it something else."

"A cover."

"There you go. From Martinique, right? What did it cost him?"

"It's worth somewhere between eight and ten thousand. I don't know if he paid that much."

"And you're keeping it."

"Well, sure. It was a present."

"I see."

"And something to remember him by."

"I guess," she said. "But don't you usually try to forget them as quickly and completely as possible? Don't you do that mental exercise, fading their image to black and white and then graying it out? Letting it get smaller and smaller until it disappears?"

"Usually."

"Oh. Are you all right, Keller?"

"I think so," he said.

KELLER'S
LEGACY

CHAPTER FORTY-EIGHT

When Keller turned the corner, he saw Dot standing on the front porch. A white flowerpot was suspended from the ceiling on either side of the old-fashioned glider, and each held a spider plant, and she was watering them. She turned at his approach, and her eyes widened, but she took a moment to finish watering the plants.

"This one," she said, "is growing faster than the other. See? It's got more babies, it's going to reach the floor sooner. I wonder if I should trim it and keep them both the same length."

"Why?"

"In the interest of symmetry," she said, "except I'm not sure it's good for the plant. What did you do, walk from the train station?"

"It's a nice day."

"I guess that's a yes. Except how did you get here so fast? I left a message on your machine less than an hour ago, and by the time you got it and caught a train at Grand Central . . ." She frowned. "It doesn't add up. What did you do, call in and pick up your messages?"

"I went out for breakfast," he said, "and I read the paper and did the crossword puzzle, and then I was going to call you but I figured I'd take a chance and just come up. I never thought to check for messages."

"You came up on your own. There's a stamp you want

to buy, so you want some of the money from our broker-age account."

He shook his head.

"You sensed that I was trying to reach you, and that's what drew you here. No? Well, I'm all out of guesses, Keller. Come on inside and tell me about it."

At the kitchen table, he drew a folded sheet of paper from his pocket. Without unfolding it he said, "I've been think-ing. I've got my share of whatever's in our brokerage account, but aside from that most of my net worth is tied up in stamps. There are ten albums, plus a small carton of odds and ends."

"In your apartment."

"That's right. Now here's what I want you to do. If something should happen to me, go straight to my apart-ment. You still have the key I gave you, don't you?"

"Somewhere."

"If you're not sure where it is—"

"I know right where it is, Keller. It's hanging on a hook by the back door. You want to tell me what all this is about?"

"What you'll do," he said, "is go to my apartment and let yourself in. You'll probably want a helper, because they're hefty albums and it's a lot to carry. Just take them right on out of there and bring them back here."

"And then I suppose I'll have to kill my helper and bury him in the backyard, because dead men tell no tales."

"I'm serious about this, Dot."

"I can see that, and I wish I knew why."

"I was thinking about that guy. Sheridan Bingham."

"The one who went out the window."

338

"He'd made arrangements. His stamp collection was going to Wayne State University, and they would sell it. Well, what would happen to my collection? It would just sit there until somebody cleared out my apartment, and then God knows what would become of it."

"And you want me to display it or something? Add stamps to it?"

"What do you care about stamps? You can sell it and do whatever you want with the money."

"But—"

"I haven't got anybody else to leave anything to," he said, "and I haven't got anything else to leave, aside from the brokerage account. And you'd get that, wouldn't you?"

"Officially," she said, "we're joint tenants with right of survivorship. So yes, it'd come to me. Keller, why the hell are we having this conversation?"

"Peace of mind," he said.

"My mind was at peace before you brought this up," she said, "and now it's not, so I have to say I think the whole thing's counterproductive."

"Just let me finish going through this." He unfolded the sheet of paper. "Three dealers," he said. "What you do, you call all three and offer them the opportunity to inspect the collection and make an offer. I wrote out a description of the material. Schedule them on different days, because it'll take them a while to look through everything and come up with a price." He went on, explaining how to negotiate with the dealers, and what sort of offer she might realistically expect. With really expensive items, a dealer could work on a narrow margin; with common stamps, you could recover only a very small fraction of the cost when you sold. On balance he figured his collection

339

would probably bring a fourth to a third of catalog value, but it was hard to say for sure.

"If you think of stamps as an investment," he said, "you're better off putting the money in the market, or even in the savings bank. But if you think of it as a hobby, a leisure-time pursuit, well, you get a certain amount back, and that's not true of fly-fishing."

"On the other hand," she said, "you can eat what you catch. Unless you're one of those catch-and-release guys. Keller? What brought this up, and don't tell me about Sheridan Bingham."

"Well, something could happen."

"Have you got a bad feeling, Keller? A premonition?"

"Not exactly."

"Not exactly. Is that a yes or a no?"

"Things happen to people, Dot. They get hit by buses."

"So be careful crossing streets."

"Or, well, the work I do. I don't usually think of it as dangerous, but I suppose it is."

"It's usually dangerous for other people. But I suppose the life insurance companies would consider you to be in a high-risk category."

"Or I could get arrested. Last time out I wound up talking to the police. I initiated it, and they never came close to suspecting me of anything, but it gets your attention, when you go and talk to the police."

"I can see where it would."

"If I get killed," he said, "go straight to my apartment and grab the albums. If I just disappear, if you don't hear from me and can't get in touch with me, do the same thing, but in that case just hold on to them for a while on the chance that I'm all right. You can always sell them somewhere down the line. Same thing goes if I get arrested."

"If you get arrested," she said, "your stamps can shift for themselves. I'm not going anywhere near them."

"Why not?"

"Because as soon as I get the news I'll be throwing things in a suitcase and rushing to catch the next flight to Brazil. I want to be long gone before you rat me out."

"You honestly think I would do that?"

"Keller," she said, "welcome to the twenty-first century. Even Mafia guys rat each other out. They'd be charging you with murder, and your only way out would be to cut a deal and give up the client, and you probably wouldn't know who that was. But you know who I am, and that might be enough to save you from the needle."

He thought it over, shook his head. "I'd rather have the needle."

"Than give me up? I'm touched, Keller, and you can say that now, and you can even mean it, but—"

"I'd rather have the needle than do time in prison."

"Oh."

"And if I did give you up," he said, "it wouldn't be for weeks, maybe months. You'd have plenty of time to sell the stamps and close the brokerage account. You could even put this house on the market."

"I wonder what it would bring. There's no mortgage, and the real estate market's sky high. It's better than stamps, and one thing about houses, you don't have to paste them in a book." She looked at him and frowned. "Keller," she said, "is there something you're not telling me?"

"I don't think so."

"You're not planning something foolish, are you?"

"Something foolish?"

"You know."

"What, like killing myself? No, of course not."

"But you think something might happen to you."

"Sooner or later," he said, "something happens to everybody."

"Well, I guess that's true."

"I have health insurance," he said, "and it's not because I expect to get sick. I mean, I never get sick. But most people do get sick sooner or later, and this way I don't have to worry about it. And now I won't have to worry about what happens to my stamps, because you'll take care of them."

"What gets me," she said, "is the way you showed up here today. I left you a message, and you never got it, but you came anyway."

"Well, I wanted to have this conversation, and—"

"What we haven't talked about," she said, "is why I left you a message."

"Oh."

"I got an express shipment."

"Oh."

"Remember Al?"

It took him a minute, but then he did remember. "He sent us money."

"He did indeed."

"A long time ago."

"Donkey's years, whatever that means. It sounds even longer than dog years."

"Prepayment for a job," he said, "but then there never was a job, and I sort of forgot about him."

"So did I. I figured either he changed his mind or he died, and either way we could just keep the money and forget about it."

"Don't tell me he sent us more money."

She shook her head. "No money. Just a name and an address and a photograph and some newspaper clippings."

"And the photograph is of somebody he wants taken care of."

"Well, it's not a postcard from the Grand Canyon. You know what I'd like to do? I'd like to send him his money back."

"You're spooked," he said.

"You're not? We don't hear from him and then we do, and it's the same day you decide your stamps are going to outlive you? No, don't explain. You've got the heebie-jeebies, and all of a sudden here's Just-Call-Me-Al with something to have the heebie-jeebies about. Dammit, you know how I feel about sending money back."

"You're against it."

"But this time I'd do it in a heartbeat, but I can't. Because I don't know who the son of a bitch is or where he lives. You know what we could do?"

"What?"

"Nothing," she said. "Zip, zero, nada. If he wants the money back, let him ask for it and tell us where to send it."

"And in the meantime we just wait to hear from him?"

"Why not?"

"And he waits for me to do the job, and I don't."

"Right."

He thought about it. "That's an awful lot of waiting," he said. "You said he sent a photo."

"And some clippings. Hang on."

He read the clippings, studied the photograph, memorized the name and address. "Albuquerque," he said.

"You've been there, haven't you?"

"A long time ago. Is that where Al lives?"

"*A* my name is Alice, my husband's name is Al, we live in Albuquerque and we raise alpacas. Don't look at me like that, Keller. It's a rhyme to jump rope to. If you'd ever been a little girl you'd be familiar with it. I don't know where he lives. He sent the FedEx from Denver."

"Oh."

"Which doesn't necessarily prove he lives there, either. Why don't I just file all this crap under *F*?"

"Why *F*?"

"So we can Forget About It. But you don't want to, do you?"

"There may be a direct flight," he said, "but you know what I think I'll do? I think I'll fly American through Dallas."

"I don't think you should go at all."

"I want to get it over with," he told her. "I don't want to sit around waiting for something to happen."

CHAPTER FORTY-NINE

There was no reason to expect anyone to meet his flight. Still, he took a long look at the dozen or so men waiting with hand-lettered signs between the security gates and the baggage claim. He read the signs, thinking he might see one with a familiar name on it—NOSCAASI, or BOGART, or even KELLER. He didn't, but he evidently stared hard at a stoop-shouldered man waiting for a Mr. Brenner, because the man stared just as hard back at him. Keller drew his eyes away and kept walking. He felt the man's eyes tracking him as he headed for the Hertz desk.

He'd made reservations at three different motels located at consecutive exits along I-40, and he went to them in turn and checked in at each one under a different name, paying cash in advance for a week's stay. He showered in the first one, left the bed there and in the second motel looking as though it had been slept in, and, in the third motel, stationed himself in front of the television set for an hour or so, flipping back and forth between CNN and one of the sports channels.

He didn't unpack, and took his carry-on with him when he returned to the car. He ate at a Denny's, then managed to find an address just off Indian School Road. All the houses were of adobe, but the neighborhood was otherwise a mixed one. Small lots held yellow-brown cubes that looked as though they'd been assembled in a weekend by the owner and a couple of his pals, while

345

other lots were several acres in size, boasting oversize homes designed by architects and elegantly landscaped.

The house he was looking for, with a shack on one side and a McMansion on the other, was more manor house than shanty, but a good deal less grand than some of its neighbors. The adobe construction allowed for curves and arches, and the overall effect was pleasing. It looked, he decided, like a house in which one could lead a pleasant and comfortable life.

Keller wondered what Warren Heggman had done to create such a pleasant and comfortable life for himself, and wondered too why someone wanted that life brought to a close. He looked down at the passenger seat, from which the man's photo looked back at him. He had a long narrow face, a high forehead. In his forties, Keller thought, or maybe his early fifties.

Keller circled the block, pulled up at the curb across the street from the Heggman house. The garage door was closed, so there was no telling if Heggman was home, but there were lights on, which suggested that he probably was.

It didn't matter. He'd seen the place, he told himself, and now he should return to one of his motel rooms and get a night's sleep. Then in the morning he could stake the place out and familiarize himself with Heggman's routine. After a few days he'd be able to work out the best way to get at the man, and in the meantime he'd have equipped himself with a suitable weapon, and then, before too many more days had passed, he could do the job.

He drove on. Then, barely aware of what he was doing, he circled the block one more time and pulled into Heggman's driveway.

346

Three motel rooms, he thought. Three different names. Pussyfooting around, trying to cover his tracks. Why?

Look at Sheridan Bingham, for God's sake. Holed up in a vault in the middle of a house full of bodyguards, and the only time he could relax was when he got out of there and flew to San Francisco. And what was waiting for him there?

He got out of the car, walked to the front door, rang the bell.

CHAPTER FIFTY

"**I** thought it might be you," Dot said. "How's the weather in Albuquerque?"

"I'm in White Plains," he said.

"That's funny," she said. "So am I. What do you mean, you're in White Plains?"

"At the train station."

"Well, sit tight," she said. "I'll pick you up."

"I'll take a cab. Really, it's easier."

The cab dropped him in front of her house, and she was waiting for him on the porch. "You pruned the spider plant," he said. "I think it looks better that way, with both of them the same size."

"The baby I lopped off," she said, "is in the sunroom in another pot. Once you start with plants it never ends. If you were going to take a cab, why did you bother calling?"

"Well, I came out without calling the other day, and it took you by surprise."

"You're always taking me by surprise," she said. "Some surprises are better than others. I'm surprised you didn't go to Albuquerque, but I have to tell you I'm just as glad."

"You are?"

"I was worried about you," she said. "All that business about your stamp collection. I kept thinking of different ways it could go wrong."

"So did I."

"But when you left here the other day you were bound and determined to go. What changed your mind?"

"Nothing."

"Huh?"

"I went."

"You looked it over and decided to pull the plug on it?"

He held up a hand. "I went there," he said, "and I did the job, and I came back."

"You did the job?"

"Sure."

"But—"

"I figured it would take a week," he said, "or maybe as much as two. And then, I don't know, I decided to take the bull by the horns."

"Do you suppose anybody ever did that? Literally took hold of a bull by the horns?"

"Probably. Anything you can think of, somebody tried it."

"Well, I guess you're right about that."

"I drove over there, I parked in his driveway, and I rang his bell."

"The day before yesterday," she said, "you were sitting in my kitchen."

"I flew out yesterday morning, and it was around dinner when I went to his house. I'd already eaten, I stopped at a Denny's. They gave me more food than I could finish."

"So you took a doggie bag to share with Heggler."

"Heggman, and no, it was this Breakfast Anytime special, and I didn't want a doggie bag full of eggs and pancakes. I rang the bell and the thought occurred to me that I'd probably be dead within the hour."

"But you rang the bell anyway."

"And he opened the door. He looked disappointed to see me."

"You must get that a lot, Keller."

"He thought I was one of his wife's lawyers. He was saying something about a prenup."

"If he had one," Dot said, "and if it was a good one, it'd do for a motive."

"I hit him."

"You hit him?"

"I didn't plan it," he said. "I didn't plan any of it. Dot, I had three different motel rooms reserved and I checked into all of them, so I could move around and keep out of sight. And then I went straight to the guy's house and rang his bell, and without even stopping to close the door I made a fist and hit him in the pit of the stomach."

"And?"

He looked away. "He folded, and I kicked him, and then, well, I got hold of him and broke his neck."

"Just like that."

"He was dead, and there were no fingerprints to wipe off because I hadn't been there long enough to touch anything. I didn't even have to touch the doorknob because the door still wasn't shut, so I walked through it, and as I did I heard a voice from upstairs. 'Warren? Is everything all right?'"

"His wife? No, you already said she was divorcing him."

"It was a woman's voice, though."

"Maybe she was the reason his wife was divorcing him."

"Who knows? I kept going. I got in the car and drove straight to the airport."

"And nobody saw you?"

"I don't think so. If anybody got the plate number, well, I rented it under another name. I turned the car in, and I got a flight to L.A. and a red-eye home."

"And here you are."

"Here I am," he agreed. "I stopped at my apartment to shower and shave and change clothes, and then I walked over to Grand Central and caught a train. I was going to call."

"You did call, remember?"

"I mean I was going to call from my apartment and fill you in over the phone. But I decided to come out instead."

"And here you are. Damn, I keep saying that, don't I? I'm evidently having trouble taking it all in. Remember that baseball player?"

"Floyd Turnbull."

"You followed him around for an entire season."

"It wasn't that long."

"The hell it wasn't. You stopped along the way to kill other people, but you took your sweet time with Turnbull."

"Well."

"This time," she said, "with both of us spooked, and every reason in the world to play it safe, you were in and out in nothing flat. I was afraid you were being set up."

"So was I."

"If you managed to kill him, there'd be somebody waiting to kill you."

"That's why I booked all those motel rooms."

"Come on in," she said. "Sit down. I'll pour us each a glass of iced tea. Or would you rather have a cup of coffee?"

"I hate the red-eye," he said. "I thought about getting a room at an airport hotel near LAX and getting a night's sleep before flying home. But I realized I wasn't going to sleep anyway, and if I was going to be awake I might as well be on my way home. I did some thinking on the plane."

"And?"

"I decided we'd picked the wrong job to worry about. We had a client who'd stayed completely out of sight. We didn't know where he lived, let alone who he is. He wouldn't have to kill me to stay in the clear, because he'd been completely in the clear all along."

"He could kill you to avoid having to pay you," she said, "but he's in the clear in that respect, too. We never discussed money. He just sent some, and if he figures that's payment in full, what am I going to do about it? It's not as though I could send him a bill."

"You think he'll pay anything more?"

"I can't imagine why he would," she said, "but that doesn't mean he won't. If he does, fine. If not, that's fine, too."

"The reason I was worried," he went on, "is that I got stirred up on the last job."

"Bingham."

He nodded. "And I couldn't stop thinking about my stamp collection. I guess I realized I was going to die someday. I mean, everybody does, right?"

"So they tell me."

"And I knew that, and I thought I was used to the idea, but then I got haunted by the idea of my stamps being left behind. What would happen to them? I don't have kids to worry about, or relatives, but it suddenly seemed very im-

352

portant to make arrangements for my stamp collection. And once I'd made arrangements, once we'd had that conversation—"

"And what a conversation it was."

"—I had this sense that it was all taken care of, and now all that was left was for me to go out and meet my fate."

"That's why you wouldn't let me pull the plug on the job."

"If it was fate, what good would it do? Instead of going to Albuquerque I'd stay home, and when I went down to the corner for the paper an air conditioner would fall out of somebody's window and kill me. That poor bastard Heggman, I don't think he ever had a clue. He must have been dead before he could figure out what was happening to him."

"You're sure it was him?"

"He was at the right address," he said, "and he looked just like his picture. But I wondered myself. Waiting for my flight, I kept thinking I should have asked him his name. And then of course I kept expecting the plane to crash."

"Which one? The flight to Los Angeles or the red-eye?"

"Both of them. But the flights were fine. The cab ride in from JFK, the driver was a maniac, cutting everybody off, driving way too fast. But he got away with it."

She nodded slowly, took a long look at him. "You must be exhausted," she said.

"Sort of."

"I'll run you back to the station, and you go home and get some sleep. And maybe we should both think about packing it in."

He shook his head.

"No?"

"No," he said. "Because we don't have enough money, not really. And even if we did, even if my end came to a million dollars, it still wouldn't be enough."

"How do you figure that?"

"I'll go home," he said, "and for the next week I'll barely leave the house. I'll sleep a lot and watch a lot of TV. And for a month or more I'll go to movies and work out at the gym and work on my stamps, and it'll be just the way it would be if I were retired, and I'll enjoy it. And then sometime in the second month I'll start feeling as though there's something I ought to be doing."

"I think I get the picture."

"And then one of us will call the other, and it'll turn out that there's a job out there if I want it. And I'll go like this—"

He pressed his wrists together.

" 'What time?' "

"There you go."

"And you'll go off to do the job," she said, "thinking all the while that you're really too old for this, and that you wish you could retire."

"That sounds about right."

She thought about it. "Well, okay, Keller," she said. "I guess I can stand it as long as you can."

KELLER
AND THE
RABBITS

CHAPTER FIFTY-ONE

Keller, idling at a stoplight, reached over to turn on the radio. A woman's voice, warm and slightly theatrical, said: "*A Rabbit Odyssey*, by Cameron Markwood. Read by Gloria Sweet."

The light turned green. He crossed the intersection, then reached to dial in another station. But nothing happened when he turned the dial, and he realized it wasn't the radio, it was the CD player, and he was listening to an audiobook. About rabbits, evidently.

That was the thing about rental cars. You got a different make and model every time, and by the time you figured out things like cruise control and the best position for the seat back, it was time to turn the car in. Evidently the last person to rent this one had figured out how to use the CD player, but hadn't remembered to retrieve his CD.

So Keller got to listen to a story about rabbits. He was going to turn it off, but he had to concentrate on the traffic and on an upcoming left turn, and by the time things settled down and straightened out, he'd managed to get interested in the story.

It was, he decided, a fable, in that the rabbits not only had conversations but also expressed philosophical sentiments that seemed a stretch for something that hopped around and ate carrots. It was an allegory, with the rabbits meant to represent humans. But at the same time they were rabbits, and he found himself caught up in the story, concerned about their survival. When one of them was caught in a snare, he got really worried, and didn't fully relax until the other rabbits managed to do some artful gnawing and liberate the little guy.

He was supposed to take a right at Rumsey Road, and damn near missed it. But he made his turn, while a rabbit named Williwaw analyzed the failure of the lettuce crop in terms of supply-side economics. That was kind of interesting, he thought, but there were a couple of boys out with guns, and Williwaw had better put a lid on it and get hopping or he was going to wind up in the stew pot . . .

There was the house, white with dark green trim, a prewar frame house with a basketball hoop mounted on the garage at the end of the long driveway. Keller circled the block, parked where he could watch the place without being too obvious about it. He cut the engine, but moved the key to a position that let you listen to the radio. Or, in this case, the CD player, where Williwaw was in desperate straits.

The side door of the white frame house opened, and two children hurried up the driveway to the garage, shortly followed by their mother, who was wearing gray sweatpants and a University of Southern Michigan sweatshirt. The garage door ascended, and a Japanese SUV backed out of the driveway and headed off down Rumsey Road. Taking them to school, Keller thought. And she didn't look to be dressed for anything more than dropping them off and coming straight home.

Would the CD player keep his place? Or would the damn thing start over from the beginning? Hard to tell, but it was a risk he'd take. He turned the key, drew it from the ignition lock, and walked up the driveway

358

she'd recently backed out of. She'd left the garage door open, which suggested a quick return, and which made it easy for Keller to conceal himself. He stood in the shadows, next to a child's bicycle, and thought occasionally about the woman, and the rest of the time about Williwaw and his long-eared fellows.

She was back in under fifteen minutes, and she was out of the car before she saw Keller. She hadn't expected this, had evidently had no idea that her husband, conveniently on the other side of the country on a business trip, was so anxious to get rid of her that he'd paid a substantial fee toward that end. Still, she was afraid, and her fear froze her in her tracks, mouth open, eyes wide.

Keller stunned her with a stiff-fingered jab to the solar plexus, then took hold of her and broke her neck.

Back in his rental car, Keller had a bad moment when he started it up. But then the CD came on, and it resumed right where it had left off, which saved having to search for his place. He thought the image of the woman's face might get in the way, that and the sense-memory of lowering her body to the ground and shoving her out of sight underneath her SUV, but before he'd gone three blocks he was caught up in the story, and the woman's image was already starting to fade from his memory.

Poor little rabbits. He hoped nothing bad would happen to them.